POISON
MEMORIES

BOOKS BY HELEN PHIFER

POISON
MEMORIES

HELEN PHIFER

bookouture

Published by Bookouture in 2024

An imprint of Storyfire Ltd.
Carmelite House
50 Victoria Embankment
London EC4Y 0DZ

www.bookouture.com

ISBN: 978-1-83790-354-2
eBook ISBN: 978-1-83790-353-5

In loving memory of my darling mum,
Pat Corkill 7/12/1936 – 7/4/2024.

The most wonderful, loving, kindest, woman I have ever known.
I miss you, Patti.
Ain't that the truth!
Xxx

PROLOGUE

Margery Lancaster checked the bolt on the front door for the second time. She could feel the draught blowing underneath the old warped wooden door. It badly needed replacing even with the knitted draught excluder she'd made, which was stuffed in front of it.

The wind was howling outside as the driving rain pelted against the single glazed wooden windows. She had taped cardboard over the most worn panes. Rain and wind once blew in through the gaps, but now the cardboard blocked out the worst of the draughts along with the daylight, making the inside of the cottage perpetually dark. Was it as dark as her soul, her mind? She doubted it. For a woman who had known nothing but sadness and torment, she thought living in a house full of nothing but shadows and darkness suited her down to the bone. This house was always cold. It had never been a happy house.

She shuffled along the tiled floor in her worn slippers, pulling the crochet blanket tight around her shoulders. She tried to remember if there had ever been happiness inside of here. She paused to look up the staircase, straining to hear if there were any strange sounds: the creaking of floorboards, the closing of doors, footsteps walking from room to room, any signs of life that didn't belong to this house of gloom. There was only the whistling of the wind coming through the gaps in the front door, so she carried on to the small room she used as her bedroom. It had been the parlour many years before she'd even lived here, and then it had been empty when she'd gone away for quite some time.

She had never imagined that she'd return here, to this exact house, but it was as if it had lain waiting for her to come back, to come home. It was like it had known she could never escape and deep down so had she. This old house could give Bleak House a run for its money. She knew the history of it, but she preferred not to think about it. The house, however, had other ideas and she believed that was all it thought about. Those past memories had imprinted themselves into the bricks and mortar.

She shuddered.

She could have changed it all. At one point she thought she was making a difference, until the house, which was like a living, breathing thing, had decided she wasn't going to do that. It was happy the way it was. Who was she to think she could bring in the light? And this place had turned from her sanctuary to her own private prison.

A small scrape from somewhere made her pause at the doorway to her bedroom. She stilled, waiting to see if it happened again. She sometimes heard things that weren't there. She lived in a house of silence, no television, no radio, no life, after all. And she was forced to live that way. She had done a very bad thing, and she knew that she had to pay. This house was her prison cell, and she was her own jailer.

The Lancaster family had suffered for centuries, some might say they had been cursed and she couldn't argue with anyone who thought it. The noise never repeated, and she put it down to her imagination or the wind brushing a tree branch against the windowpanes. Which was likely the explanation with the stormy weather outside. She stared at her bed, her one comfort in her life, her one luxury. In the past, she had spent twelve long years sleeping on a mattress so hard it had given her back pain that made her take pills every day now, to keep it bearable, and she didn't like to take pills or medicines because she knew what could happen when you trusted someone to make you better. She sighed as she climbed into the bed, it was warmer than the kitchen and the only place she felt safe. Margery wondered if sleep would come easily tonight, or if it would tease her with a brief respite of unconsciousness before her nightmares would wake her fully to lie there for hours listening to the wind and the rain battering the outside of the ramshackle cottage. As she closed her eyes, she felt the over-whelming tiredness tugging her down into the darkness and once again prayed for forgiveness.

———

An hour later her eyes opened at the sound of footsteps in the narrow hallway. Someone was creeping around. Fear lodged itself like a lead ball in the pit of her stomach and the back of her throat. She clutched the covers in panic; she didn't want to see who it was should they open the door. Sometimes she thought she heard the ghosts of the people who'd died here before, going about their business as if nothing had happened and they were still alive. The footsteps paused outside of her room, and she knew then that this was no ghost. They were too heavy.

She had no phone in her bedroom to call for the police, the old-fashioned house phone was in the hallway. Not that they would rush to come to her rescue. She lived in the middle of nowhere. And she deserved nothing. Whoever was out there had a reason to be inside of this godforsaken cottage in the early hours of the morning. There was nothing of any value to steal, no gold, no jewellery, no antiques, not even a decrepit computer. She knew they were looking for her.

There was no point in reaching for a weapon. She had no energy to fight, whoever this was, and she wondered if she already knew deep down who it might be. Had they finally come to exact their revenge?

Margery decided that she was ready to face it if they had. She was surprised it had taken this long. Pulling the covers down she swung her legs out of the bed and sat on the edge of it, hands folded neatly in her lap. If and when the intruder decided it was time to come and get her, she was ready.

1

Detective Constable Morgan Brookes was dripping puddles of rainwater onto the tiled floor of the changing rooms of Rydal Falls police station. She was fuming that she'd been forced to park in the very last spot in the car park. Her car was as far away from the station as it could be. She may as well have left it in Ambleside. Cain, her colleague and friend, walked past her and asked, 'Did you decide to walk to work today with no umbrella?'

She didn't even give him the benefit of an answer because it would have been far too rude for this early in the morning. She glared at him, and his laughter echoed around the room.

'Now, if you'd just come ten minutes ago, you could have got the space I'm in, right next to the doors.' He smiled. 'And it wasn't even raining then. Unlucky, Brookes, hope you have a change of clothes in your locker.'

She ignored him and walked to the ladies' toilet to survey the damage; her hair was sodden, and her winged eyeliner was smudged. Her jacket was stuck to her arms, and it was supposed to be showerproof too. Grabbing some paper towels, she began to blot herself dry, starting with her hair and then her face. Giving up she used the hair dryer someone had left plugged into the socket and blasted herself, the warm air taking away the chill. A few adjustments and she was almost passable as human except for her wet clothes. She hung her jacket on the rack in the drying room with all the soaking wet uniforms that had been hung in there once the nightshift had ended, and got herself a fresh set of clothes out of her locker. Stripping quickly, she was glad she kept a spare set in case of emergencies. Once she was dressed, she threw her clothes on the bench in the drying room too, not bothering to hang them up; they would smell musty after being in here and need washing again. Ready for a coffee and the chance to warm up in the CID office, she had made it to the bottom of the stairs, when her boss and partner, DS Ben Matthews, came running down, with Cain and Amy following behind.

'Ah, Morgan. You have excellent timing, we're off out. Sudden death near High Wraith Cottage; you might as well come along.'

'You've got to be kidding me? I've only just got here.'

He shook his head. 'Paramedics say it's suspicious and patrols haven't got there yet, better to be safe and attend.'

She didn't argue with him – of course it was – and she wasn't one to shirk away from any jobs that came in, it's just that she really needed a coffee to get her brain cells working.

'I need to grab a jacket, give me a minute.'

She went back to her locker and took out her old fluorescent yellow waterproof coat. It might not look pretty but it was functional, and she knew that High Wraith Cottage was at the top of a hill in the middle of nowhere. She'd been there once on a call when she was on her probation. The owner had thought there had been an intruder in the house. There hadn't but she was scared and lived alone so they'd checked it out and ensured her it was okay. The weather down here was bad enough; up there it would be horrendous. Grabbing her old waterproof baseball cap with earflaps off the shelf, she tucked it in her pocket then slammed the door shut and went back to where Cain was waiting for her.

'Where's the others?'

'Don't know what you gave Ben for breakfast today, but he's off on one. Practically ran out of the door dragging poor Amy with him, and he said to wait for you and go up in a separate car. Why do you look so sad, Brookes, are you missing him already?'

'Bugger off, Cain, I'm cold and miserable. I slept in, Ben left without me this morning, and I need coffee.'

'I promise you I'll buy you coffee on the way back. Hopefully, it's nothing and the paramedics are being overly cautious. We could be on our way to The Coffee Pot in thirty minutes.'

She smiled at him. 'Hopefully.'

Morgan directed Cain as he drove at speed along the narrow roads that would take them to the old cottage at the top of the hill.

'I wonder who phoned it in. It's so desolate up there I can't see any walkers being out so early in this weather at this time of year.'

He shrugged. 'Diehard dog walkers always find the bodies. Or maybe one of the farmers, they have to be out in this weather regardless.'

As he turned onto the road that led to the cottage, they both let out a gasp. A body dangled, mid-air. It was suspended by a rope hooped around a gnarled branch on the old oak tree that edged the property. A black cloth covered the head, making them unidentifiable, and a thick chain was wrapped around both wrists, binding the person's hands together.

Morgan closed her eyes for a moment. She was taken back

to the very first call she'd attended on her own after finishing her training. The beautiful Olivia Potter had been hung from a tree in her perfectly landscaped garden.

She looked at the overgrown garden surrounding High Wraith Cottage; it was the complete opposite of the Potters' – this garden had been sadly neglected for years. The only clear path was from the front door to the gate. The door of the cottage was open, blowing in the wind, a repetitive thudding as it smashed against the wall inside. The rain was still lashing, making it hard to do anything. The paramedics were huddled by the back of the ambulance, and Ben was talking to them. Amy was tugging on a pair of gloves. She had ripped open a packet to pull on a disposable crime-scene suit, when it got whipped out of her hands by a gust of air – packet and suit took off into the grey sky. It filled up with air like a strange, person-shaped balloon and flew off into the distance as Amy cried out, 'Shit.'

Both Morgan and Cain watched as it gathered speed, wind-milling through the air.

Ben looked at the three of them and shook his head. 'This is no good,' he shouted over the wind. 'No chance of forensics out here. We need to get them down before it gets any worse.'

Morgan was staring at the body which was dressed in a pair of men's pyjamas; it was also gathering speed as it swung from side to side. 'How?'

She didn't need to finish her question as an ear-splintering crack filled the air.

Ben shouted to the paramedics, 'Move,' just as the branch holding the body slammed to the ground, hitting the front of the ambulance and cracking the windscreen on its way.

Cain was watching the scene with a look of horror on his face.

Morgan couldn't help it, she leaned over and cupped a hand to his ear. 'Do you still think the paramedics were being overly cautious?' She shook her head, then walked into the wind and rain to get to the body.

Ben was now peering down at it with a look of wonder on his face. He shouted, 'We're never going to keep a tent over them. Morgan, can you phone Wendy and ask her to get here ASAP? I saw her on my way into work so she's around.'

She pulled out her phone and turned to go back to the car, the driving rain and howling wind making it hard to hear anything other than the storm that was raging around them on the side of High Wraith Fell. She got into the car and was relieved to be temporarily out of it.

Wendy answered straight away.

'I'm just about to set off, on my way up to you. I saw Ben rushing out and went to check the log.'

'It's a mess. I think it's a she but there's some kind of cloth bag over the head and they're wearing men's pyjamas. Wendy, the branch snapped under the weight with the wind and rain, and she fell to the floor. What should we do?'

'Nothing, I'm assuming she's dead and beyond help?'

'Yes, paramedics said so.'

'Then, as horrible as this is, best to leave them where they are, don't touch anything. You could see if there is some tarpaulin to put over them. I highly doubt there will be anything I can get forensically from outside in this weather, depending on how long she's been exposed to the storm, but inside should hopefully be salvageable.'

'I'll tell Ben, thanks.'

She glanced out of the window. The old tree was taking a beating with the storm and so were her colleagues. She wished that the rain would stop, and the wind would drop so they could help this poor victim, but it was like fighting a losing battle against Mother Nature and at the moment she was winning hands down.

Morgan got out of the car and braced herself to join her

colleagues. If they were out in the elements then she was too. They would use all they had to find the person who did this.

2

Forensic Pathologist Declan Donnelly was leaning on his elbows staring out of his office window at the rain as it bounced off the paving slabs outside. It was like a tropical storm washing over the greyness of the hospital. 'It's a shame we're in Lancaster and not the Bahamas; it would be a lot more fun watching this somewhere hot and humid with a large cocktail in my hand.'

Susie, his assistant, joined him. 'Jesus, is this ever going to end? The entire month of December has done nothing but rain and it looks like January is going the same way. It's usually starting to get all frosty and fresh like, and this is just dreary.'

He glanced at her. 'Dreary? I like that, I think I'll use that for my word of the month. Thank you for reminding me such a word exists, Susie. How's your love life by the way? Managed to scare off any more potential partners lately?'

She elbowed him in the side. 'Nope, I'm single, it's just me and the dog for the foreseeable. I can't be bothered with the hassle.' She tucked a strand of loose emerald-green hair that had fallen out of one of the short bunches she was wearing behind an ear.

'Yes, I completely understand that, especially with your track record. I mean it's not that great, is it, to be fair. Have you considered joining a convent? I'm sure they would love to have someone with a sparkling personality such as yourself helping out at morning mass.'

'Ouch, you are such a mean person at times, Declan, and it's not as if you can talk. How many lovers have you had in the last twelve months?'

He reached out and patted the top of her head. 'Sorry, I didn't mean that. I couldn't manage without you. Your hair alone brings life to my theatre of the dead. I'm just feeling sorry for myself. It's the thought of these long, cold nights, it always makes me all maudlin.'

'What's up? Did you and Theo split up?'

'No, just a bit of a falling out but we've kissed and made up. But I keep thinking, is it going to work out with him being a priest and all that? They get moved around a lot and I'm worried he might have to move to the Outer Hebrides or somewhere like that, and you know it's impossible to keep up a long-distance relationship.' He sighed. 'I really like him, he's funny, kind, caring and just an all-round nice guy. They don't come around very often. He's so uncomplicated, it's refreshing to say the least.'

'You could always go with him if he had to move.'

'What, and leave my little colourful fairy friend all alone to work with a grumpy old doctor who would probably want to snap at you all day long and feel your bottom every time you bent over? I wouldn't do that to you and besides, I like it here and I love my old mates Ben and Morgan. I couldn't imagine leaving to go and do what? Pass out Bibles in a wooden shack on some island where the weather is even worse than here.'

Susie smiled at him. 'You think I'm like a colourful fairy?'

'Oh, dear God, are you feeling extra sensitive today, Susie? If you are I didn't mean that as an insult.'

She laughed. 'Not at all, I like that. It's a compliment. Did you know that the fae are real? I would have thought you would, being of Irish descent and all that. I saw some guy on TikTok talking about putting fairy houses in your garden so they have somewhere warm to go, especially in weather like this.'

He swiped a hand across his brow, miming the relief he felt. 'For real?'

She nodded. 'And you should have been an actor, Declan, you are so dramatic.'

The pair of them laughed as the phone on his desk began to ring. 'I have a feeling that is bad news, that Morgan or Ben is going to drag me out to some awful crime scene right in the middle of this storm.'

Susie shrugged. 'Don't answer it then. It could just be the lab with the tox results for Marvin Hartley.'

He turned and reached for the receiver. 'It could, but I bet you a bacon roll that it's not. Hello, Pathology.'

'Declan, are you free?'

The familiar voice sounded a million miles away and as if he was calling from inside a wind tunnel.

'Bloody hell, Ben, I just said to Susie I bet it's you or Morgan.'

He could hear the wind howling down the phone and knew it was going to be awful.

'We have a suspicious hanging; victim, I think is female, had a hood over their head and hands tied together with chains. The tree branch they're suspended from snapped and they are currently on the floor in a puddle of mud and rainwater. What should we do?'

'Ideally, get them out of this weather and on their way to me. How bad is the mud damage? Is there anything of forensic value left?'

'They seem to have fought back, hands are a mess. Nails are

all bloodied and broken, and there's bruising on some of the fingers.'

'I'll come out, where are you?'

He wrote down the address on a scrap of paper and then typed it into the search bar on his computer. 'It's going to take me at least an hour in this weather, probably a lot longer because the roads will be flooding and visibility poor. Look, is Wendy there?'

'Yes.'

'Good, bless her soul, the best thing is to preserve what's there; get her to bag the hands for me, to keep them from getting any wetter or soiled, and get the body moved here. I'm not busy, I can start straight away. If you're free come along, and if you're not send two of the others to attend.'

'Thanks, Declan.'

Ben hung up.

Declan turned to Susie. 'I best go get those bacon rolls.'

She rolled her eyes at him. 'I think you're a little bit psychic. Do you see dead people when you're not in the mortuary?'

'Absolutely not, except for in my dreams. Then I do, but, thank God, I can't see them following me around, that would be a bit difficult, don't you think? Especially after I'd cut them open and sewn their organs inside their stomach cavity in a plastic bag. I feel a bit bad, you know, not going to the scene, but there's nothing much I can do. By the time I get there any evidence will have washed away, if it hasn't already.'

He sauntered off to the canteen to fulfil his end of the bet. The dark corridor, painted a sickly, faded yellow, ran underneath the whole of the hospital from the mortuary into the main building. He felt a cold chill run down his spine and shivered. It was eerie down here at the best of times, and now Susie had put the idea of ghosts into his mind he couldn't stop thinking about them. All the tortured souls whose bodies had been wheeled along here in body bags to his mortuary for their final indignity before being put to rest. He never usually thought about it, but the weather and Susie had put his mind on edge. Of course, this was before they made an entrance where they could be brought straight into the pathology suite instead of this long way to it. If Stephen King saw this corridor, he would call it the long, yellow mile. This was an old hospital and that was a lot of dead people.

He picked up his pace and decided not to use this shortcut on the way back from the canteen. He would rather go out in the rain than walk back down here today.

3

The undertakers muttered under their breaths and to each other the entire time while trying to battle against the wind and rain to get the body bagged and into the back of the private ambulance. Wendy and Joe, the other CSI on shift, supervised the undertakers. Amy and Cain were inside the cottage, and Morgan and Ben were outside to help if needed. Once the body was in the back of the silver van with tinted windows and the doors slammed shut, Morgan said a little prayer for the woman who had been left this way, so out in the open for the world to see. It was just as well she lived in a remote cottage on the side of a fell, and there were not many people around, which meant...

She turned to Ben. 'This was someone who knew her; it's personal, Ben,' she shouted above the wind.

He nodded. 'Maybe, this is far too remote of a place for an opportunistic killer. Come on, let's go inside and see if there is any evidence of a struggle.'

They wouldn't normally all go into a crime scene before Wendy had finished – the fewer people inside the less chance of compromising any forensics – but the weather was driving them in. Cain and Amy were searching the upstairs for signs of a struggle, and Wendy, who was trying to warm herself up a little, was ready to document the scene. She stared at the pair of them as they stood in the doorway.

'Stay there and don't move another inch.' Then she called out, 'Amy, Cain, can you make your way back down here, please, and get out of the house. Unless you're going to tell me you found me something good?'

Amy popped her head over the small banister at the top of the stairs. 'Nothing up here, except for junk. It's a hoarder's paradise, and it doesn't look as if anyone has been in these rooms for years. Everything is thick with dust.'

As if to prove a point Cain sneezed so loud it felt as if the entire cottage shook with the force of it.

Morgan felt sad, what a way to exist. Whoever lived here must have been so lonely and scared when their assailant got inside then attacked them.

She told Wendy, 'I'll go and check the back door, see if that was the way in.'

She braced for the rain once more, though she was glad to be out of that small, dreary space that was so depressing it made her want to cry. She hurried around the perimeter of the house and found a broken window by the kitchen door. There were no trees nearby, no branches or debris that could have been thrown against the window by the wind. At least they had a point of entry. It seemed the killer had to break in, so they probably didn't know the victim well enough to have a key. There were footprints in the mud, and she stopped as soon as she saw them, retracing her steps to the front door.

Breathless, she stepped inside, almost knocking Ben over. 'Kitchen window is broken, and there's some footprints in the muddy soil underneath it.'

He grinned at her. 'Hallelujah.'

Wendy said to Joe, 'Go get some footplates to cover them, try and preserve as much as you can.'

He squeezed past both of them to go to the van.

Morgan's phone was vibrating in her pocket, and she pulled it out to see her aunt Ettie's name on the screen. A warm rush of love coursed through her entire body; it had been too long since she'd spoken to her aunt but now was not the time. She would ring her back as soon as she could. Closing her eyes, she silently told Ettie this and the phone stopped ringing immediately. Ettie had got the message or so she liked to believe. Her aunt was a full-on kitchen witch, living the dream in her own cottage in the middle of Covel Wood. She even had a pet raven called Max. She was badass, and Morgan couldn't love the woman any more than she did. One of Morgan's favourite films was *Practical Magic*, and she loved that Ettie reminded her a little of Aunt Frances, a tea drinking version of the woman. She couldn't imagine her aunt drinking midnight margaritas, but then again, she'd never slept over at her house, so for all she knew she did on a regular basis.

'Everything okay?' Ben was looking at her, and she realised she was smiling to herself.

'Fine, just Ettie. I'll ring her back when I can.'

He nodded. Ben and Ettie had had a few run-ins with each other, but they were okay now. Morgan knew that he'd sought her help when he'd been struggling with the pressures of work, as she'd found a black obsidian crystal that had tumbled out of his pocket one day. She had popped it back inside and kept quiet, happy that he had sought help and stopped keeping all his guilt and worry bottled up, because he carried far too much of it around with him.

'Right, enough of this. You lot can either go wait in your cars or go back to the station because I'm struggling to think with you all breathing all over my crime scene.'

'If it's okay with you, I'll go speak to the DI and then me

and Morgan will go to the post-mortem. There are no other houses for miles and no CCTV; the only witness we have is the guy who found her. He was on his way to an Airbnb and missed the turning. The satnav brought him along here, poor bugger.'

Morgan didn't know this; she'd assumed it was a farmer who had found the body. 'Where is he now?'

He shrugged. 'On his way to the house.'

'Who spoke to him? Because we didn't, and he wasn't here when we arrived.'

'Paramedics. He gave details to the Control room when he rang it in, said he couldn't wait around. He had a small child asleep in the back of the car and didn't want them to see anything.'

'Oh, right. I suppose that's okay then, bit weird though.'

'Why?'

'I don't know. I would want to know what had happened and see if the woman was okay.'

'Morgan, you don't have kids. If you did, would you want them to see something so horrific?'

She shook her head. 'How do we know he had a kid with him? Did the paramedics see the child? Are we certain there was a child there?'

He crossed his arms. 'Well, I suppose we can't be.' He turned towards Cain and Amy. 'Can you two find him and go take a statement from him? See what he has to say for himself. I don't know the address, but it will be on the log. Control will pass it on if you ask them.'

Cain looked relieved to be escaping, so did Amy.

Wendy was watching the four of them with her arms folded across her chest. 'Are you lot quite finished? I need you out of here now.'

Ben held his hands up. 'Sorry, we're leaving now.'

He ushered them all out of the tiny hallway back into the rain. Cain and Amy headed to Cain's car. Morgan didn't think

she'd ever been so wet and miserable in her life. She followed
Ben to his car, and managed to tug her wet coat off after a
struggle and throw it in the back. Ben removed his outside and
clambered in. The white cotton of his shirt was now sticking
to his chest, and she was glad it wasn't her wearing a wet
white cotton shirt this time around or everything would be on
show.

'Turn the engine on and whack the heater up, I'm freezing.'
As if to prove a point her teeth began to chatter.

Ben reached out for her hand. 'Should we go home and get
changed before we head off to the mortuary?'

She shook her head. 'It's only going to add another twenty
minutes on, just head there. The heater should blast us dry
soon, and Declan will have some scrubs we could borrow.'

'Yeah, you're right. We can feel sorry for ourselves later
when our noses are running like taps and we can't stop
coughing our guts up.'

'All part of the service I suppose. What do you think has
happened here? Seriously this is horrible. I mean all sudden
deaths and suspicious deaths are awful.' She stopped as she
thought about their most recent serious investigation, of
Evelyn's, Bronte's, and Lexie's horrible deaths. She hadn't slept
without bad dreams since the day she'd watched as Bronte had
been run over and killed on that country road a couple of
months ago. All three women haunted her nightmares; they
were the reason she felt so tired lately. She knew she should get
some counselling.

Ben didn't answer, and she turned to him. 'Why didn't you
wake me this morning, by the way? You let me sleep in and I
was late for work.'

'You looked peaceful for the first time in weeks. I didn't
have the heart to wake you up. I was going to either let you work
a late or put some time off in lieu to make up for it.'

All the anger and frustration she'd been feeling since she'd woken up and realised she was late for work melted away. 'I was?'

Ben nodded. 'You were, it's been a tough time for you, everybody knows that. I just wanted you to catch up on your sleep a little. You look worn out.'

'Thank you. I was thinking you were being an arse.'

Ben laughed. 'Thanks for the trust, Morgan.'

She shrugged. 'I sometimes wonder if you're too good to be true and then I catch myself and remind myself that you are and I'm a very lucky woman to have you.'

He picked up her hand, which was still frozen, and kissed it while he was driving, the sound of the windscreen wipers swishing treble time to keep his vision clear on the narrow roads.

'Not as lucky as I am. You know I still find it hard to believe that you could see anything in me, but I'm glad that you do. Now enough of this, we need to focus and figure out just what the hell is going on here because it's got me stumped. Can you ask someone back at the station to run a background check on the occupant of High Wraith Cottage while we're on the way to the hospital?'

'I went there on a job once; it was a woman who lived on her own and thought there was someone in the cottage.'

'How long ago?'

'Four years ago, never heard from her again. It's probably the same woman. I don't remember her name, but there'll be an incident report on the system.'

'Was there anyone inside?'

'No, and no sign of anyone either. I think she scared herself and panicked.'

Morgan shouted up for Control to check the quick address system to see who their victim could be, and then she rang Mads who she knew without a doubt would be sitting in the sergeant's office. There was no way he'd be out in this weather.

'*What do you want, Brookes?*'

'Charming, who said I wanted anything?'

'*Do you not?*'

She smiled. 'Yes, I do.'

'*See, point taken. What is it?*'

'Have you got anyone who can do some background checks on the occupant of the cottage we're at?'

'*Where is that big lout Cain? Can't he do it and make himself useful? All my staff are out, busy chasing escaped sheep and closing off roads that are flooded.*'

'Never mind, he's gone to speak to the witness.'

Mads let out an exasperated sigh.

'*I'll do it and ring you back.*'

He hung up, and she muttered, 'Rude.'

Ben smiled at her. 'Well at least he didn't offer to give it to Amber.'

Morgan thought that wouldn't have been too bad. She was beginning to warm to the woman who'd been a bit nicer than when she first started in her role as a police officer, after getting dragged into cases they were working.

'She's not so bad.'

He arched one eyebrow in her direction. 'Isn't she? I'll have to remember that next time you start to roll your eyes at her.'

Morgan declined to comment and closed her eyes. She was starting to get feeling back into her fingers at least, but her toes were still sodden and frozen. She realised she hadn't returned Ettie's call and now was the time before they got to the hospital.

'Morgan, how are you, darling? I had this feeling I needed to call you, so I did.'

She smiled to herself. 'I'm very wet, but apart from that I'm good thanks, how are you?'

'Oh, you know, just the same old cantankerous woman you know. How have you been sleeping?'

'Not so great, lots of bad dreams, Ettie.'

'I knew it, which is why I've made you a special batch of Sleep Well tea. I would drop it off for you, but my van is in the garage.'

'That's okay, I'll pick it up later. I'm on my way to Lancaster Infirmary now so will be in a few hours.'

'Are you hurt, sweetie?'

'No, I'm fine. It's not for me, it's for work.'

Ettie paused before she spoke.

'Morgan, where were you when I phoned earlier? I don't want any details, but I need to know. I couldn't settle and knew something terrible had happened, and I got this urge to call you that wouldn't go away.'

Morgan wondered if it was okay to tell Ettie the location. She'd been about to but not the details. 'I was at a job at High Wraith Cottage.'

Ettie let out a small gasp.

'Oh dear, I knew it, I had this feeling you might be there. You don't have to tell me how, but is she dead?'

Ben couldn't help but overhear Ettie's conversation because it was so loud, and the radio wasn't on. He looked at Morgan and nodded.

'Yes. Do you know the owner, Ettie?'

'I know her, yes. Terrible what happened, what she did, but desperate times can call for desperate measures. She's a bit of a recluse like me, I suppose, but I try and help people. I had a feeling this was going to happen; I haven't been able to get the woman out of my head. I suppose I could have warned her that something was going to happen, but that would be a bit awkward, wouldn't it? Just knocking on her door to tell her that I saw something bad happening to her in my tea leaves.'

'What is her name and what exactly did she do?'

'Margery Lancaster. You're too young to remember, in fact you probably weren't even born, but she was the talk of the town for months after it happened.'

Morgan couldn't imagine doing anything that would deserve the punishment Margery had been given. She repeated, 'What did she do?'

'She poisoned her little boy and her husband; the husband was quite poorly for some time, and they almost lost the child, but he clung onto life, the poor lamb, and fought to survive. She didn't phone an ambulance. The husband realised what had happened and managed to reach the phone to call one before he collapsed.'

'Jesus.'

'He had nothing to do with it.'

Morgan smiled. 'No, I meant...'

'I know what you meant, I'm just teasing. It was a long time ago.'

'What happened to her?'

'She got sent to prison and then transferred to a secure mental health unit. I'm not too sure but I think she did about thirteen years then got released. Nobody expected her to go back to the family home, but she did, as bold as brass. Of course, people move on, they forget. I think the News & Star printed an article on her release, detailing her crimes, but nobody lived around here was affected.'

'What happened to her son and husband?'

'I'm assuming he got put into foster care; he was only a toddler. Her husband, I have no idea.'

'Thank you for that, it's really helpful.'

'Good, I'm glad to be of help. Don't forget to call in for your tea. I'd love to see you, darling.'

'I won't. Bye, Ettie.'

'Goodbye, Morgan.'

The line went dead, and she looked at Ben. 'Did you hear that? I think we might have just found ourselves two suspects without even trying.'

'I did, good old Ettie. How did she know to ring you though, at the exact time you were at the cottage?'

'She had a feeling and please don't say she should be a suspect, Ben; there is no way on earth that she would do anything so horrid and violent to another person, and her van is in the garage so let's not even go there.'

'I wasn't even thinking anything of the sort. I'm kind of getting used to her strange ways and she's not strong enough for a start. Whoever hauled Margery up to hang her from that tree would have had to have been capable of doing that; even though she isn't a big woman, she would still have been a dead weight.'

Morgan leaned forward and began to untie her Dr Martens boots. Unlacing them she slipped first one foot and then the other out of the soggy leather, pulled off her socks and dropped them on the floor of the car and sighed, wiggling her wrinkled toes beneath the heater.

'That's better.'

Ben laughed. 'I'm glad it is, whatever you do don't leave those socks in this car or we'll get Mads chasing us down.'

'In her defence she's a witch, she knows things.'

'Do you really believe that?'

'What's not to believe? She's been reading tea leaves and making her teas for longer than I've been alive. She knows her stuff, and I would have no reason not to believe her. Anyway, Google will confirm everything, won't it? Not to mention the police records. Mads is going to have a field day when he investigates Margery Lancaster's background.'

'I suppose he is.'

'Do you not remember it? Were you in the job back then?'

'Morgan, I'm old, but I'm not *that* old. I vaguely remember something, but it could have just been in the news.'

He drove carefully along the steep, waterlogged roads, and she stared out of the window. It seemed as if the rain had been falling for almost forty days and nights, making Morgan wonder if it was some biblical sign from God. Whatever it was she wished it would go away. She liked the rain, especially when she was inside, curled up with a book and a mug of coffee, but this was something else.

She tried to get Google to load on her phone, but she had no signal and sighed. Living and working in the Lake District was all fine until you needed a bit of technology, and then you might as well be living in a cave the Wi-Fi was that sketchy out on the fells.

4

MAGGIE

Maggie watched in horror as her son pulled himself up, hanging precariously off the side of the coffee table next to her burning-hot tea. He had been crawling around on the faux sheepskin rug with the cheap plastic egg cup that he'd play with rather than the expensive Fisher Price baby toys she'd bought him for Christmas. She'd placed her mug of freshly brewed piping hot tea on the table just moments ago. She had only gone to take the chicken out of the oven that she'd forgot about until the smell of charred chicken began to fill the room.

'David, get down.' She screamed the words at him so loud it made him lose his balance, and he fell against the table.

Dropping the Pyrex roasting tray, the chicken smashed to the floor, hot juice and fat splattering all over her legs. It was burning through her jeans, and she gritted her teeth, her bare feet sliding on the burning grease that coated the tiled kitchen floor as she skidded at the same time as yowling in pain, scaring the fucking kid to death. She watched it all in slow motion: he was rocking unsteadily, the table was shaking, and the liquid in the mug was sloshing about ready to tip all over him. She dived over the sofa, reaching out her hand, and pushed him away from the table. He fell to the floor with a loud scream of terror, but at least the tea, which had toppled over and was now spilling all over the carpet, hadn't touched him.

'What the hell are you doing, Maggie?'

She wanted to scream at him to bugger off, at the pair of them.

'Stopping that little sod scalding himself, that's what, and I've given myself third degree burns in the process.'

Her husband was a big man, and he strode into the room to scoop David up into his arms, shushing him and rocking him. He put him over his shoulder and looked into the open kitchen door to see the mess on the floor.

Without another word he leaned down and slammed his fist into her stomach, winding her.

'Get that mess cleaned up now.'

She let out a gasp of pain as the wind was knocked out of her, and she rolled off the sofa onto the floor to try and get to her knees before he decided to put the boot in as well.

George was no stranger to violence and would think nothing of kicking her as if she was a stray dog begging for scraps. David had stopped wailing and was now sobbing. She glanced at him and not for the first time wished the kid had never been born. Her legs were burning, and she needed to get her jeans off, soak the skin in cold water to stop blisters forming, but she didn't have time for that.

She managed to stand up, but not straight. She had to walk doubled over to get to the kitchen. She looked at the mess and wanted to cry, to scream how unfair it was. She was tired and had only wanted a cup of tea, five minutes peace, and the horrible boy hadn't even afforded her that.

George left the room with David, and she began to pick up the pieces of the smashed-up chicken. The dish had survived its fall to the floor, but the dead bird hadn't. Hot tears fell down her cheeks as she wished for the tenth time that day that she'd never met George, never got pregnant and never given birth. She shouldn't have told him she was pregnant in the first place and got rid of it, but she had and here she was. Stuck in this cottage in the middle of nowhere, with a kid she didn't like, a husband she hated and nobody to hear her screaming for help if she needed it. Ever since she'd given birth, she hadn't felt what the baby books and her mother had told her she would. There had been no instant bond. She'd looked at the baby and could only see the pain he had caused her up to now and the pain he would bring in the future. She had hoped to feel the sudden rush of love that women talked about on the television, and instead she had felt a rush of distaste, an unpleasant feeling that she didn't think would leave anytime soon. He had cried so much she had practically begged the midwife to take him away, as far away from her as possible. George had been so happy to see his son. He had smiled at the baby more than he'd ever smiled at her, and she knew she disliked the pair of them even more than she could have imagined.

When Maggie had finished cleaning and mopped the grease from the floor, she took herself upstairs to the small bathroom and peeled off her grease-stained jeans. Standing there in her washed-out grey big knickers from M&S, and the baggy black T-shirt that she'd shrunk in the wash that belonged to George, she stared down at her legs. There were angry red blotches all over the lower part, and they stung like mad; a couple of watery blisters had formed on some of them and then ripped open as she'd removed the soggy denim that had stuck to them. It hurt so much, she should really go to the hospital and get them cleaned up, but George would only scoff at her and tell her to stop being soft.

Biting her lip, she put the plug in the bath and began to fill the tub with cold water, enough to cover the burns on her legs. Gritting her teeth, she swung them over the side, plunging them into the icy water, and tried not to make a noise. She didn't want him coming in and seeing her like this. He would take one look at the mess her skin was in and remember next time he lost his temper to slap her or kick her where the blisters were. He was an evil man at times, and she wondered what she'd ever seen in him; of course, he hadn't been like that in the beginning though.

As she swished her feet in the cold water, she remembered how he had done his best to win her over. She had been head over heels for a guy called Tommy, who was a copper, but had been too shy to do anything about it. George had known she had a soft spot for him and would purposely ask her to dance. She didn't even like dancing, but the monthly disco with pie and peas at the church hall was about the only thing that gave any excitement when she'd lived in Rydal Falls. Tommy hadn't paid her any attention; he had been too smitten with a girl called Samantha with long blonde hair and pale blue eyes. Maggie was the complete opposite, with black hair and brown eyes. George had been the booby prize and she'd accepted his flirting and offers of dates, now look where it had got her. A kid she didn't want and a husband she hated. Out here there were no neighbours to gossip with, her friends all hated George so didn't bother coming to visit, and her parents were both dead.

Maggie closed her eyes and wished she could turn back time, or that the pair of them were dead, too. She wouldn't miss either of them; being a wife and mother wasn't what she'd wanted, and it was far worse than she'd expected.

5

They reached the mortuary ninety minutes later, which was slow for Ben who normally drove like a Formula One race car driver even around the twisty Lakeland roads. The rain in Lancaster was a steady drizzle now. They had left whatever storm it was this week behind in Cumbria, and Morgan was glad. Ben parked in a reserved spot which wasn't for them, but she could tell he was past caring, then he pointed to her feet. 'Are you going to walk barefoot, or would you like me to give you a piggy back?'

'Would you mind, I'm not that heavy.' She smiled sweetly at him, and he shook his head at her.

'What are you going to do? You can't wear those boots with no socks, you'll rub your feet to pieces.'

Morgan eyed the damp socks. 'I'll manage, Declan might have a spare pair I can use.' Tugging her boots on, she didn't even bother to lace them up.

When they reached the mortuary entrance, she pressed her finger on the bell far longer than needed until she heard Susie's voice calling, 'I'm coming, hold your horses.'

The door opened and she stared at the pair of them. 'Oh, man. You two look like a pair of drowned rats.'

Morgan smiled at her. 'We do and we are, please tell me you have some warm, dry scrubs we can wear? I'm frozen and can't stop shivering.'

'Yeah, of course we do. You know where the changing rooms are. Go knock yourselves out. In both rooms there is a cupboard with a sticker on that reads "clean scrubs", not hard to miss really. I'll tell Declan you're here.'

'Thank you, Susie. I love your hair.'

Ben was smiling at her, and Susie blushed, one hand reaching up to tuck a stray strand of green behind her ear. 'You do? You're being genuine and not sarcastic?'

He nodded. 'I certainly do.'

She punched him gently in the arm. 'Ooh, you're all soggy and I knew I liked you, Ben, thank you.'

Morgan liked Susie a lot. It was nice that he had managed to contain his shock at the two-tone black and green hairstyle she was wearing this time. He was getting better at accepting things that weren't what he was used to, and she felt proud of him for a moment, until Susie asked, 'What books are on your to-be-read list this month?'

Morgan wondered what white lie he was going to tell her this time and waited for his reply.

'Actually, Susie, I'm not that into reading and haven't had time. It's Morgan here who is the bookworm. You'd be better off asking her.' With that he walked off and dipped into the men's locker room.

She turned to Morgan. 'Boy, that took him long enough to confess to, didn't it? I've been waiting for him to tell me to sod off for months.'

'You have? I mean, you knew he didn't read yet you still kept asking him?' Morgan laughed. 'That's wicked.'

Susie shrugged. 'No, I was only trying to get him to pick up a book and read something to help him chill out a bit. He is always so work orientated, and I figured if between the two of us we could get him reading, it might take away some of the stress he's always under.'

'Susie, I take that back, it's actually really sweet of you.'

'Ah, it's nothing. I just like the pair of you that's all, so what about you give me something juicy, please, and make my day.'

'I've just finished reading *The Haunting of Hill House*.'

'By Shirley Jackson? Really, you only just decided to read one of the best classic horror stories of all time?'

'Better late than never.'

'Suppose so, I bet you've never read *Hell House*, by Richard Matheson either?'

Morgan shook her head.

'You have some serious catching up to do. Please read that next and tell me what you think of it.'

'Susie, what in the name of God are you doing holding up Morgan when she looks as if she's about to succumb to hypothermia?'

Morgan waved at Declan. 'I'm just going to strip off and put something warm on then I'll be ready; it's wild out there. I don't suppose either of you have a spare pair of socks I could borrow?'

Susie shook her head. 'No, but I'm sure we could grab you a pair out of one of the fridges.'

Morgan felt faint at the thought of having to wear a pair of socks that someone had died in.

'Away with you, Susie, behave yourself.'

Susie winked at her and rushed towards the mortuary, leaving her with Declan.

'I have spare socks; I have a set of spare clothes too if you need them, but if you're happy to wear scrubs then we have plenty of those. Ignore her, she's been a mischievous little devil all morning. I blame it on the weather.' He winked at her.

'Thank you, socks are more than enough. I just really hate cold feet.'

He disappeared into the men's changing room and came back less than a minute later with a ball of rolled-up socks. 'They're not pretty, they've been worn, but they are clean.' He tossed them at her, and she smiled to see Big Bird from *Sesame Street* staring up at her.

'Thanks, I appreciate it.'

He gave her a curt bow, then went back into the mortuary.

Morgan wasn't looking forward to this. She was cold to her bones, and it would be even colder inside, but she needed to be certain it was Margery Lancaster who had died. The only way was to observe Declan and Susie as they unwrapped and undressed the victim in order to be able to identify her.

Morgan pulled a clean pair of scrubs out of the cupboard, taking an extra top because she was so cold. It wasn't as if she could ask Declan to whack the heating up; it didn't work like that. She was thankful for the spare pair of white rubber boots Susie had told her to wear. She stuffed her own boots under the radiator and hoped that the heat wouldn't shrink them too much, but in all honesty, she didn't care as long as they were dry when the post-mortem was finished.

This case was different to how they usually worked, as the weather had thrown them all over the place and it felt as if they were working backwards. Normally there would be a briefing first, where tasks were handed out to investigate, but the location of High Wraith Cottage was so remote there were literally no leads to follow up. First, they needed to identify their victim. Morgan's phone pinged with a WhatsApp message from Wendy. She opened it up to see a passport photograph of Margery Lancaster. The woman staring back at her had dark hair with strands of white running through it, brown eyes, a furrowed brow as if she had spent her entire life scowling, and an expression on her face that made Morgan feel sad for her.

She wasn't a happy woman, which to be fair was a blatantly obvious observation. They say a picture can speak a thousand words and this one did. It told Morgan that Margery was angry, sad, lonely and probably mistrusted most people, which was why she preferred to live alone in the middle of nowhere.

Morgan tucked her phone in her pocket. Could you ever repent for the crimes that you committed? If this was the same woman waiting to be cut open from her breastbone to her pubic bone in the mortuary, had she ever forgiven herself for almost killing her husband and baby? She didn't know if you could unless she was a pure psychopath and had no empathy for anyone.

Morgan closed her eyes and tried to imagine how she would feel if she ever did something so terrible. She had come close to extreme violence a few times, but that had been in self-defence. She had been put into circumstances that dictated her actions and whether because of them, she would live or die. That was different, wasn't it? She was pretty sure it was. She didn't feel any remorse over them; she would rather be here to tell the tale to the judge than the one waiting on the table to be dissected like a lab specimen.

'Morgan, are you good to go?'

Susie's voice startled her. 'Yes, sorry, just trying to warm myself up.'

'Oh, you're not going to feel any better going in there. Here.' She threw Morgan a bright yellow cardigan with purple stripes that only Susie would wear. 'It's gonna clash with your hair, but you'll thank me for it. It's that cold in there today I've had to put an extra thermal vest on to stop my nipples from standing to attention.'

Morgan grinned at her. 'Thank you.' Then followed her inside, where everyone was waiting. Claire, the Barrow CSI, and Ian, the Crime Scene Manager, who was a waste of time and hadn't made a very good impression on the team so far, had been given the honour of attending to document the procedure, with Wendy and Joe both still working at the scene.

Ben smiled at her, and she gave him a thumbs up. Declan's radio had Classic FM playing in the background. He was very good at choosing music to work to that he thought the victims might enjoy. Morgan wasn't sure if Margery would thank him for it if she was alive. It didn't seem as if she found much pleasure in anything judging by her cottage.

Declan clapped his hands, and everyone looked at him.

'Are we all ready, are we focused? Let's see who we have here, shall we? Claire, I'm going to wait for you to finish photographing the body as it is before I begin to weigh, measure and the rest of it. It's a bit like that game show where they show you around some rich person's home and ask you: "Who lives in a home like this?". Only we're going to be asking who it is under the hood.'

'*Through the Keyhole*,' said Ian.

'What is?' replied Declan.

'The game show, it's called *Through the Keyhole*.'

'Yes, that's the one. Very good.'

Morgan stood next to Ben while the preliminaries were carried out. She showed him the photograph Wendy had sent over. He looked at it and shook his head.

'I don't recognise her. It could have been when I was in training or working in London – I did a secondment down there, or maybe even earlier.'

Eventually it was time to remove the black hood that had been tied around the victim's neck, and Morgan felt her heart begin to race a little. *What if it wasn't Margery Lancaster under there and somebody else? What if she had killed again?* Morgan watched, unable to tear her gaze away as the rope was cut away from the knot that secured it and photographed in detail. Then the hood was removed, and the terrified face of Margery Lancaster stared back at her.

Margery's eyes were wide open, protruding from the sockets, her tongue lolled at the side of her open mouth. Morgan thought that it would make a terrifying death mask. A killer had once sent her some that he'd made of his victims, but somehow their expressions hadn't been as haunting as Margery's.

Everyone in the room let out a low murmur or gasp of horror.

Declan was shaking his head. 'If her heart didn't give out first, I'd be surprised; that is a look of pure terror in those eyes. Although it can't have done because she was gasping for air when the noose was tightened around her throat, that much is clear without me telling you.' He bent closer and whispered, 'I am truly sorry you have suffered this way. I'm Declan, the pathologist, and I'm going to be looking after you now, along with my assistant Susie. We will take care of you and hopefully find the evidence we need to track down whoever did this to you, my love.'

Morgan felt sad, those were probably the kindest words anyone had ever spoken to Margery Lancaster in a very long time, and she couldn't hear them because she was dead.

6

Declan nodded at Susie. 'You can reunite Margery with her heart and kidneys now.' Susie took the bag of carefully weighed and measured organs that had been removed and placed it into Margery's stomach cavity ready to sew up.

Morgan had survived this examination, unlike the last she'd attended, when she had passed out cold on the floor. Not because of the brutal procedures that the bodies were put through – because she was a little hardened to that part unfortunately – but because she had known the victim, Lexie White, a little too well.

Declan began to strip off his mask, then apron and finally his gloves. 'I'll meet you guys in my office, I need a bathroom break.'

Morgan was still cold, but not as much as when she'd first arrived. In the changing rooms she took off Susie's cardigan and hung it up on the peg. It had been a couple of hours since they'd first gone in and she was hungry, also still in dire need of coffee. She hadn't eaten or drunk anything, and she felt queasy. Her boots had gone stiff as they'd dried out, but at least they were no longer soggy and for that she was relieved as she pulled them on, tucking the legs of the scrubs into them. By the time she walked into Declan's office, he was already in there sitting behind his desk.

'What do you know then? Are there next of kin who are going to want to come and see her or are you happy we identified her from the photo and prints?'

Ben nodded. 'The prints don't lie, and I'm not sure she had anyone to come and see her.'

There had been no wedding band or engagement ring on her fingers – there had been no jewellery at all. The only thing of sentimental value to her had been the fine gold crucifix around her neck. A smaller version of the one Morgan wore herself; she felt sad for the woman and couldn't stop thinking about her.

Declan had a filter coffee machine in his office, and it smelled like heaven to Morgan as he filled it up and the water began to drip through into the coffee pot.

'Have you got anything to eat? I didn't make breakfast this morning and feel a bit sick.'

Ben turned to her. 'Why did you not eat something before you came to work?'

'I was hoping to grab a bacon roll from the canteen. I didn't know we would get called out straight away.'

Declan tutted at her. 'Morgan you should never presume that you won't be getting called out. I'm surprised you didn't faint watching that on an empty stomach.'

'I'm relieved I didn't.'

He opened a drawer and rooted around until he found a chocolate bar and tossed the chunky KitKat her way. She caught it and sighed. 'Thanks, this is great.'

Ben's phone began to vibrate. He answered it and excused himself, leaving the office to talk to Marc whose voice Morgan would recognise anywhere. He had a light Manchester accent and spoke louder the more animated he got.

Declan passed her a chipped mug of fresh coffee, and she took a sip, savouring the first hit of caffeine as it entered her body.

'How are you anyway? It feels like forever since we saw you out of work.'

'Good, does it? We better remedy that then. Why don't you and Ben come to mine for supper at the weekend if you're not working.'

'That would be lovely. Are you and Theo still a thing?'

'A thing? I don't know if we are. What is that, Morgan, is it some kind of affliction, disease or are you referring to our loving relationship, which, in that case it is definitely not a thing.'

She laughed. 'Sorry, the relationship part, that's what I meant.'

'Mmn, apology accepted but only because I love you so much. To be honest, I'm surprised myself at how well it's going. I was telling Susie this morning. He's a good man; he's everything I could wish for in a partner. He's independent, funny, kind, considerate in and out of bed.' He winked at her. 'I suppose he's like my version of Ben, and seeing as how I never got the man of my dreams because some red-haired harlot beat me to it, Theo will have to do.'

Morgan's mouth dropped open and she didn't know whether to laugh or cry. 'I am not a harlot, and you never said you were in love with him.'

He shrugged. 'I didn't have to, did I? It was never going to happen; he's straighter than that ruler on my desk. He's my best friend though, so that was enough for me. Don't tell him that, by the way, it's our little secret.'

Ben walked in. 'Don't tell him what?'

Morgan shook her head. 'Not my story to tell, just some gossip. What did Marc want?'

'Us, back at the station for a briefing. He said the DCI is

having a meltdown that we decided to do the post-mortem before discussing anything else.'

'Oh, God. What did you say?'

'That we had very little else to do due to the extreme weather situation and that I called it. At least we have a positive ID of the victim and managed to preserve what little forensics there might be. He shut up then and started listening, but said there is going to be a huge news story when it breaks; the press are going to be all over it.'

Declan passed him a mug. 'Well, death was by asphyxiation that much is positive. I didn't see any obvious signs of drugs in her body, but it doesn't mean that there aren't any. We're going to have to wait for the toxicology results to come back for that one. I'm hoping the scrapings from underneath her nails will give us a DNA profile that you can match on the database. It looks as if she put up a fight at the last minute, probably when she realised exactly what was happening. That hood over her head was a good old Asda pillowcase; might be useful, but again we're going to have to wait for the tests to come back.'

Morgan couldn't stop thinking about Margery's hatred for her husband and son; they had the most to gain from killing her so brutally; had they come for their revenge after all?

7

Ben drove them home to get changed. Morgan had never had so many changes of clothes in the space of a few hours. They rushed inside still wearing the scrubs that they had borrowed from the mortuary; their neighbour, Mrs Walker, who was standing at her front door gossiping with the post lady, did a double-take at their attire, her mouth forming a perfect oh shape. She knew they were coppers, made a point of talking about the latest crimes reported in the *News & Star* to them when she caught them going in and out.

Ben waved at her, shouting, 'Good afternoon, Mrs Walker.' Then turned away before she could question him. Morgan had to stifle the laughter as she pushed him inside the hallway and slammed the door shut behind them.

'You're awful.'

'I know, but I couldn't resist it. She thinks we don't notice her watching us? At least it's going to give her something to gossip about for the next week. Did you see her face?'

Morgan nodded, kicked off her boots and ran upstairs. Ben followed and in less than ten minutes the pair of them were in fresh sets of clothes, dry shoes, and munching on cheese,

tomato and onion sandwiches that Morgan had thrown
together.

When they left in their usual work attire looking more like
the detectives they were, Mrs Walker was peering out of her
large bay window.

'She's good, you know, a one-woman neighbourhood watch
system. Maybe we should be a little nicer to her,' Morgan said
as she slammed the car door closed before the woman could
come out and call them over for the third degree.

Ben shrugged. 'We could and probably should. You're nice
to her all the time.'

'Yeah, but you're not. She doesn't know how to take you.'

'Enough about Mrs Walker, we need to get back to work
before Marc has a meltdown. He was getting close when we
spoke last time.'

The rain had finally stopped by the time Ben parked outside the
station, though the sky was still grey. Morgan felt as if she'd
forgotten how good the sun felt on her fair skin, even though it
did burn her. As much as she loved all things dark and Gothic,
she also loved warmer, drier days where she could get up early
and watch the sun rising over the background of the mountain
tops, or setting over one of the many beautiful lakes.

Cain and Amy were back in the office, empty sandwich
cartons and crisp bags on the desks. As Ben and Morgan walked
in, Cain waved a bag of salt and vinegar crisps in their direction.

'Want some?'

Morgan shook her head, but Ben held out his hands and
caught the packet as Cain launched it through the air towards
him.

'How did it go?'

'Same as always: crap. We managed to ID her though. It is
Margery Lancaster. And we can confirm it wasn't suicide. It

was murder. How did you both get on with the caller who phoned it in?'

Cain glanced at Amy then back at Ben. 'We didn't get that far, sorry. Marc was pretty keen that we return for the briefing.'

Amy was bent over her keyboard and began typing Margery's name into the intelligence system. A small square with a picture of the dead woman appeared in the corner. She double clicked on it to open the file.

'Wow, I thought it was her when I sent you that photo; I knew the name was familiar. They nicknamed her "The Iron Lady Killer" because she crushed up a load of the iron tablets the doctor prescribed her after having a baby and fed them to her husband and baby boy in their food.'

Ben scrubbed his hand across his face. 'Jesus, for real?'

Amy nodded. 'For real, look.'

She turned the computer monitor so they could see the headlines on the newspaper articles. He leaned over to read them. 'Send these to me, please. What happened to them, her husband and baby afterwards, does it say?'

'They were both seriously ill, but he realised what she'd done when he found the empty bottles in the bin and got help for them both. They survived. The baby was in hospital a long time; the husband didn't do too well either.' She turned to back to the screen. 'You just don't know if something like that is going to affect you in the long term, do you?'

Morgan shook her head; she was busy writing notes.

Iron poisoning, husband, son where are they now? Do they live in the area, family?

Marc popped his head through the door. 'Right then, blue room when you're ready because I've got heartburn with this cock-up of an investigation, and I can't cope with how it's all screwed up and arse about face. I want the details, facts and some kind of clarification that you lot know what you're doing and haven't royally screwed up a murder scene.'

Then he was gone, leaving everyone staring at Ben. It was Amy who swore under her breath.

'Is he for real? Did he bother getting his arse wet to come and attend the scene? No, he didn't, he stayed in that nice warm office while we all got bloody pneumonia.'

Cain patted her arm, mimicking Marc. 'Calm down, our kid, it's all right, the boss will get him told. Won't you, boss?'

Ben nodded, and Morgan could see he wasn't in the right frame of mind for any of this. Marc's mood swings were the last thing any of them needed.

'Come on, let's go put him straight.'

He led them out of the office, the major investigation folder under his arm, towards the blue room, his loyal team following. They would put their lives on the line to protect their boss and friend. Morgan wondered if Ben knew just how loyal they all were to him. She hoped that he did because it was a rare thing to have a group of people so focused on catching the criminals and all liking each other at the same time, who would defend you to the last and not stab you in the back.

8

Marc was pacing up and down the briefing room like a panther stalking its prey, and Morgan had a feeling Ben was his victim.

'Boss,' Ben and Cain both said at the same time, nodding at him. Both Morgan and Amy ignored him and sat down as far from him as possible; neither of them in the mood to be bollocked after the day they'd had so far. Wendy and Joe filed in behind them, along with Al and the rest of the task force team that were on duty. Claire, the detective chief inspector from the murder investigation team up at headquarters, was dialling into the meeting, and her face appeared on the smart board.

'Claire, glad you could join us.' Marc waved at her then continued. 'Are we all here? Looks like it. There's no point in wasting any time. Ben, you might as well talk us through what the hell is going on.'

Ben's cheeks were a little pinker than usual as he stood up, and Morgan got the impression that he was wishing Marc would crawl back into his office and leave them alone.

'Well, as you know, the body of a female was found by a guy who got lost looking for his Airbnb. She has been identified as

Margery Lancaster by her driving licence and fingerprints, and this has also been confirmed at the post-mortem.'

A couple of murmurs went around the room. It was Al who asked, 'The iron lady? It was her?'

Ben nodded. 'So it seems, yes, it was. For now, let's forget about her past and focus on the present. We have clear indications of foul play. We're here to give a voice to Margery because hers was taken away and for the time being I don't care what she did in the past. Judging by her lifestyle, I'm sure she suffered her whole life. I care about finding the person who killed her. Somebody decided to kill her. Tie a noose around her neck and put a bag over her head. She must have put up a fight once she realised what was about to happen, as she's left us some nice forensics in her fingernails, which Doctor Donnelly is analysing.'

Heads were nodding in appreciation of Margery's bravado and potential DNA capture.

Ben continued. 'There are no neighbouring properties to High Wraith Cottage, and absolutely no CCTV close by. The closest potential for CCTV is the farm at the bottom of the valley. Cain, can you go there and speak to the farmer? If the road is captured on a camera we might see a vehicle passing some time last night. We don't have any tyre marks leading up to the house because of the storm, but one thing to do is to figure out how our killed gained access to the cottage.

'Amy, can you check ANPR to see if the cameras that cover entry into that area of the fells captured anything useful? I'm not hopeful, as there are numerous small back roads the killer could have taken.

'Shortly after arriving on the scene, the branch holding Margery's body snapped under her weight. She fell into a wet pool of muddy water. I consulted the home office pathologist who advised us to preserve her hands then get her moved out of the rain ASAP before all potential evidence was lost. By doing just that we did preserve what little evidence was left'—Ben glanced over at Marc as if to defend his actions—'If we hadn't moved her body then, we would have lost any forensic evidence.'

Marc nodded, and Claire, who hadn't spoken yet, held up her hand. 'Well done, Ben, team. You did the right thing as far as I'm concerned. It sounds like you salvaged the DNA evidence under the fingernails, so well done. This weather has been horrendous, we all know that and to work out on a fell in the middle of a storm that's raging around you was brilliant teamwork. Excellent work, wouldn't you agree, Inspector?'

Marc nodded. 'Yes, I do. It was just a bit of a shock; I'm not used to that kind of improvisation.'

Morgan couldn't stop herself. 'Yes, I suppose working in an inner city like Manchester doesn't mean you have to stand out for hours in the middle of a raging storm trying your best to do what's right.'

Both Cain and Amy sniggered behind cupped hands. Ben looked mortified, but Morgan didn't care; they had done what they could, and he was all too ready to slam them down for it. That was the one thing she hated about this job: management would rather tear you down and criticise than give praise where it was due, except for Ben. He really was the exception, and she knew that if she ever did decide to go for promotion then it would be his leadership skills she would follow and not Marc's.

'Thank you, Morgan. Right, where was I?' Ben continued. 'Yes, as I said, the body had a bag over the head. Wendy, could you get a photo up for me?'

Wendy moved across to where Marc's laptop was set up on the desk and brought up the images that had been taken when she'd first arrived at the crime scene. It didn't matter how many times Morgan looked at them it still gave her the same shock value, they were awful. In fact, she would go so far as to say they were terrifying. The body was dangling precariously from the branch of the old oak tree, the hood over the head making it look like something out of a horror film, along with the chains around the wrists. Margery's bare feet dangled towards the muddy earth, and Morgan felt a cold shiver run down the full length of her spine, thinking how Margery's feet must have been so cold. Wendy brought up another image, this time the body was lying on the ground in a puddle of muddy rainwater, the branch still attached to the rope half stuck in the sodden earth, the other half embedded through the windscreen of the ambulance.

'Bloody hell,' said Al out loud. 'That's awful, I bet the paramedics were well pissed off with that result.'

Ben was nodding. 'They were a little bit miffed to be fair. The bag, which is actually a pillowcase, is black and has Asda tags. Where is the nearest store that sells bedding? I can't say I shop there much apart from the one in Barrow if I'm passing through.'

Amy was counting on her fingers. 'Kendal, Barrow, Lancaster, Morecambe, Blackpool, Preston.'

'Six, that's a lot but not too bad. I think we're going to have to speak to each store, concentrating on Kendal and Barrow, initially, to get a list of recent purchases. I'll get Lancs police to do the enquiries their side of the border, maybe get the PCSOs on it; they'll know who to speak to in store.'

'Bit like looking for a needle in a haystack that, boss.' Amy said.

'Can you think of a better way of tracking down who bought that pillowcase?'

'It might have been one from the cottage.'

Ben nodded, then looked to Wendy. 'Do you know if there were any missing pillowcases out of the cottage?'

She shook her head. 'Not out of Margery's bedroom, but I'll be honest the rest of the house is like a hoarder's house, so I didn't notice upstairs because the bed was covered in clothes and books. Didn't look as if it had been touched in years.'

He smiled encouragingly, and she nodded. 'I'm going back after this anyway; I'll take another look around.'

'Thanks, Amy, that's a valid point. I still want PCSOs going to the Asda stores to follow it up. Who is to say we won't get a nice clear image of the killer walking out with a pair of black pillowcases in hand.'

Morgan knew the likelihood of this happening was probably a million to one, but it had to be done because occasionally suspects weren't that bright or clever. They could mess up, not all of them watched every crime documentary on the television or listened to true crime podcasts, unlike her who thrived off them. She'd been prepping to be a detective as soon as she realised that the bookshop had a whole section on true crime books. Her first serious book had been *The Stranger Beside Me* by Ann Rule, inspired by Ann's relationship with Ted Bundy, and she still had the well-worn, dog-eared copy on the bookcase in Ben's spare room.

'The chains around Margery's wrists weren't, as far as we could see, branded, but Wendy will send photos out to the PCSOs. Ask them to visit all the hardware stores in the county to see if anyone has purchased any similar chains recently.'

Claire was taking notes, and she looked up, into the camera. 'What about Margery's son and husband, do we know where they are? It's pretty obvious they both have a good enough motive, but would they wait years before exacting their revenge? Would they really want to risk the lives they're leading now over getting revenge for something that happened a long time ago? That would be my question.'

Ben was nodding his agreement. 'I'm taking Morgan with me, and we'll visit her ex-husband and son, see what they have to say, if they have contact with her and if they want to go see her now. I'll keep you updated.

'Wendy, did you get anything from the cottage? We found

evidence of a purposefully broken kitchen window and foot-prints in the earth beneath it.'

'We found some partials off the broken window. Could be Margery's fingerprints, but we'll find out. There were also a couple of drops of blood, so whoever broke it cut themselves, only a scratch though because there was no further trail. Joe managed to salvage one of the footprints, the rest were smeared with the mud and not clear enough, but they were facing towards the cottage so I'm going to suggest that they didn't leave that way. Although it's pretty obvious they didn't, since the front door of the cottage was wide open. It seems clear Margery was taken out through there. It would have been logical, since the tree was closest to that exit, and her body would have been heavy to carry around.'

Al was nodding. 'So, you want a full search carrying out?'

'Yes, please.' Ben glanced at Daisy who was leaning against the wall with her arms crossed. 'And, Daisy, if you can take a look, too, that would be appreciated.'

Daisy was watching Morgan, and she lifted her eyes to his and smiled at him. 'Yes, boss,' she said in her soft voice.

'Right, well that's it, I think, for the time being. Be careful out there, the roads are waterlogged, there's a lot of water coming down off the fells and some parts are flooded. If you can't get past, don't risk it, turn around and come back. Thank you all.'

Everyone began to leave the too small room that was still pink and not blue, but the name The Iron Lady Killer used in the blue room had stuck just like nicknames stuck on certain coppers – once they were given, they were never forgotten.

9

Morgan went back into the office. Dragging her chair as close to the radiator as possible, she huddled next to it. The light drizzle had now turned back into a steady downpour, and she could think of many things she would rather be doing than having to go back out in it. Amy came in carrying a tray with four mugs on it.

'You are a lifesaver.'

She laughed. 'I think that might be a bit over-appreciative and dramatic, Morgan, it's only Gold Blend and milk with a little hot water.'

Morgan shrugged and took a mug off the tray. 'I don't know what to think about all of this, it's just awful what has happened to her, but she can't have been a very nice person. I suppose I can understand some sort of motivation to poison her husband, if he was abusive or threatened her? If he was horrible? But her own baby?'

'Yeah, but she could have had major post-natal depression, and nobody realised? I've never wanted kids; my sister has three and they are amazing, but honestly, for the first four years of their lives she was severely sleep-deprived. That's torture, actual torture used to break people. Was she extremely unwell and totally forgotten by society? Did we fail to help her back then?'

Morgan nodded. 'You're right. What if she didn't have support? What if she was at breaking point? What if she was unwell? Did she see a red mist and make one terrible mistake? I think we need to find out a lot more about her circumstances before I go around judging her. She's still a victim of a horrific crime regardless of what she did in the past.'

Morgan scooted back to her desk and logged on to take a look at Margery's intelligence records. There were markers for mental health and violence on there. She brought up the reports about her and began to read through them, but there was nothing until the day her husband and baby got rushed to hospital. There wasn't much after either. She pled guilty so there was no trial, which was probably the reason it hadn't been as much of a long-running scandal in the newspapers. According to this she had served thirteen years in a low secure mental health unit, then was released under licence for two years.

She never broke the conditions of her licence, except for one episode. The offender management team had visited and found her smashing the cottage up with a hammer. She was taken to hospital, kept in Dane Garth Mental Health Unit for forty-eight hours then released with a new prescription for medication.

'Blimey there's not much on here is there? It's like nobody bothered with her before or after her crime. She was diagnosed with a mental health disorder and then left to rot. No social worker. No check-ins? I wonder if it was a cry for help?'

'What, trying to kill her family or smashing her house up?'

'Both.'

Amy shrugged. 'In my experience you don't serve your whole sentence unless you show no remorse for what you've done. If she'd been crying and sad, they would have probably released her after a couple of years.'

Morgan wrote down the name of the doctor who had prescribed Margery's most recent medication. She wanted to talk to her to see what kind of woman Margery Lancaster was and find out if she had any medical conditions that would have made her act the way she did. Then she clicked on the file for her husband and began to read the long list of violent offences he'd been arrested for over the years. He smashed someone over the head with a glass bottle in the pub, had numerous drunken fights; there was a domestic violence marker against his name but not for Margery, it was for his previous partner, Lynn Scott. He had broken her nose, blacked her eyes and dragged her out of the pub by her hair in front of an audience. 'Wow, he is a nasty piece of work. Did you look at his file?'

Amy shook her head. 'Not yet.'

'He beat his ex-partner several times, got in lots of drunken fights. There is no way he didn't hit Margery; he didn't meet her and decide not to be violent anymore. I wonder how many injuries she sustained at his hands and kept quiet about. If he abused her then perhaps that's why she poisoned him.'

'Maybe, but what about the baby? There is no reason to poison the kid too.'

'Unless it was an accident. Or she thought he was going to turn out just like his dad and she was trying to stop another bully going out into the world, repeating the same kind of violence over and over. I'm not saying it's justified what she did to the baby, but what I'm saying is she had her reasons, and if she was mentally unstable, she probably thought that she was stopping anyone else from being hurt the way she was. Now I do feel bad for her.'

'Morgan, you need to speak to the kid and the husband. She might have been a total psychopath; would she not have reported him if he hurt her so badly? Did Declan pick up on any old injuries, broken bones that had happened a long time ago?'

'Not reported yet, but it doesn't mean that he didn't hurt her. Maybe he got clever and didn't cause injuries that needed hospital treatment.'

Ben came in, his cheeks red, his tie loosened along with the top two buttons of his shirt. 'Don't let me interrupt you, what's this discussion you're both having?'

Amy pointed at Morgan. 'We're discussing Margery's crimes and if they were the motivation for her murder or if this was a random act of violence.'

'What did you conclude?'

Morgan shrugged. 'Nothing yet, I don't think we can make assumptions until we've spoken to her doctor, ex-husband and son.'

'Have you got the addresses?'

'I've got her husband; there is nothing on the system about her son or what happened to him after the poisoning.'

He rolled his eyes. 'There's a surprise.' He picked up a mug of coffee and drank it down like it was a cold pint of beer. 'Jesus, Amy, don't go offering your skills as a barista anytime soon that was awful.'

Amy glared at him. 'You cheeky sod, make your own next time.'

'Joking, it was okay, well it was drinkable. Morgan?'

She was on the phone to the PNC bureau and passing the names to them to see if they had any more recent addresses. 'One minute.' She scribbled down the address passed to her and hung up.

'Guess where her husband lives?'

'No idea, put me out of my misery.'

'Kendal.'

Ben groaned. 'It's going to be a right pain trying to get back there.'

'Yes, but what else is there in Kendal?'

Amy grinned. 'Asda.'

'You never know. If we could get a hold of his bank statements, we could see if he's been shopping there and what date, time.'

'I like that train of thought. You two are good, has anyone ever told you that?'

Morgan smiled at him. 'We don't need telling, we know.'

She stood up, re-energised and ready to go meet George Lancaster. She imagined he wouldn't be sad at the news of Margery's death, and there was even a chance he already knew about it.

10

George Lancaster lived in a brand-new assisted living apartment in a complex that was situated near to the River Kent. He had a ground-floor flat. Morgan rang the communal doorbell for George's flat.

'*Who is it?*' The voice was gruff and breathing heavily through the intercom.

'Police, we need to talk to you.'

There was no reply, but the door clicked, and Ben pushed it open so they could get inside of the communal hallway. It smelled of new paint and plaster which was a refreshing change.

Morgan led the way to number nine. The door was ajar.

'Come in.'

They stepped inside, and Morgan was surprised to see George Lancaster only had one leg, his other had been amputated above the knee. He was sitting in an armchair with a pair of crutches leaning against the wall next to him.

'I think I can guess why you're here, so tell me what the crazy bitch has done now? Have a seat.'

They both sat down on the sofa. Ben took the lead. 'I'm not sure what you mean. Who are you referring to, George?'

George rolled his eyes. 'Let's not play games. She has been the pain in my backside my entire life. I rue the day I ever met Margery. I should have known she wasn't wired right.' He tapped the side of his temple with a finger.

Morgan took a dislike to George; she couldn't help it and she knew it wasn't very professional of her, but there was something about him that got under her skin.

Ben was nodding. 'I'm afraid we have some bad news for you.'

This made George look up from the TV remote he'd been playing with. 'You do, is she dead? Christ, please tell me she is. Do you have any idea how long I've waited for someone to tell me that she died and is out of my life for good?'

Morgan answered before Ben could. 'Yes, she is. She was murdered, and I'd like to ask you where you were last night.'

He laughed so hard it took him a couple of minutes to compose himself. Then he looked at Ben. 'Is she for real? Is she a copper or one of those pretend ones who volunteer for the thrill of it?'

'Let's start again, George. I'm Detective Sergeant Ben Matthews and this is my colleague Detective Constable Morgan Brookes. Margery was murdered in the early hours of the morning, and we do need to know where you were last night.'

He was still shaking his head. 'How did she die?'

'You tell us where you were, and I'll tell you the circumstances.'

'I was here, where do you think? Trying to kill her with my prosthetic leg? I can only get around here on crutches because it's so small. I am not an Olympic athlete in case you hadn't worked that one out.'

Morgan asked. 'Do you have a car?'

'Well, yes I do.'

'What kind is it, make, model, registration?'

'Is she taking the piss?' He was asking Ben, who nodded at him to answer the questions.

'It's a Vauxhall Mokka, blue, PEO 72.' He paused. 'I can't bloody remember, it's out in the car park in a disabled bay. You can get it yourself on the way out. So, what happened? You said someone killed her. How?'

Ben gently nudged Morgan's elbow with the slightest movement, and she knew he wanted to ask the questions, which was fine by her because George Lancaster was a dick.

'She was hung from the tree in the front garden of High Wraith Cottage.'

Finally, a reaction from the man whose mouth dropped open. 'She was? Well, I can't say I'm sad about it. Shocked a little, but there is no love lost between me and Margery.'

'Why is that?'

'If you'd done your homework, you would know that the bitch tried to kill me and our baby boy. That's why.'

'Why did she do that?' Morgan continued. George would have had years to consider this, and she wondered if he'd mention any disagreements, any fights... his violence.

'How do I know? She always had a screw loose. She just decided she didn't want the pair of us in her life, so she thought she'd poison us instead. The doctor said she was anaemic after the boy was born, and he put her on iron tablets. What she needed was Valium or something, but he didn't prescribe those when he should have. She never remembered to take the iron tablets though and had a stack of them in the cupboard. She ground them up and laced our food with them one day.'

Morgan was writing all of this down. She looked up at him. 'Could you not taste the poison? It can't have been nice to swallow.' She stared at George, and he stared right back.

'She was a good cook, I'll give her that much. She made a syrup sponge pudding with homemade custard then sprinkled the tablets all over it and must have covered it in sugar and syrup, so we didn't taste it. Only I knew when I was eating it something wasn't right with it. Not at first, I ate half of it, but then I got this horrible metallic taste in my mouth as if I'd been sucking on a two pence piece. I didn't finish it like I normally would, which is probably what saved my life. She was standing in the kitchen watching me, and by this time she'd fed David his pudding; poor little bugger had eaten it all. It took a while but then I got the worst stomach cramps I'd ever had in my life and ran to the toilet thinking I was going to explode. By the time I'd come out the baby was screaming and vomiting. I don't know if she felt bad, but her face was white. I began to vomit and could barely move, I rang for an ambulance but it could have taken hours to find the address; back then there was no GPS. Margery put us in the car and drove us to the hospital. I never did figure out if it was guilt that made her drive us there. I don't remember much except that I was burning up and in agony with my stomach. I could hear the baby screaming too in the cubicle next to me and I couldn't do anything to help him.'

'When did you find out it was an overdose?'

'The next day, the doctor came and told me that Margery had confessed to a nurse who was trying to look after David what she'd done. By this time, she'd been arrested and put in prison or wherever. I didn't care, I never wanted to see her again.'

'But you did?'

'Well of course I did, her face was all over the newspapers at the time, but she didn't make us go to court. She had the decency to plead guilty.'

'What happened to David?'

'I was ill for a long time; it took a lot longer to recover

because I'd ingested a lot more than he did and I got blood poisoning. He got put into foster care.'

Morgan was shocked. Why didn't George take over custody? 'You didn't want to look after your boy yourself?'

George paused before shaking his head. 'I didn't want to upset him anymore than what he'd been through. I wasn't fit enough to look after him. I got sepsis and had to have my leg removed below the knee, and his mother was in prison for trying to kill him. I thought it was best to leave him be, let him forget all about it and start a new life as far away from me and Margery as possible.'

Ben nodded; Morgan was taking notes. 'That must have been hard.'

George shrugged. 'It was but I knew it was for the best.'

'Do you ever see him now; did he ever try and find his birth parents?'

'I've met him once; he came looking, asking all sorts of questions. I answered them the best that I could then I sent him on his way.'

'Did you not want to restart a relationship with him?'

'What's the point? He's a grown man. Too much time has passed. All I am to him is a reminder that his mother hated him and me so much she would rather kill us than live with us. Who knows how that would mess with your mind?'

'Why did she want to kill you both? She must have had a reason,' Morgan asked, she couldn't help herself.

He looked her up and down before answering. 'Because she was crazy, and she decided she didn't want a family. She found being a mother too hard, and she disliked being told what to do. She had a mind of her own, did Margery, and it did her no good at all.'

Morgan didn't like being told what to do either, and she wondered just how much George pushed Margery about. 'Have you got an address for David?'

'No, I told him I didn't want to know where he lived. I didn't want to know anything about him really. What was the point? He stopped being my son the moment he was taken away. She took him away from me and at the time I wished that she'd killed me instead. I've never loved anyone like I loved him, but I couldn't look at him after that, all I saw was Maggie when I looked into his face, and I couldn't do it. I was so angry with her; I didn't want a daily reminder. Not knowing that Maggie had tried to kill us both. Plus I didn't want to have to bring him up on my own, it's woman's work looking after kids; I had nobody to help me do that. Bloody shame I married a woman who didn't realise that was the deal.'

'Did you hurt your wife, George? Did you abuse her?'

'I did what was necessary, nothing more or less. Back then you could give your wife a good slap if she deserved it, same as you could have sex with her without her being able to cry rape. That was what a marriage was, you put up with it. It's ridiculous now, I don't know why anyone would bother getting married.'

Morgan felt the skin on the back of her neck crawl. She disliked George Lancaster and his almost Puritan thoughts on marriage more than she imagined she would and wanted to get out of there. She was beginning to understand how Margery would have wanted to poison him, but she didn't understand why she would have done that to her baby.

'Could I use the bathroom please?'

George rolled his eyes at Ben but pointed to the little corridor past the kitchen area. Morgan had to clamp her lips shut, he was horrible. She saw the bathroom door was ajar, but ignored that and pushed open the bedroom door, taking a cursory glance at the bed to see if there were any black pillow-cases or bedding on it.

'Next one, love, not much happens in there anymore.'

George laughed and she felt the hairs on the back of her neck bristle, but she pulled the door shut and walked into the bathroom closing the door. She didn't want the toilet, but at least she knew George wasn't sleeping in a bed with black coloured bedding or missing a matching pillowcase.

11

MAGGIE

David had been crying for hours, nonstop crying, and Maggie was about ready to launch him at the wall. She was overwhelmed with feelings of hatred towards him. All she could think was that she hadn't wanted him, but she knew no one would understand. Who could she tell? What could she do?

She closed her eyes, thinking back to the time when she'd just found out she was pregnant. Her mum told her before she died that now she was married, the next step was kids. When she'd started feeling sick she had known the cause of it was going to be a baby. The smell of coffee which she loved so much now turned her stomach and made her feel queasy, so she had gone to the chemist and bought a pregnancy test. Too scared to do it at home, she'd gone to the public toilets in Windermere. She hadn't wanted anyone she knew to see her.

She had sat in the cubicle and cried after the plus sign had finally appeared. She had thrown the test in the bin and wandered out onto the main street. The number six bus was making its way down the main road and for a split second she had considered throwing herself under it and ending it all. Then she'd seen the group of school kids on the top deck and realised she couldn't do that to them; they didn't deserve to have their day and the rest of their lives spoiled by the selfish woman who had decided to kill herself while they were on a school trip.

She had wandered around in a daze, then finally realised she only had a few hours before George came home. She hadn't told him when she left the house, or he wouldn't have let her; he liked her to be at home all day cleaning and cooking. When she'd talked to her mum about him just before she'd moved into the retirement home, she'd told her that was all part and parcel of being a wife. She was there to look after him regardless of whether she wanted to or not. Too late Maggie had realised that she most certainly did not want to. She wanted a life of freedom, not this. Some days he was okay; he could still be nice if everything went how he wanted it to, if she didn't argue or disagree with him. She was learning not to argue back with him because it didn't help her situation at all and made her dislike him even more, and it hurt too much to tell George how she felt about him – the bruises would last for days.

It wouldn't be so bad if she had a friend to talk to about it, but she didn't have anyone. Her best friend had moved away to go to college, and she had never been a people person. She felt so utterly lost.

While she waited for the bus, she looked in the newsagent's windows and saw a white card that said:

Want to know your future? I can read your tea leaves and tell you what you have in store. If you prefer to have your cards read, then I offer that and can make any kind of tea you need.

It was just the direction she needed. She felt out of control, but this might tell her everything was going to be okay.

Maggie took a pen out of her handbag and scribbled the telephone number down on her hand. She would write it somewhere when she got home where George wouldn't see it. Then she spied a telephone box and before she knew it, was rooting around in her purse for some change to feed into it, feeling scared and a little nervous; she didn't talk to strangers; she didn't talk much to people she *did* know. She picked up the receiver and pressed the numbers into the keypad. The phone on the other end began to ring but was picked up straight away.

'*Hello.*'

'Hello.'

'*Can I help you?*'

'I saw your number in the shop window. Could you read my tea leaves or cards? I don't care which one.'

'*I can do that, of course I can. When would you want to do it?*'

'It has to be after ten in the morning and before two in the afternoon. Where are you based?'

'*I have a room above the hairdressers a few doors down from the newsagents in Windermere, where I suspect you just read my card. I was going to call it a day, but can you come now? I have a feeling it's urgent.*'

Maggie looked around the street and saw the hairdressers. 'I can come now; how much is it?'

'*We will sort that out when you come here.*'

'Okay, thank you.'

The pips began to beep, and she hung up. There was no point putting another ten pence in as they had finished talking. As she stepped out of the phone box she felt as if she was breaking every single rule in the book. Don't talk to strangers about your marriage. Don't tell anyone your business.

Putting her head down she hurried towards the hairdressers. Pressing the handle down, it didn't budge, and she realised it was shut. All the hope she'd been feeling washed away as she looked up at the small window on the first floor that was open slightly; it was all in darkness. Then she heard a voice shout through the gap, 'Won't be a sec, I'm coming down.'

Relief flooded her veins. She wasn't sure why, but she knew she needed to talk to this woman before she spoke to George about anything. The door unlocked, and the most beautiful woman Maggie had ever seen stood there smiling at her. She had magnificent red hair, creamy skin with a smattering of freckles across her nose and the greenest eyes. She was wearing a black velvet cloak.

'Come on, quick, before anyone realises that I haven't shut up shop for the day.'

Maggie was ushered inside the dark, narrow hallway that smelled strongly of incense. The sweet smell was overpowering, and she felt a wave of sickness roll over her. She moved to one side so the woman could lock the door behind them.

'Go on up, shan't be a moment. I'm Esther, and you are?'

Maggie thought about lying and telling her the completely wrong name, but she had a feeling that Esther would know. 'Maggie.'

She turned and rushed up the stairs eager to be somewhere that wasn't as potently overpowering. There was a room at the top of the stairs, where the floor was covered in brightly coloured silk cushions. There was a small round table with a purple cloth on it and a spread of tarot cards.

Maggie sat at one of the two chairs both scared and fascinated at the same time. If George could see her now, he would kill her. He would drag her out of here by her hair.

Esther appeared in the doorway and smiled at her. 'You are a strange one. I never saw you coming today, yet here you are.'

Maggie smiled. What did that even mean? 'I never knew I was coming here either until three minutes ago.'

Esther laughed and took a seat opposite her. 'That makes two of us, so I don't want you to tell me what's wrong. I want to take a look at your cards, if that's okay with you, and we can take it from there. I feel the cards will be the most useful to the both of us.'

Maggie nodded and then watched as Esther picked up the deck of cards and began to shuffle them so fast, they looked blurry. A couple of them sprang out and Esther picked them up. She looked at them and said, 'Aha.' Then carried on shuffling, before spreading the pack out in front of her. She asked her to pick three. Maggie did just that and passed them to her. 'I normally need more than three, but I'm going to be honest with you. I don't even need to read these cards, it's so obvious.'

'What is?'

'That you're pregnant, you don't want it and you don't know what to do about it.'

Maggie gasped. 'How?'

Esther shrugged. 'I can read people; I know things and you are easy to read.' She glanced at the cards then quickly put them face down on the table. 'Do you want to tell me what the problem is, and I can see if I can help.'

Tears pricked at the corner of Maggie's eyes. 'You're right, everything you just said. I don't want the baby because I hate my husband and now, I don't know what to do.'

'Can you not leave him? How far on are you?'

'I have nowhere to go, my mum died a couple of months ago, and I have no money. I should never have married him.'

Esther was shaking her head. 'No, you shouldn't have. He is not the man for you.'

'Then why did I? What made me think he was?'

'I'm afraid I can't answer that. You already know yourself that you've made a mistake and it's time to put it right before things get any worse.'

Maggie noticed the Welsh dresser along one wall filled with jars of teas and dried herbs. 'What are those for?'

'They are for medicinal reasons; I make teas to help people with their problems.'

'Could you make one to help me with mine?'

'It depends which problem we're talking about. If you want

something to help induce labour to rid yourself of the baby that is growing inside of you, I can do that, but only while it is so early on. I don't particularly like to do it, but sometimes it's better for the woman carrying the child not to have it if there are valid reasons that could put your own life at risk or the risk of the child coming to harm after birth, and I feel as if you are in that particular predicament. If you want something to help rid you of your husband, I can't give you that.'

'Why not?'

'Because I don't do dark magic. What you put out into the world comes back threefold, and if I were to give you something to poison your husband it would not bode well for either of us, and by that I don't mean the police involvement either that would surely come. There are greater forces out there at work that most people would never understand, and there are boundaries that mustn't be crossed.'

Maggie began to cry. 'I don't want a baby or George; I want to take back time and be myself again. I wish I'd never met him; I wish I'd never married him.'

Esther stood up and patted the top of Maggie's head. 'There, there, is he really that bad?'

Maggie nodded.

'There are many household items that are poisonous, prescription medicines are deadly as are some cleaning fluids, but take it from me this line of action is not going to solve your problems. Not that I'm suggesting you use anything of the sort – it's against the laws of humanity, Maggie. Why don't you pack your things and go to a women's refuge? There's a shelter in Kendal. I can take you there. You could have the baby and start a new life without your husband in it.' She passed a handful of tissues to her. 'My advice to you is to sleep on it, think about the positive circumstances to having the baby you're carrying. If you decided that you still can't carry on being pregnant and living with your husband, then come back here in three days. I will brew you some tea to help induce the baby and then drive you to the shelter myself.'

'You would do that for me?'

'Yes.'

'Why? I don't have much money.'

'I don't want your money; I want you to be happy. I can sense you haven't been happy for a long time and life is too short not to enjoy every precious moment. Now go home and think very carefully about the consequences any of the actions we've discussed could have on your life. I'll be here when you decide to return, if you decide to.'

Maggie stood up. 'Thank you.'

'My pleasure. Maggie, where do you live?'

'High Wraith Cottage on the outskirts of Rydal Falls.'

Esther paled at the name. 'Is the house yours or your husband's?'

'Mine, my mum signed it over to me when she went to live in the retirement home with the stipulation that I can only stay there if I'm married. If I leave, I could lose the house and it's all I have.'

'Then you are in a predicament, but, Maggie, that cottage is not a happy place. I know it isn't. Has it been in your family long?'

'Since it was built, some distant relation lived there and it was passed down through the years.'

'Do you know about the history of the place?'

She shook her head. 'I'm not interested, it's a horrible, dark little house, but it's my home until I can take it no more, and I'm seriously thinking about your suggestions.'

Esther rubbed at the side of her temple. 'I'll let you see yourself out if that's okay. I feel exhausted.'

Maggie went back downstairs, let herself out of the flat and closed the door behind her. Wondering what had just happened. She had asked a stranger to help her kill George.

What was she thinking? She felt shocked and ashamed of those thoughts that had entered her head inside Esther's flat. Was that what she wanted? She didn't know but she was struggling to put the idea out of her head now it had popped into it.

———

When Esther was sure the woman had left and was outside, she picked up the three tarot cards. Slowly turning them over she spread them out and a sigh escaped her lips. She knew they weren't good, which was why she hadn't turned them over in front of Maggie.

Looking back at her was the ten of swords, the death card and the four of swords. That woman was walking into a lot of trouble. She wasn't sure if it was Maggie, the baby, or her husband but the cards were telling her that one or possibly more of them was walking into death, and it was beyond anything Esther could control. It wouldn't have been so bad if the cards had been reversed, but they hadn't.

She stood up and crossed to the window, just in time to see the bus pulling away from the stop with Maggie on it. She crossed herself and hoped that she wouldn't see the woman again. She should never have let her inside, but she had and now she was going to have to live with the knowledge that something terrible was probably going to happen. She could phone the police and tell them what? that she saw a terrible destiny in some tarot cards for a woman she'd only known for around ten minutes? They would laugh at her and tell her not to bother them again.

She opened the window and picked up the white sage stick she kept nearby. Lighting it from one of her many candles that were burning she began to wave it around the flat, then down the stairs to the front door. She didn't want whatever bad energy that was attached to Maggie to linger in her home.

Opening the front door she wafted the sage around, pushing everything out then closed the door again and said a little prayer and blessing to rid her of the guilt she knew she was going to carry around until whatever was going to happen imploded, and it would.

High Wraith Cottage was a bad place, the land had been tainted with death and murder back in 1672, and whatever plagued the land had lain dormant for a very long time, but not, it seemed, for much longer.

12

Morgan was relieved to be out of George Lancaster's flat. She scanned the car park for the blue Vauxhall and saw it parked in the disabled bay near to the front entrance. She wrote down the full number plate and asked PNC to check the driver details to be sure. Ben opened the car door for her to get inside out of the steady drizzle that had started again. She smiled at him; he was too cute, old-fashioned with excellent manners. Her mum would have called him a proper gentleman, which she loved. He would never not hold a door open for anyone; it was just how he was.

As Ben started the engine, PNC confirmed that the vehicle belonged to George Lancaster, and she opened the door and jumped out, quickly checking the car to see if the tyres or chassis were covered in mud. There was some under the wheel arches, but nothing excessive and besides if there was, the rain would have washed most of it away.

'Sorry, just thought it was worth checking to see if he'd been anywhere muddy, like the roads up to the cottage.'

'You think that a guy with one leg could do that? Break in,

drag her out of bed and hang her from that tree. Which I was thinking about. How did they get her up there?'

'I think George is a big strong man and he probably could do all of that if he had a prosthetic leg on or a bit of help, he could have had an accomplice he may be lying about his relationship with his estranged son. I imagine he hoisted her up into the tree, though it would take some strength if she was struggling but look at Olivia Potter's murder, the killer wasn't as strong we'd originally thought. It could be done if you were determined enough I suppose.'

Ben shrugged. 'I don't think it was him, not in the rain and the howling wind, but I'm not ruling him out completely. He may well have had an accomplice. He certainly has motive; he still hates her, even now. He's on the list.'

'He's top of my list.'

Ben laughed. 'Well, if you put it that way, he's also top of mine because right now we have nobody else on it except for her son, who is a bit of a mystery. We need to find David Lancaster or whatever he's called now and speak to him. He's younger, probably a lot fitter than his dad and has a good reason to take out his revenge on Margery. She was supposed to take care of him, keep him safe and she didn't. She tried to kill him, made him sick and because of her he was put into the system and was probably forgotten about. His own dad didn't want anything to do with him. That's a lot of rejection for anyone to take. Margery clearly wasn't mentally stable at the time of the poisonings, and maybe he takes after her in that respect. Anyone would struggle finding out that the parents who gave you up for adoption didn't do it for your own sake, but for their own twisted reasons, leaving him with nothing but poisoned memories of a childhood he was robbed of.'

'I feel sorry for him, it's so sad. He was only a baby; he had no control over anything, and he didn't ask to be born.'

'It is sad, but it doesn't justify killing someone.'

'No, it doesn't, and maybe it wasn't him, but it gives motivation, don't you think?'

Ben nodded. 'I guess it does, but look at what you've been through. You were adopted, your mum was murdered by your dad in front of you, but it didn't turn you into a killer.'

'Not me, but it affected my brother Taylor and look how his story ended.'

'I suppose it depends on what kind of person you are anyway.'

'Maybe. I always wondered if you are exposed to extreme violence when you're very young, does that mean you are predisposed to it. Because look at me and Taylor. What do you think?'

Ben shook his head. 'Tough question that I'm not qualified to answer, but going back to David Lancaster, why though, why now?'

'Maybe he just wanted revenge for being abandoned.'

'Maybe. I don't envy anyone having to sort through that hoarder's paradise, as Amy called it. It took me a couple of years before I was able to face going through Cindy's stuff. I suppose it was the guilt, I couldn't bring myself to pack it up and remove everything. It felt so wrong that I was still living my life and Cindy was gone.'

She reached out and touched Ben's hand briefly. 'It was a bit different for me with Stan, he didn't own much, and it was rented flat, I had no choice but to bag it all up and get rid of it, bless him. If we can't find him, you can bet that whoever deals with her estate can.'

Morgan's phone vibrated and she put it on speaker. Amy's voice filled the inside of the car.

'Cain said to tell you there's a knackered silver pickup caught on camera at eleven p.m. last night, passing High Wraith Farm on the road up the fell. Impossible to get the VRM though, but it's a start. I'm going to check the ANPR cameras now to see if it got picked up coming through any of them.'

Ben lifted a hand and high-fived Morgan. 'Good work, that's great. Hopefully it's picked up by one of them so we can get the registration. Did you ask if the vehicle belongs to the farm or if they know of anyone who drives one?' Morgan thought of George's blue Vauxhall.

Amy paused.

'Er, no because Cain is the one who is there. I'm still in the station.'

'Oh, yeah. Sorry, I'm getting mixed up. I'll ring him now. Thanks, Amy.'

Morgan asked, 'Why didn't Cain ring you himself?'

Ben shrugged. 'Maybe he hasn't got a good signal, you know how rubbish it can be. Can you ring him for me?'

She did and it went to voicemail.

'Let's get back to the station, see if the search team have found anything useful. You could ring around the local solicitors too, see if anyone has dealt with Margery so we can find her next of kin. Maybe that will help us find David.'

Morgan looked at the clock on the dash – it was just past five. 'I'll try, but I don't think they'll be open now.'

'You're right.'

'Should we go to the cottage and see if we can find anything?'

'Al and Daisy were going through it—'

'Nobody mentioned a will to the search team, though, did they? So they wouldn't have been looking for that. And given she was a hoarder there will be a lot of paperwork to go through.'

'Can do.'

. . .

The roads to High Wraith Cottage were waterlogged in places, the steady drizzle not helping them to clear. In the distance Morgan could see a solitary car parked outside the gate. The van with the search team had left and she wondered if they had found anything useful. Al hadn't phoned Ben to update him, though, so there was a chance they hadn't. As Ben's car climbed the steep road, she wondered who had got the crappy job of scene guarding this place. He parked behind the white unmarked car, and she saw Tina sitting inside.

Morgan zipped her coat up and waved at Tina, who wound the window down but didn't get out.

'You drew the short straw?'

'Yep, search team left about ten minutes ago.'

'Already? Did they have much?'

'A few evidence bags, it didn't look like a lot though. Any luck finding the killer?'

Morgan shook her head; Ben was up at the front door, putting shoe covers on his feet. 'There are some forensics, which is a great start, but we need the DNA results back from Declan so we can make some real headway with finding our suspect.'

'Terrible if you ask me. I keep looking at the broken branch lying on the floor and seeing a body lying there. It's dark up here, and I'd rather not be here all night. Do you know how long it's going to be?'

Morgan didn't tell her she had seen the body both hanging from the tree *and* lying there on the muddy floor. 'Ben, how long do you need the scene guard on for?' she shouted up to him.

'I'll take a look around, then see what Al has to say. If the DI agrees we can lock it up and leave it. I'll let you know, Tina.'

Tina nodded. 'Aye, suppose so.' Then she put her window back up and looked down at the book she was reading on her phone, making Morgan grin. She'd quite like to sit up here on her own and read, although she wasn't sure she'd feel the same in the dark. It was lonely and eerie.

She caught Ben up at the front door to the cottage. 'Do you think we should have a PCSO sitting here on their own while the killer is still at large?'

'No, bloody hell. Absolutely not, I'll get Mads to send an officer to take over. You're right, she has nothing to protect herself with.'

'Do you think they'll come back?'

'Depends on if they are looking for something.'

She followed Ben inside. The cottage was even gloomier than it had been this morning and that was with the single bulb illuminating the narrow hallway. It smelled of damp. There were two rooms and a kitchen downstairs, and all the doors were opened. What used to be the parlour was now a bedroom. Margery had moved herself down here. Did she have bad mobility and struggle with the stairs? The staircase was steep and curved.

'I'll go take a look upstairs if you want to do down here.'

'Whatever you prefer is fine by me.'

She flicked the light switch on and made her way to the narrow landing, where there were three doors and what looked like an airing cupboard. Morgan checked the airing cupboard first, tugging open the door and slamming it shut again quick. It smelled musty. There were stacks of towels and bedding on shelves inside of it. Not the kind of place to keep important documents. Working her way along she pushed open the bathroom door. There was an old-fashioned clawfoot tub in the middle of the room that looked directly out of the window onto the desolate countryside, and it was amazing. She could imagine having candlelit baths in the dark, watching the velvety black night sky flicker to life as each star revealed itself to the world. It wasn't cluttered; in fact it was clean and tidy unlike the rest of the house – or the downstairs anyway. There was a tube of moisturiser on the sink, a single toothbrush and tube of toothpaste. She opened the small, mirrored cabinet; it had paracetamol, cough medicine and tweezers. Nothing else. Margery lived a very simple life, and she wondered what she did with all her time. Stuck up here alone, it must have been boring as anything. She went into the next room and her question was answered. It wasn't exactly a library, but there were stacks and stacks of books piled up on the floor, covering every square foot of space. There was a single bed that was covered in books too, and this made her feel a little better. As long as there were books you were never alone, she knew this. The years she'd spent locked away in her bedroom after her adoptive mum Sylvia died and then her best friend Brad's unexpected death, books had been her best friends and her saviour. She had lost herself in alternative worlds, visited tropical places and found herself chasing through the streets of New York City, and nothing could ever replace the pleasure reading a well-written story could give her. She tilted her head to look at the stacks of books: Jane Austen, Charles Dickens, Emily Brontë, Jilly Cooper, VC Andrews, Jackie Collins; she noticed there were no crime thrillers as such, though she wasn't sure what she'd label *Flowers in the Attic*, but it looked as if Margery didn't like anything too violent. The complete opposite to her own bookshelves that were overflowing with true crime books about serial killers, and crime thrillers that had her racing through the pages desperate to finish the story yet at the same time reluctant to finish the story. Her go-to favourites were Angela Marsons and Lisa Regan, but Margery it seemed didn't enjoy anything of that nature. Then again, she had attempted familicide, the ultimate crime of trying to kill her own family, no fiction book could compare to living that for real. Morgan picked up a few of the books at the top of the piles and flicked through them to see if any papers had been pushed between the pages, but all she succeeded in doing was releasing a cloud of dust motes that filled the air and made her cough.

She closed the door, feeling sad, wondering what was going to happen to all those books. She hoped whoever inherited this house gave them to a charity shop and didn't just throw them into a skip. That would be a complete waste. The third bedroom had a double bed that was covered in boxes, dusty boxes and clothes. This time she pulled her T-shirt up to cover her mouth and nose before lifting the flap on the boxes that had already been disturbed by the search teams, more books and some clothes. She looked around and saw a chest of drawers. If Margery kept personal documents like letters or old diaries, it seemed the best hope of finding something up here, unless Ben had struck lucky downstairs. Although she doubted that because surely, he would have shouted to tell her if he had found anything of interest.

The stripped pine chest of drawers had blue and white porcelain round knobs, and it was beautiful; a lot of the furniture in this cottage was old pine and probably worth a bit of money to someone who wanted original country cottage furniture to go in their newly renovated houses. It was a shame it was hidden underneath all the clutter. Morgan lovingly pressed her hand against the top of the drawers. She loved pine, not sure why, but it reminded her of her childhood bedroom, her safe haven when the world around her had all gone horribly wrong. Tugging open the first drawer she saw it was full of loose photographs and picked a handful up. They had all been taken with a 35mm or Polaroid camera. Lots of photos of who, she assumed, was a very young-looking Margery and George, standing outside this cottage, which looked in much better shape, with an older woman, her grey permed hair cut short. She looked a little like Margery, and she wondered if it was her mum or maybe her gran.

Then she came to a stack of baby photographs. The kid was

cute, he had lots of dark curls and big brown eyes that would melt anyone's heart. It made her think of *The Omen*, that kid Damien looked cute on the outside but had been pure evil on the inside. Was that how Margery had perceived her own perfect little boy? As someone to be feared and not loved? She definitely needed to speak to whoever dealt with the case when it happened, the coppers investigating, the hospital staff, somebody who knew what went on because she was sure whatever started the chain of dreadful events was the reason Margery was dead now.

Tucked underneath the drawer liner underneath all the photos was the corner of a small book, she peeled back the liner to reveal a couple of old style savings books, one with seventy-two pounds in and the other she had to look at twice. There was over five hundred thousand pounds in it. Morgan looked around the cluttered room – judging by the fresh marks in the dust nothing had been touched in here until they had arrived en masse this morning and trampled through the house. Al and Daisy had done a good job with their search, it had been pure luck that she had decided to go through the photographs and seen the edge of the book. How had she got so much money? From what little they knew about her, Margery Lancaster lived frugally, didn't work, didn't go out to socialise, had very few if no friends that they were aware of, didn't use social media. Pulling an evidence bag from her pocket she dropped the savings book inside of it. Maybe the bank could help them, although that would take time. From her experience banks were worse than doctors for getting information about their deceased patients. Even if they didn't find her will, this to her was proof that someone may have thought Margery was worth killing. Who would know about it? The bank. The person who gave it to her. The only other person she could think of was George. Did he know she had it? Even if her son had turned up out of the blue looking for her, she wasn't likely to tell him *I'm sorry, one day you can have this house and half a million pounds to make up for being a crap Mum*, or had she?

She took the bag downstairs to Ben who was looking through a plastic box full of papers. He glanced at her. 'What did you find?'

'Margery has over a half a million pounds in her bank account.'

Ben straightened up, looking around the room. 'She does? Yet she lived like this.'

Morgan shrugged. 'Some people are scared to spend money; they keep it for a rainy day. Have you found anything?'

'Nothing really, bills, hospital letter for an MRI scan of her back. No will anyway.'

'No journals, diary?'

'Nope.'

'That's a shame, I bet it would have been interesting reading.'

He finished rifling through the papers and put the lid back on it. 'Come on, let's get back. You have something, when was the deposit made?'

'Oh, I didn't look at the date just the balance. It completely threw me. I imagined she was struggling the way she lived.'

She managed to open the book inside the plastic bag and lifted it closer so she could read it. 'That's weird, it was ten months ago. I wonder where she got a lump sum of money like that, and why now.'

Ben shrugged. 'I guess we'll have to go ask the bank. Which one is it?'

'Furness Building Society, there's a branch in Kendal. I think that would be the nearest one to here.'

'Add it to the list. Margery, you are full of surprises,' he said aloud to the room as if she could still hear him.

Morgan felt a cold shiver run up her spine. Maybe she could, she could still be here watching them, perplexed as to what all these strangers were doing inside of her house. Sometimes she wished she was gifted and could see the dead people they dealt with. Imagine how much easier it would be if they could whisper the name of their killer directly into your ear. It would be amazing. They left the house, locking the door behind them. Ben went straight to the car with Tina in, and she rolled down the window.

'An officer is coming to take over, Tina. You shouldn't be out here on your own.'

'Praise the lord. I need the toilet.'

Ben grinned at her. 'Sorry, we shouldn't have sent you here alone.'

She shrugged. 'Same shit, different day.'

Morgan and Ben strolled to the car smiling. 'She's right you know,' said Morgan. 'But at least we have money as a motive for definite. If we can find out where it came from and who she told about it, we might be able to find the killer. I wish there was some way to speed up the DNA. Even though it's been fast tracked it still takes too long.'

Morgan knew that the turnaround was far faster now than it had ever been, but still it felt as if it took too long.

13

Morgan had been right; every local solicitor was closed for the day. Cain had come back and managed to print off the worst CCTV still she had ever seen in her career, and she had come across some right belters. It was nothing but a silver pickup-shaped blur and by blur it looked as if it had been taken by some drunk wielding an old-fashioned camera that they had been waving around the dance floor while trying to break dance. Cain was beaming with pride at his piece of evidence, and Morgan didn't want to be the one to upset him, but it was totally useless. Amy on the other hand strolled in, straight to the whiteboard, leaned towards it screwing up her eyes then turned to him and said, 'What the fuck is that supposed to be?'

'It's the pickup that went past the farm gates last night.'

'It could be an alien spacecraft, Cain, it's just a blur. There's no definition, no driver, no number plate.'

He was no longer smiling, his mouth now set in a straight line. 'What have you got?'

She shrugged. 'Nothing yet, waiting on the results from the ANPR to see if there's a hit.'

'Precisely, you have nothing. I have something and regardless of the clarity of the subject matter it's still a silver pickup. Even without the number plate or driver we know that if any suspects have a silver pickup that bumps them up the list.'

Amy was standing with her arms crossed, and she gave a curt nod. 'Yes, we do. But seriously, Cain, that is going to go down in the history of the worst CCTV captures ever. It's worse than the time Scotty came back with a still of that burglar's naked arse and not his face.'

Morgan felt bad for Cain. It was true, and Amy was right, but she didn't have to be so hard on him. 'At least we have a car, well a truck to look out for. You did good, Cain.'

He glanced at her and beamed. 'Thanks, Morgan, at least you agree with me.'

Ben came in with a mug of coffee and joined Cain and Amy at the whiteboard. He shook his head, muttered, 'Jesus,' then headed into his office and shut the door behind him.

'Ungrateful you lot are, except for you, Morgan, who is a team player unlike some people I could mention.'

Amy laughed. 'I'm not being mean, or ungrateful. I'm stating a fact. It's a crap photograph, that's all.'

'You tell me how many times do we get CCTV footage that is actually clear enough to identify suspects? Almost every job I attended on section, the cameras didn't pick anything up, the images were blurry, the cameras weren't working – nobody knows how to work the cameras. Rarely did I get something that could not just identify a suspect but be used in court.'

Amy turned to Morgan. 'He's taking this super personal, isn't he?' She looked back at Cain. 'You're right, I'm not arguing with you. Do you need a snack, Cain? Are you hangry or something?'

Cain began to laugh. 'Yeah, I am. I'm bloody starving. What are we having for tea? We should have gone home an hour ago, well not you, Morgan, you wandered in late. Perks of sleeping with the boss I guess.'

Morgan's cheeks turned a deep fuchsia. 'I thought I was on your team yet here you are dissing me. I'm working late to make up for it. It wasn't my fault my alarm didn't go off.'

'I guess there's life in the old dog yet if he tired you out that much.'

'Cain,' she admonished him and turned to Amy. 'Feed him before he gets himself into serious trouble.'

He was laughing at his own joke. 'I can feed myself, thank you. I'm not some kind of animal that needs taking care of.'

Amy rolled her eyes. 'Oh, really then why are you acting like a pig? I fancy pizza, a great big, cheesy pizza from Gino's, smothered in onions, ham and mushrooms.'

Cain leaned over and high-fived her. 'I'll have a meat feast; Morgan, what do you want?'

'Meat feast and Ben will have a Margherita.'

Cain nodded. 'Leave it with me, I'll sort it out. I get a police discount.'

Both women looked at him. 'Since when?'

'Since lockdown. Gino started giving emergency services a discount but only to us hard workers in uniform though, not you softies up in the offices who got to work from home most days.'

'Erm, Cain, where is your uniform?' asked Amy.

'Doesn't matter, I could go in wearing my gym shorts and he would give it to me. I'm not easily forgettable.'

Amy rolled her eyes at Morgan. 'You can say that again. Go get food so we can talk about how crap your still is without you listening and getting all upset about it.'

He pouted, then began to laugh. 'You're so mean, at times, it's a good job I love you.'

'You're gonna make me puke, Cain, will you get out.'

Morgan was grinning at the pair of them. They were like an old married couple the way they bickered.

'See ya, wouldn't wanna be ya,' were his parting words.

'He's been watching *Gimme, Gimme, Gimme* again.'

Morgan grinned. 'Kathy Burke was so funny. I remember watching that when I was a kid, I was too young really, but Stan never cared what I watched or read.' A wave of sadness rolled over her. Stan, her adoptive dad, had been both her defender and her enemy rolled into one and it broke her heart that he'd been killed just as they were finally beginning to appreciate each other for who they were. That was one thing nobody told you about grief: the guilt, the what ifs, the missed opportunities and the sudden memories of fond moments that seconds later broke your heart when you were least expecting it. Out of the blue you'd be okay or think you were okay and the next a song, or a certain smell would have you sobbing in the car on your own. Morgan's entire family had died far too young, and she had nobody but Ben and her aunt left; there was Taylor, but she would never give him the satisfaction of even acknowledging his existence. He'd chosen the path he went down and as far as she was concerned he was nothing to her. Sibling rivalry at its best or maybe its worst, even though she had no idea she had a sibling at the time because all her early memories had been blocked out after seeing her mum so brutally murdered in front of them both.

Amy was staring at her. 'Are you okay? You've gone all quiet.'

'I'm fine, just remembering a lot of stuff that I shouldn't because it does nothing but cause me heartache and sadness.'

Amy nodded. 'You've had a much tougher time than the rest of us. Good job you're not soft like Cain.'

Morgan laughed. 'He's not soft, he's just sensitive and likes to be praised even if he brings back stills like that.' She pointed to the whiteboard and the blurry streak of silver. Both of them laughed too loud, so loud it brought Ben out of his office.

'What's going on? You're not supposed to be happy or enjoying yourself you know, you're at work.'

Morgan pointed to the whiteboard. 'Cain's masterpiece.'

Even Ben smiled. 'Are we eating tonight or are we starving?'

'Cain has gone to get pizza, apparently he gets a police discount.'

'Does he now? Make up for that.' He pointed at the board. 'I'm not sure what else we can do tonight until we get details of David Lancaster's whereabouts. I've spoken with PNC who have sent a list over of all males in the area called David Lancaster – and there are a few – but he got adopted out of the county so there's a good chance it's not even him.'

'What about a press appeal, ask him to come to us?'

'Could do, probably will do if we get no luck going through this list, but I don't want to spook him if he thinks we're looking for him in connection to the murder. He might go to ground and leave the area.'

'Surely he'd only do that if he was guilty though, boss,' Amy said.

'Depends on how well he likes the police, how much he knows about his birth mother and if he's guilty or not.'

Morgan had a feeling that he might be responsible. Her phone beeped, and she saw Ettie's name on the screen. 'Oh no, I forgot to go see Ettie. Are you okay if I nip out now? Do you need me for the next hour?'

'No, but you'll miss your pizza.'

'I can warm it up when I get back. Thanks, I'll be as quick as I can.'

She left them to it, excited to go see Ettie and her pet raven, Max, if he was around. It had been way too long since she'd visited the pair of them.

Ettie was standing at her front door waiting for Morgan. It was dark, and she'd needed to use the torch out of the car to light her way, but she knew it like the back of her hand by now. She also had the best guide a girl could ask for. As she'd got out of her car

Max had swooped down and landed on the roof. She found one of those little Biscoff biscuits in a clear packet that he loved and unwrapped it for him. Holding out her hand, he'd hopped onto her arm and gently taken it from her.

'Don't tell Ettie okay, because I have no idea how many biscuits you've eaten today already.'

His shiny black eyes stared at her, and she was sure he winked before taking off in the air ready to guide her to the cottage in case she got lost.

Her aunt was on the doorstep as she arrived at the gate.

'Morgan, I've been waiting all day. I know you've been busy, but I had to see you, darling. I see Max kept you company.'

Morgan smiled at her aunt who then drew her in for a hug; an Ettie hug was the closest she could get to a mum hug, and she didn't break free. She embraced it and held on tight, her aunt swaying from side to side with her, rocking her gently. When Ettie let her go, she sighed.

'You needed that, my sweet girl. I wish you wouldn't leave it so long between visits. I miss seeing your beautiful face.'

Ettie took her by the hand, leading her into the small, open-plan living room/kitchen/diner. It was compact, but it was perfect. Morgan used to dream about living in a little house like this and it was the kind of home she would make for herself one day. When she'd first walked in here on enquires for another murder she'd fallen in love with it, unbeknown to her that Ettie was her aunt and that this could be her lifestyle if she really wanted it. And the more she dealt with the depravity of humans and the way they treated each other, the harder the yearning became for a much simpler way of life that didn't involve violent killers and grieving relatives. For now, she was content chasing down twisted criminals, but one day when it all got too much it made her happy, deep inside, to know she could come here and ask Ettie to teach her everything she knew.

Morgan never really thought about children, or having them. She didn't feel as if a child would be an extension of herself, and did she really want to bring one into the world when her job was so demanding? But she could picture herself working alongside Ettie, making teas, drying herbs with a little girl by her side, standing on a little footstool helping as Ettie guided them both. The vision was so strong that she wondered if it was some long-forgotten memory.

'Ettie, did my mum ever bring me here when I was a toddler?'

Ettie nodded. 'She did; several times a week we would work in the kitchen making the jars of tea to sell at the market. You loved it, you were a dab hand with the mortar and pestle. I would pass you dried rosemary, lavender, fever few, whatever was called for in that particular recipe, and you would grind away until your heart's content.' She sighed. 'Those were the happiest times of my life; I loved your mum. She was like a younger sister, and I adored you. When Gary did what he did he tore a hole in my heart bigger than a black hole. When I found out that he'd killed Janet in front of you both, and that you had been taken into protective custody, I almost gave up. I cried for what seemed like forever. I wanted you to come live with me, but I wasn't allowed access to you. I applied to foster you both, but they wouldn't listen. I lived alone, I didn't have a proper job, had no savings, they didn't want to know and told me it was in my best interest to let you both get fostered with strangers. That a fresh start was what you both needed.'

Ettie brushed a tear away with her sleeve. 'I have never forgiven myself for listening to that bloody old bitch of a social worker.'

Morgan reached out and clasped hold of her aunt's hand. 'You weren't to know.'

'I wasn't, but I should have made it my priority to.'

'We have each other now, that's all that counts. What did

you need to see me about?' Morgan changed the subject, hoping to take Ettie's mind off the past.

'Oh, yes. Sorry, I got carried away. I wanted to tell you about Margery Lancaster. Somebody has to stand up for her because she has nobody else. I knew the day I first met her that she was troubled. I guess getting older makes you realise that at some point you have to grow some balls and do the right thing.'

Morgan felt her stomach do a funny little summersault wondering what Ettie was about to confess to her.

14

He spent a lot of time watching. He was good at it and always had been. He should have trained to be a private investigator, that would have suited him to the ground. Getting paid for sitting around in cars for hours watching the world go by, it was a pretty decent gig if you asked him.

The door to the retirement complex opened and at long last out came George; big, blustery George, whose bark was worse than his bite now, although it hadn't always been this way. He remembered how fond he was of using his fists, had heard the stories about what a mean bastard he was. There was no love lost between him and the man who was supposedly his dad, supposed to be the loving parent to take care of him. The only person George took care of was himself, putting his needs before others, and he was a selfish man.

It took George some time to manoeuvre himself into the car, but it was okay, there was no rush. He'd taken a chance and driven past the cottage earlier; the police had gone. Locked it up tight and left because there was nothing there for them. They could rip it to pieces board by board, and they wouldn't find anything to tie him to Margery. There was no evidence. *Are you sure about that?* A voice whispered in his ear, and his fingers reached up to touch the scratch on his cheek that she'd inflicted in a blind panic. He hadn't expected her to be so ferocious. He'd thought she'd give in and accept her fate, just like she'd given up on her own existence.

She had until she'd seen the tree and realised what he was about to do – someone had to serve justice. Thirteen years for attempted familicide was not good enough, not in his eyes. She had poisoned her own kid. George he could understand, but not her own flesh and blood. It ran in the family, that much he did know, and sometimes it skipped generations, but then it would rear its ugly head and happen again. It was a well-kept secret that High Wraith Cottage was cursed, whether it be the land or the house he wasn't sure, but whoever lived there would never lead a happy life. It just wasn't possible, not with the ghosts that haunted the walls and had never left, not even to go to the after-life. Not with the misery those walls had watched as the deaths had unfolded inside, one after the other, trapping so many people in one place. How could anyone live there? How could they be happy, that was the question. Would he be able to live there when the time came? He wasn't sure, but he would rip it to pieces stone by stone and rebuild it if he had to, or he could sell it; if new owners took over maybe that would break the curse. He had a feeling that Margery hadn't even known about the history of the cottage when she'd decided enough was enough and that she'd rather poison her own family and watch them die slowly than carry on living with them. It would make a great TV show, one of those bingeworthy Netflix series that would have everyone sitting on the edge of their seats the entire time.

Finally, the reverse lights came on in the blue car as it slowly began to back out of its space. He was surprised that George was even going to do this, but he was also relieved that he was. There was no point waiting around. The best chance he had was now. The police had only just left, they shouldn't be coming back tonight. It was too dark for one thing and the rain was due to start in the next hour. Whatever else it was they needed could wait until tomorrow. When the car turned onto the main road, he began to follow it. Once it hit the dual carriageway he would overtake and get there first, a one-man welcoming party. He wondered if old George would be happy to finally be going home, or if he'd put up a fight just like the once meek and mild Margery.

15

Ettie made them both tea, not any of her lovingly handmade herbal tea but a big pot of M&S Gold Blend tea that Morgan loved so much. There was also cake; another thing she loved dearly about her aunt – no matter the occasion there was always cake or biscuits. As Morgan watched from the comfy sofa that seemed to envelop her into a hug when she sat down as much as one of Ettie's hugs, she sighed with contentment. Ettie's cat jumped up on her lap, purring loudly.

'I envy you,' she said to Ettie, 'you are living the life I would love to live.'

Ettie turned to her. 'You do? Well one day this could be you. It probably will be you, but I'd need to read your tea leaves to be sure.' She looked down at the cups on the table. 'And it's not the same when I use a tea bag.'

Morgan laughed. 'One day you can, and you can tell me the good news.'

Ettie winked at her. 'I will, now let me tell you everything I know. I'm hoping by telling you this it might just absolve some of the guilt I have been carrying around with me since the very first time I met Maggie. And you can see if it's of any importance to your investigation, but first.' She leaned over and poured out the tea, passing a cup and saucer to Morgan, then sliced the Victoria sponge cake into generous pieces and passed her one of those too. 'Eat up, you need the extra calories. I'm sure you don't eat enough; I worry about you.'

'I eat like a horse and there is a huge pizza waiting for me back at the station.'

'Good, I'm glad to hear it. You need sustenance when you work as hard as you do. Now, where was I? Oh, yes that poor, poor woman. It breaks my heart how alone she was all her life.'

'But you live alone, in a cottage in the middle of nowhere. Are you lonely?'

She laughed. 'I am never lonely. For a start I have those two pesky free-loading things following me everywhere.' She pointed to the cat and the raven, the most unlikely of friends. Max was perched on windowsill, preening.

'I also have a lot of visitors; I have many friends and I have you, dear. Maggie had only herself. It was partly her fault because she wouldn't let anyone get close to her after she came out of the secure unit. As far as I know the only person who ever visited was me, and I never went as often as I could have. I don't know if it was her or the house, but it would drain me so completely of my energy; a visit to Maggie's house would take me days to recover from. I would have to come home and cleanse myself with sage, take a long hot soak in a crystal-infused bath to ground me again. I would wear smoky quartz and obsidian bracelets to protect my own energy; it was so all-consuming inside of that house.'

'But you went and saw her which was kind of you. Who else used to go?'

'The grocers on the high street had a delivery boy before he went off to university. He would go once a week and take her the essentials, bread, milk, you know everything to keep her going. He was such a nice young man; nothing was too much trouble. He would bring my groceries to me too. Of course, I didn't need it. I used to drive to M&S in Kendal, but I liked to support Mr and Mrs Patterson. They were nice people, and nothing was too much trouble for them. I know Dorothy would slip an extra packet of biscuits into Maggie's box; she told me that she felt bad for the woman all on her own living in that awful house.'

'Are they still there?'

Ettie shook her head. 'No, they retired and moved to Tenerife, said they'd had enough of this climate. There wasn't much money to be made once the big supermarkets opened those little chains in Ambleside.'

'Who was the delivery guy?'

'Matthew, Mattie, no idea what his surname is though. I'm sorry I don't know much more about him other than what we chatted about, general stuff. He did live with his mum though, in the village, so you could ask around. I doubt he's been to Maggie's house since he went to uni though, Morgan. He wouldn't have had any cause to.'

'No, I was wondering if he'd be able to fill me in on if she had any other visitors that he knew about.'

Ettie shrugged. 'Possibly.'

'How did you come to meet Margery?'

'She came to me. I used to live above the hairdressers on the main street back in my younger days. I didn't always live here. It was a cosy flat, and I did quite a bit of business reading people's cards back then or their tea leaves. It depended on the vibes I got from them. One day I had this feeling in my gut that I was going to get a visit from a woman needing help and just as I was about to call it a day my phone rang. It was Maggie asking if she could make an appointment. I told her to come straight away. She was nervous and polite, but there was this air about her of, I don't know how to describe it, other than doom. Her aura was so dark. I knew she was tired and upset, there was no light in it at all. I shuffled the cards, and one flew out immediately. I turned it over and knew this was not going to be a good reading. I told her to only pick three because I already knew they were going to be bad, and when she passed them to me, I put them face down. I didn't want her to see them. I didn't want to read them in front of her; there are some things that people should not know, as it's not always in their best interests. That was a hard decision, but one I feel was right. She told me that she was pregnant, that her husband was an abusive man and could I give her something to make the problem go away. I think she thought I would brew her up a batch of poisonous tea she could give him.'

Morgan's mouth was wide open, and she had to pick up the tea and take a sip to register what she was hearing.

'She wanted you to give her something to kill him?'

'I guess she did. I told her I couldn't and wouldn't, that it was a bad idea, that whatever we put out into the world comes back threefold. I told her I could help her with something to bring on an early labour. This is not something I do very often, and I will only ever do it if the baby is going to make someone's life situation far worse than it already is. I also will only do it before they get to eight weeks. I'm not proud of this, and I no longer do it because there's no need. There is no stigma attached to it anymore and medical help is relatively easy to access if there's a problem. But I could see Maggie was in distress and not sure what to do about the baby. I told her to think it over for a couple of days then come back. She never did. The next time I saw her she was pushing a pram. I smiled at her, but she didn't look at me. She put her head down.'

Morgan was stunned by all of this. 'She had the chance to abort the baby, but she didn't want to, yet she tried to kill him a year later. I don't understand it. I wonder what gave her the idea to poison them?'

'Me, most likely. I casually happened to mention that there were plenty of household items that were poisonous. I'm not proud of that. I've felt bad ever since. I was trying to help her in my own way without getting too involved. When she left my flat, I turned over the cards and knew she was walking into death. I wanted to call her back, but she was already on the bus. I thought about calling the police, but they wouldn't have listened, and then I never heard from her again. I'd offered to take her to the women's shelter in Kendal so she could escape from George, but she didn't take me up on it. I saw her pushing that pram and thought that maybe things had worked out better than I could ever have foreseen for Maggie Lancaster. That maybe this time the cards had been completely wrong, and I had been worrying over nothing. Then I saw the headlines about the attempted murder, and everything came crashing down.'

Morgan reached over to pat Ettie's knee. 'You weren't to know what she was going to do two years later. None of this is your fault, so if you're still holding on to guilt that it was, you have to let it go.'

Ettie squeezed her hand and smiled at her. 'I have, but I'm an empath just like you and we feel bad for people anyway. I was her only visitor while she was in the secure unit.'

'You went to see her?'

'Once a month, without fail, for the whole time she was in there.'

Morgan stared at her aunt, wondering how she could have done such a thing when there was no reason to other than some guilt. She felt for something that had been out of her control.

'She didn't speak much, just passed pleasantries really, but I couldn't bear the thought of her being stuck inside there with no one to talk to, who might understand what she was going through. I never judged her; it wasn't my place. I just wanted Maggie to know that if she needed someone I would be there to listen when the time came to talk about what she did. She never, ever did talk about it. After around six years I asked her why it had come to that, and do you know what she said?'

Morgan shook her head.

'That the ghosts had told her to.'

'I knew then that she was poorly. I also knew that it was a possibility they had. I mean that many people murdered in one house, there was bound to be some kind of haunting, don't you think?'

The teacup Morgan was holding slid from her fingers as she loosened her grip without even realising what was happening. It hit the stone floor and shattered into pieces, sending tea and porcelain everywhere. Max let out a loud squawk and took off out of the window, the cat ran for cover and Ettie jumped up to clean the mess.

'I'm sorry, Morgan, I thought you would have known about High Wraith Cottage. I thought everyone knew of its history.'

'I'm so sorry, let me clean this up. I know nothing about it. I had never even heard of it until this morning.'

Ettie shooed her to sit back down. 'I'll get this, don't worry, it will only take a minute. Once I've cleaned it up, I'll tell you the rest.'

Morgan sat with her feet up while Ettie picked up the pieces of broken china. Her entire body was tingling with a fraught energy of being on the verge of some huge discovery. What murders? How long ago was this and how did it impact on what had happened to Margery Lancaster? Did it cause her murder? There were so many questions and she just hoped that Ettie could give her the answers.

16

Morgan tried not to run because she hated it and wasn't very good at it, but after Ettie's background information she was desperate to get back to the station. Her phone signal had been crap at the little car park at Covel Wood near Ettie's house, and she wanted to research the cottage Margery Lancaster had spent most of her life in. She had driven back to the station a lot faster than she'd driven away from it. As she opened the office door her stomach let out a loud growl when the smell of pizza hit her nostrils. She was hungry, even though Ettie's cake had filled a gap.

Cain pointed to the box on her desk. 'It's still full, we didn't eat it.'

She gave him a thumbs up. 'Good job or I'd have choked you with the empty box.'

He turned to Amy. 'Now who's hangry?'

'How was your aunt?' asked Amy.

'Good, she had some interesting stuff to tell me about Margery Lancaster.' Morgan had torn off the biggest slice of pizza, and she took a huge bite, sighing in delight. It was still warm enough to taste good.

She waved at Ben, beckoning him to come out of his office. He stood up, blotting his mouth and brushing crumbs off his shirt but smiled at her, and she felt her heart do that little skip a beat thing. He was so handsome, but he looked tired, and she thought maybe a little gaunt. When she'd first met him, he had been a lot heavier, and she missed that. She loved that he was all soft and cuddly. It pained her to think he had lost weight because of her, despite her telling him how much she loved him exactly as he was.

'How's Ettie?'

'Good, she had some stuff to tell me about Margery, but first of all, did any of you know that her cottage has seen more murders than any other house in Cumbria? Probably more than any other house in the UK to be fair.'

All three of them stared at her, mouths open, heads shaking. Ben perched on the end of Cain's desk, so he was looking straight at her. 'What? How, wouldn't we have heard of them? Is she winding you up, Morgan?'

'Nope.' She was typing into the internet search bar but very little came up. 'Oh, bugger. No wonder nobody knows about them. The first happened in 1672. Thomas Lancaster married into the Braithwaite family who owned the cottage which was part of a larger farm back then. He lived there with his wife; the rest of the family lived in the farmhouse further down the valley. The whole family had gathered at the cottage for a meal, and he laced all of their food with arsenic, killing his wife's dad, his wife and her three sisters.'

Amy was staring at her. 'He killed five people inside of that house?'

Morgan nodded.

'What happened to him?'

'He was taken to the Assizes at Lancaster and the judge declared he was to be taken back to his own house bound in chains and hanged at the door until he was dead.'

They all looked at one another. They could all see the link to Margery's death. Poison. Hanging. Chains.

'Wow, that's just unreal. Why did he do it? Does it say?' Ben asked.

'Money. He wanted the farm and properties for himself. They took him back there to hang him, wrapped him in chains. Whoever killed Margery knew this, they copied Thomas Lancaster's execution; it's possible they had the same motivation.'

'So, we're looking for someone who knows about the history of the Lancasters. Did Margery know about this, do you think?'

Morgan nodded. 'I think so. I think that's why she put up a fight. She realised what was about to happen. History was repeating itself. She didn't get life in prison for her crimes and whoever wanted to kill her must think that is what she deserved.'

Amy was shaking her head. 'But George and David didn't die. They survived, so why leave it till now?'

'It has to be her son, who else would wait this long? Maybe he did a family tree or something on Ancestry, trying to find out about his real family and this came up. He's been waiting until he's an adult, and has all the resources to make it happen, plus Margery had a recent windfall and half a million pounds was paid into her building society account, maybe he'd found out about it.'

Ben smiled. 'Good work, I'd never heard of this at all.'

Cain clapped him on the shoulder. 'That's because it's a little before you were born, boss.'

'A little, are you saying I'm old?'

'Older than the rest of us for sure.'

Ben stood up. 'We need to find her son. As soon as the solicitors open tomorrow, I want them checking, we need to know if she had any dealings with them and who she had down as her next of kin; and Amy, you can try and find out who dealt with his adoption at social services.' He strolled to the whiteboard and began to write a list – adoption paperwork – then he stopped. 'Would they have given Margery any paperwork about this, he was taken from her because of the situation. I wouldn't think she would have had a say in any of what happened to him next. It was out of her control?'

Morgan smiled at him. 'I doubt it, I can go speak to Angela, the retired social worker who has helped me in the past. She might know who dealt with the case. It could cut down on all the phone calls and red tape.'

'Amazing, yes please. I suppose now we have nothing else we can chase up, we should call it a day and be back here bright and early.'

'Fine by us, isn't it, Amy?' Cain was already edging towards the door.

'Yes, great. See you in the morning, hopefully we'll have a hit on the forensics tomorrow to give us half a chance.' She placed her palms together as if she was praying and winked at Ben.

Then the pair of them were out of the door in less than ten seconds.

'Ettie said the only person who ever really went to Margery's cottage was her and the local delivery kid from the grocers on the high street. The owners closed it a few years ago and moved to Tenerife, but I wonder if it's worth tracking him down? He left to go to university, but his parents are still at the same address, and he might have come back after he graduated.'

'Absolutely, anyone who can give us the slightest bit of information about her lifestyle and anyone who was involved in it might be able to help.'

'I'll do that tomorrow too.'

He shook his head. 'No, you won't. You're going to speak to the solicitors and Angela, remember. Cain can do that; you're not doing all the work.'

He wrapped his arms around her, pulling her close, and she

relaxed against him, their lips brushing against each other just as the door slammed open and Cain whistled. 'Get a room, the pair of you, please, my eyes are hurting.'

They pulled apart to the sound of his laughter.

'Sorry, forgot my phone.' He grabbed it off the desk and was out of the door. 'You may continue.' He was grinning, then he was striding along the corridor, and they both smiled after him. They didn't usually do public displays of affection and to be fair to Ben he had thought they were on their own.

'I hope you continue where you left off when we get home.'

He was grinning at her. 'You can bet a million pounds on that. It's been a long day.'

He wasn't wrong. As they put their coats on to finally leave, she picked up the pizza box off her desk. She wasn't letting it go to waste. They would eat it for supper and get an early night.

17

Ben was still asleep, but Morgan had woken up after the worst dream ever. She could still see the image of herself hanging from the branches of the oak tree where they had found Margery Lancaster yesterday and, somehow, she was watching her own body sway in the breeze while Margery was standing next to her, arms folded across her chest, shaking her head.

'I suppose it's true what they say, what goes around comes around, even though it's taken hundreds of years; you just can't clean bad blood.'

What did that even mean? Whose bad blood? Morgan's or Margery's? She turned on her side away from Ben. Grabbing her phone she opened up the notes app and typed it in, so she didn't forget it. Bad blood ran in her family, she supposed that was true, look at Gary and Taylor, but it didn't mean she was going to end up the same way, did it? She supposed if there was one fear that lingered in her darkest thoughts it was that in the end, she would turn out to be just like them. Had Margery Lancaster been cursed with bad blood too? If so, did that mean she wasn't at fault for what she did because of a generational curse? Was she trying to warn her in her dreams that she was destined to end up the same way, killing the people she loved? That thought was like a knife in her heart – the pain it caused was so sharp and physical. She would rather die than hurt Ben or Ettie, and they were the only family she had in the whole world. Maybe Margery was trying to tell her something about her own family. As far as she knew there was only her son, and George. Was she letting her know it was definitely one of them? Maybe it was George, he was her killer? About to tuck the phone under her pillow it began to vibrate, and she knew it was work. No one else would be ringing from an unknown number at six a.m.

'Brookes.' She coughed; her throat was dry.

'Good morning, it's the Control room. We have a missing person's report come in and the patrol sergeant requested you look at it ASAP.'

'What, me specifically? I'm not on shift until eight.'

'I know, I told them that when I looked up your duties; however, Mads was quite adamant you would want to know about it.'

'Who's missing?'

'George Lancaster was last seen getting into his car at approximately eight o'clock last night. He drove out of River View car park and hasn't returned. According to the duty manager there it's most unlike him. He never goes out that late and he has never stayed out all night. He's high risk because of his disabilities and because of yesterday's log about his ex-wife.'

She felt Ben's warm arm snake around her waist as he turned and listened to her conversation. 'I'm guessing the patrols have checked out High Wraith Cottage in case he's gone there feeling bad about Margery?'

'They've driven past and there is no sign of his car.'

'Okay, I'm on my way in. Tell Mads thanks.' She hung up not thankful at all; in fact quite the opposite.

'What's up?' Ben's voice sounded hoarser than hers.

'George Lancaster is missing; left his apartment around eight last night and hasn't come back.'

He sat up. 'Christ, do you think it's linked?'

'No idea, but he's high risk.'

The pair of them got out of bed at the same time. Morgan dressed quickly and went downstairs to make coffee because there was no way on this earth she was leaving the house today without a dose of caffeine. Ben came down, dressed in joggers and a thick hooded sweatshirt, not his usual office attire.

'You need to go put something warmer on. We are not, I repeat not, trailing around the fells and country roads in shirts and ties freezing our tits off again.'

'Yes, boss.' She passed him a mug and disappeared upstairs.

She put her hair in a messy bun, and did a super quick make-up job. Torrential rain and howling winds or not, she wasn't leaving the house without her eyeliner. Her eyebrows were good; she'd finally had those tattooed on, and she had semi-permanent lashes which saved her faffing around with mascara every day. Little luxuries that saved her precious time at moments like this and made her look half human when she was in a rush. Taking off her black trousers she pulled on some thermal-lined leggings, vest, long-sleeved top and a warm 50 States of Madness hoodie from her favourite podcast website. She felt better, almost ready to start the day.

Back downstairs Ben nodded in approval. 'That's better. I made you some toast too.'

She took a slice off the plate. 'Would you look at us, all bright eyed, dressed for inclement weather and caffeined up ready to go searching for that awful man.'

'Yep, we are good and, awful or not, we still owe him a duty of care.'

She nodded. 'I know, I just didn't like him or get a good vibe from him. I think he was probably violent towards Margery and could have been the reason she was pushed to her limit to do what she did.'

Morgan didn't feel good to go, she felt tired and worried, but she wouldn't tell Ben that. George Lancaster might be horrible, he also might be in trouble and regardless of her feelings towards him she would not ignore anyone who needed her help.

Morgan and Ben went straight to the sergeant's office where Mads was about to put his coat on. 'Ah, sorry to call you out but I thought you'd want to know.'

'Have you found him?'

'Not yet, but he can't be far, can he? I mean he's only got one leg and relies on his vehicle for getting around. It's not like he's gone hiking up the fells or anything.'

'Who went to his flat?'

'Amber.'

'Where is she now?'

He pointed to the report writing room. 'Uploading the details onto the system.'

Ben looked at Morgan who turned to go speak to her, leaving him with Mads.

The report writing room was quiet – everyone was out looking for George.

'Hey.'

Amber turned to Morgan. 'Hey.'

'How are you getting on?'

She shrugged. 'Not a lot to go on. I went inside his flat – the warden let me in. It was clean, tidy, no sign of a struggle, no long note telling whoever he was feeling bad and off to end it all. Perhaps he's on the run to escape prosecution for Margery's death?'

'Was there anything out of place?'

'I don't think so. The warden said it looked all okay and

looked the same as it was when she checked in on him yesterday after the police left.'

Morgan hadn't realised there had been a warden on site, she supposed that was nice. 'Did she say how he was after we left?'

'A bit quiet, looked as if he was in a world of his own and didn't really engage in much conversation with her. He told her his ex-wife had died and that was it. She left him to it and told him to ring if he needed to talk.'

'Hmn, can't get fairer than that. Did you ask about CCTV, if anyone else visited him after we left, if anyone followed him out of the car park?'

Morgan sensed that Amber wanted to roll her eyes at her, but she didn't. 'I viewed it. Look I'll show you. She emailed a copy straight over.' Amber moved the mouse around and brought up a screen showing George Lancaster walking out of the building to his car. Nobody followed him, he was alone, he got in his car and drove off. He wasn't looking around; he didn't look upset or in distress. She watched a few minutes more; no other cars left or entered the car park.

'Strange.'

'Maybe he went looking for his son to break the news,' Ben's voice said from behind her. 'Any luck on ANPR, Amber?' he asked.

She shook her head. 'He's seen leaving the Kendal Road, heading towards Ambleside, but the Ambleside camera is down, so there's nothing after Main Street.'

'He could be anywhere, or he could be at High Wraith Cottage. Has anyone actually bothered to get out of the car and go inside to check?'

Amber shrugged. 'I'd say not because it was Scotty who got sent there and he did a drive by; you know what he's like. He said it didn't look like anyone was inside, no lights on, no vehicles around.'

Morgan looked at Ben. 'I think we should go check inside of

it, just to be sure. He could have a key. He lived there long enough with Margery, and I doubt she was the kind of woman to have the foresight to get locks changed while she was detained. She probably didn't think they'd ever let her go home again.' That thought made her feel sad for the woman who had led such an unhappy life.

Morgan went back to speak to Mads. 'Have you got the key for High Wraith Cottage?'

He pointed to the desk, where there was a keyring with three keys on it. She scooped it up into her pocket.

'Thanks.'

He shrugged. 'Sorry, I thought you would want to know.'

She smiled at him. 'I did, I would have been annoyed when I turned up at eight completely unaware. You did the right thing.'

She waved the keys at Ben. 'Come on then, let's go check and make sure he's not there.'

They left in Ben's car; it was easier than going on the app to book out a hire car for the day; they didn't have time to waste.

18

Morgan knew as soon as she unlocked the door that something had changed inside this house since yesterday. She could also detect the faint, all too familiar, earthy odour of blood. She put her arm across the doorway to stop Ben from going any further.

'He's here.'

'Christ, Morgan, what are you, some kind of psychic now?'

She shook her head. 'Can't you smell the blood?'

Ben lifted his nose up and sniffed the air a couple of times. 'Not really, I'm starting with a bit of a cold after being outside in that storm yesterday.'

'Should I go in and see, then come get you if there's anything we can do?'

'No, you're not going in there alone. We don't know what the situation is.'

'George, it's the police. Are you okay, do you need help?'

Her voice was so loud it echoed around the walls of the cottage and seemed to bounce back towards her, and she looked at Ben for guidance. He shrugged. 'We better at least put shoe covers and gloves on, until we know one way or the other if he's okay.'

They did and returned to the entrance. 'George.' She called out louder this time, but silence greeted Morgan that was only broken by the relentless ticking of an antique clock on the wall. She led the way; upstairs was too cluttered. The only place with room for a guy the size of George was probably the bathroom. She didn't think he'd have gone upstairs. She was sure if he'd come here to take his own life, which is what she suspected, that he would have done it down here. Why make it even harder than it had to be by struggling up those stairs? She stared at the closed door that was Margery's bedroom then strode towards it. Keeping to one side of the wall she pushed open the door with the crook of her elbow and then jumped, a small screech emitted from her lips.

Ben peered over her shoulder. 'Oh, God.'

The pair of them stood staring at the contorted face of George Lancaster, his eyes bulging so far out from their sockets it looked as if they had been about to explode from his face. His partially severed tongue lolled to one side of his mouth, and there was a thick metal chain wrapped around his neck. George had put up a fight. Margery's small bedroom was in a state of utter disarray. The small chest of drawers by the bed was overturned; the ceramic lamp on it was smashed to pieces; and it looked as if George had cut his hands to shreds trying to defend himself. The metal bedframe was broken with the weight of George – and possibly his killer – fighting on it. Ben was looking around in horror.

'We need to backtrack out of here. Whoever did this must be injured. There is no way that George didn't cut him or hurt him. Some of the bloodstains could belong to the killer.'

Morgan was speechless; she couldn't tear her gaze away from George's body.

'Are you good, Morgan?'

Ben's voice sounded as if he was speaking to her from

outside it was that distorted. He gently shook her shoulder. 'Morgan.'

She turned to look at him and nodded but her voice came out as a soft whisper. 'I'm good.' She had disliked the man immediately after meeting him yesterday, but he didn't deserve to die like this. It was brutal not to mention torturous, and all she kept thinking about was that this house had taken another soul to add to its collection. A cold chill settled over her at the thought.

She followed Ben outside, where an arctic blast of freezing air hit her in the face, making her shiver and snap her out of the fog her brain was steeped in; he was giving orders over the radio to the Control room.

Where was George's car? How did he get here? She began to walk around to the back of the cottage. There were tyre marks in the long grass, two tracks where it had been flattened. Thank God the rain had finally stopped overnight. She followed them to the back of the garden where there was a steep drop down the side of the fell. Halfway down the fell was the blue car, the front end all smashed to pieces.

She walked back to find Ben sitting in the front of his car.

He got out. 'Are you okay? Did you have to go be sick?'

'No, I found his car. It's been pushed down the side of the fell. There's a steep drop off at the end of the garden. There might be evidence inside it, prints, DNA if the killer was bleeding and took George's car, or was in it. He could still be in the car. What if he didn't know the garden had a steep drop?'

Ben pressed his palms together, fingers pointing upwards. 'Dear God, I don't ask for much but the killer's body in the front of the car would be pretty decent. Amen.'

Morgan couldn't help the smile that broke out across her face. He was right, it would be decent and also a miracle.

'Someone needs to go down there and check?'

She turned, and Ben followed her to the edge of the sodden,

grassy drop. The car was quite some way down the fell, there were deep grooves in the ground where the tyres had rolled down at speed and flattened the scrub on the way down, it was much steeper than she'd first realised.

'I'll go down,' she offered.

'Let me see, steep drop, muddy, slippery conditions, you have a dodgy ankle anyway. That is a definite no, absolutely not. If your ankle gives way and you go tumbling down there, by the time I can get help to you, hypothermia could have set in. We're going to have to call out Langdale and Ambleside Mountain Rescue. They're better equipped than either of us to get to that car.'

'But that could take some time for them to scramble and get here. I could be down there in ten minutes.'

'If our guy is in that car, he's not going anywhere, is he? He's already been out there all night and probably dead. Have you seen the state of the front end of it? He'd have been crushed like a Coke can. I'm not risking you or me falling down there and getting hurt. This time you can do as your supervisor advises.'

She knew he wasn't being mean, and he rarely pulled rank on her, but she desperately wanted to know if this was the end of two days of horror or whether it wasn't over yet.

19

A paramedic arrived on a motorcycle at the same time as Marc and CSI. Wendy got out of the van and headed straight for Morgan, avoiding Marc who headed towards Ben.

'What's the craic then? Is this place cursed or what? Two bodies in two days, I don't get it, and excuse my being ignorant but who took the scene guard off yesterday?'

Morgan held up her hands. 'Hang on, this is nothing to do with me. I think the boss'—she arched an eyebrow at Marc— 'agreed it because it's such a remote location; nobody expected this to happen.'

'Sorry, Morgan, I'm not having a go at you, I'm just shocked. This is a record even for us.'

'At least you didn't get a tree branch with a dead body through your windscreen like the poor paramedics did. They sent a biker today.'

'I don't blame them, probably can't afford to have another van off the road if something else happens. He looks a bit worried. Had you not better put him out of his misery?'

She nodded. 'Yes, I'll take him in. He's going to wish he hadn't drawn this short straw though, it's horrid.'

Wendy crossed her arms, tilting her head. 'Average horrid or like horrid, horrid?'

'Horrid, horrid.'

'Why am I not surprised?'

'Crime scene is a mess too, but there should be plenty of trace evidence or at least I'm hoping so.'

'Bless you, don't ever lose that spark of hope you carry inside of you unlike the rest of us old and jaded doubters.'

'I'll take the paramedic in, then you can get started.'

'Is Declan on his way?'

Morgan nodded. 'He is, but he said he might be some time.'

'Ball's in your court then, Morgan.' Wendy winked at her; Morgan turned to go and speak to the paramedic.

'Hi, thanks for coming. The body is on the ground floor. Do you need me to show you?'

'Yes, please, you better had. I don't like attending crime scenes on my own, accidents are okay but, you know, when someone has been murdered it kind of freaks me out a little. It's easier when you're double crewed in an ambulance and have a partner to go inside with.'

He wasn't wrong there; she would hate to deal with this mess on her own.

She led him into the dark hallway and pointed to the room where George was. 'He's in there.'

The guy who looked as if he'd rather be anywhere but here walked into the room and said, 'Jesus.'

Morgan smiled. How many of them had taken the Lord's name in vain in the last hour? 'Definitely not Jesus; this is George Lancaster.'

The paramedic had hold of George's wrist in one of his gloved hands, feeling for a pulse in the stiffened limb. He shook his head at her. 'You didn't need me to tell you that he's dead, did you? I mean he's stiff as a board.'

'No, we didn't but the paperwork we're going to have to submit did. You know how it is?'

He gave her a look of commiseration. 'Unfortunately, I do. Wasn't his wife found murdered here yesterday? They were calling her the iron lady back at the hub, gossiping about it for hours.'

It made her sad to think that her nickname preceded Margery's real name. Nobody knew anything about her. 'Yes, she was.'

'Yeah, caused a right to do that branch smashing the wind-screen on the van. So, have you got the killer in custody, or should I warn tomorrow's shift to be on the lookout for another one?'

'We haven't and no, you don't need to. There are going to be no more murders here.' She tried to sound confident but knew that her voice wasn't as strong as it could be.

He shrugged. 'You lot have your work cut out for you then.'

She watched him walk out of the cottage into the daylight and thought she heard a whisper from somewhere upstairs, the quietest of voices calling her name. Every hair on the back of her neck stood on end, and she slowly turned to look up the staircase, terrified in case she saw Margery Lancaster's haunted face staring down at her. It was dark up there despite it being daytime, but she couldn't see anybody watching her much to her relief. Looking around to make sure nobody else was in hearing distance, she closed her eyes and whispered, 'I hear you; I'm going to try to help you all.' She wondered if George's pres-ence here had upset the balance. He was, as far as she knew, not a nice man when he lived here. How was that working out? Had he moved on or was his soul stuck here with the others?

'Morgan, how the heck are you?' Declan's voice startled her.

'Oh, I'm sorry, my love, I didn't mean to make you jump. Ben said you were already inside so no need to hang around. What have we got?'

'I'll let you see for yourself.' She pointed to the makeshift bedroom. Declan stopped to look at her. 'Are you okay, you look a little lost?'

'I'm good, there's a lot of history with this house and I guess I'm feeling the sadness.'

'Ah, that definitely makes you an empath. Susie was telling me all about them today. She said that you were probably highly empathetic whereas the pair of us not so much. Well, I do feel for every single patient I deal with, but I don't often take it home with me. You should probably speak to your aunt and see if she can give you some black tourmaline or maybe some smoky quartz to protect yourself.'

She stared at him open-mouthed. 'I should?'

'Most definitely, I know a thing or two about crystals. I have a book all about them.' He winked at her. 'Susie said she's a well-respected witch who knows a thing or two. You should tap into what she has. I would be doing that if I was you.'

He blew her a kiss and walked to the entrance of the door, leaving her staring after him, shocked that Susie knew so much about her personal life and wondering if they had been gossiping about her, or was it a general conversation?

'Well, I'll be damned. What a terrible way to die.' He stepped into the room, and Morgan watched from the hallway.

'George, I hope you don't mind me using your first name. I'm Declan, a forensic pathologist, and I'm here to help find out what happened to you.'

He turned to Morgan. 'Bloody hell, this is a mess?'

She nodded.

'Well, George, I'm going to say that you put up one hell of a fight, so well done because I would not let someone try to choke me to death without one either. I'm sorry that you didn't make it.'

Morgan watched as Declan began to bag George's hands up to preserve any DNA that might be captured underneath his nails. 'I'd say he definitely hurt his killer; there looks like a lot of dried blood under his nails. Rigour is fully in force, so he's been dead at less than twelve hours. I think this scene is going to be a goldmine and I'm hoping that George will be too, lots of nice evidence so you can nail the sick bastard who is doing this. You know if another body turns up you have yourself a serial killer.'

Morgan knew this, knew that technically two murders that were connected as part of a series could be classed as a serial killer, but she kept quiet.

'Not that we want another body. Dear God, these two are more than enough for the time being.'

'I think so too. Although his car went down the side of the fell and is all smashed up. Me and Ben are both kind of hoping the killer was inside it, but we don't know yet until mountain rescue come to take a look.'

He arched an eyebrow at her. 'Really? That would be interesting, wouldn't it? Save us all a lot of hard work and tie it up nicely. I hope that your guy or gal is in there too, although that makes more work for me but I'm team Morgan all the way, so whatever makes you happy makes me happy too.'

She laughed. 'You're too funny, I keep telling you stand-up comedy would be a great side hustle for you.'

'A side hustle. Are you mad? The number of bodies you send my way I'm lucky to get home for my supper each evening.'

'Wouldn't want you to get bored.'

'Bored, absolutely not, my love. Not with you around. Anyway, I digress and I'm sorry, George, please excuse my temporary distraction. I'm going to let them move you when they're ready, and I'll have my mortuary all ready for you.'

He finished taking samples and packed them away in his case. 'I'll go tell Ben I'm happy for him to be moved.'

A floorboard above them creaked, the sound loud in the small room, and Declan's face paled as he pointed a finger up at the ceiling. Too late Morgan realised their mistake – they hadn't searched the house as soon as they'd arrived, but they had done a thorough search yesterday and when they had left last night it had been clear. They had been so thrown by finding George that it had slipped their minds. She lunged for Declan, grabbing his arm, and dragged him out of the room, down the narrow hallway and outside.

Ben watched, a puzzled look on his face, and then he came jogging over. 'What's wrong?'

'There's somebody upstairs.'

'Fuck.'

He looked around, and Morgan knew there was nobody else for backup until he requested cops to come. The only police officers on scene were her, Ben and Marc.

He shouted, 'Sir,' loud enough that Marc turned away from Wendy with a scowl on his face.

Ben waved him over, and he strode towards them looking pissed. 'What's up?'

'There's somebody upstairs. We heard movement, the floorboard creaked.'

Marc had the audacity to roll his eyes. 'I take it you searched the place when you discovered the body?'

They both shook their heads. Morgan spoke. 'It was secure last night when we left, and it threw us seeing George like that.'

'Christ almighty. Morgan, go and guard the back door so they can't escape. We're going to have to go in.'

She opened her mouth to argue with him, but the look on Ben's face warned her not to. It wasn't happening, so she wouldn't have to go inside unarmed.

'I think you should call for a taser officer,' she whispered.

'No time, I'm sure me and Ben can handle him, there's two of us. I can't be the only one who used to spend my weekends fighting with drunken louts when I was a section officer, it's a rite of passage.'

A wave of sickness began to rise up her throat. This wasn't some drunken lout, and she didn't want Ben to go in unprotected to apprehend a violent killer, but she nodded instead then turned to go.

Marc waved Wendy over. 'Stay in the van, please, and can you get officers travelling ASAP? Tell Control the suspect might be in the cottage.'

Morgan watched the pair of them disappear from view as she headed to the back of the cottage. If she heard so much as a shout of surprise from either of them, she was going in, permission or not.

20

MAGGIE

The burns on Maggie's legs were painful, and as she prodded at one of the blisters, a yellow pus seeped out, making her wince and want to be sick at the same time. She needed antibiotics, and knew she should phone the doctors. Only she couldn't because right now there was the big, shiny, bruised black eye that George had given to her last night after he'd put David to bed. The doctor would ask lots of questions, too many questions, and she didn't want to try and make up more excuses as to why she had got a black eye in the first place.

It hadn't been her fault, she was doing too much: cooking, cleaning, looking after David. She needed eyes in the back of her head, and she just couldn't handle it. How she wished she'd gone back to see the kind woman above the hairdressers to stop this before it had even started. She had offered her a way out; had told her she'd drive her to the women's refuge in Kendal, but she wasn't about to leave her house with George living inside of it. It wasn't much, but it was all she had in the world. Even though it had never been the kind of house that was filled with love and laughter, she wouldn't give it up. It was quite simple really; the thought had been lingering inside her mind for a long time, always there hiding behind the curtains and peeping through every time she wished she wasn't married to him. He had to go. There wasn't anything hard about it and he could take David with him. She didn't care where they went as long as they did and left her alone. She could make them both sick, make them really sick, and when they got better George would leave her because he'd know she was the reason they'd got sick in the first place. She might get in trouble with the police, but that was okay. She'd never done anything wrong her entire life. She wasn't worried about getting arrested or going to prison even, as long as they were out of her life before she came home.

Rubbing some Germolene on the burn, she bit her lip at the sting, then took a clean strip of the linen tablecloth she'd cut into pieces to wrap around it to stop it weeping onto her trousers. When she was done, she stood up and opened the medicine cabinet. There was a packet of paracetamol that was nearly empty, and a brown bottle half full of pink ibuprofen pills; she didn't think they would do much harm except turn his lips pink and cure him of his hangover. The only other thing that might be of any use were the three packets of ferrous sulphate tablets the doctor had prescribed after she'd given birth. She'd hated the taste of the iron tablets so didn't bother taking them. Picking up the packet she squinted and tried to read the back of it, but the writing was too small. Pushing them into her pocket she went downstairs. David was still asleep, and George wasn't due home for another two hours.

In the kitchen she took out all the tablets and the old mortar and pestle that was in the cupboard. Carefully she ground down the tablets into a fine dust and lifted the bowl to her nose. It smelled funny. Dabbing her little finger into it she licked it and grimaced. They were terrible, how was she going to disguise that? George would taste it straight away in his tea or in a can of the cider he drank every night in front of the television. She crossed her arms and leaned against the kitchen side. Sugar, she needed to hide it in something so sweet it wouldn't be tasted straight away.

Opening the cupboards to check she had the right ingredients, she smiled to see the tin of golden syrup that she'd bought last time she had gone shopping. She would make his favourite syrup sponge pudding, sprinkle the crushed tablets on top and put lashings of the gooey, sticky sauce over the powder to hopefully disguise the vile taste. For the first time in forever she hummed as she mixed all of the ingredients together. She had a plan, she was going to be free very soon and she didn't care one little bit about the consequences.

21

'How do you want to do this?' whispered Ben.

Marc paused at the entrance to High Wraith Cottage then replied, 'Loudly.'

Ben had spent many a Saturday nightshift fighting with the drunks on Cornwallis Street in Barrow, which was once famous for its brawls. Had learned a thing or two about fighting and he had never been afraid to dive right into the middle of a fight. At one point Friday and Saturday nights on the street had become world famous and there had been a few documentaries filmed down there and a whole television series.

Marc shouted, 'Police, come down with your hands above your head,' so loud that it vibrated down Ben's ears and left them ringing.

Marc was inside.

Ben muttered, 'Bollocks,' under his breath and followed him in. If whoever was hiding upstairs hadn't been deafened by the voice, the pounding of his feet as he ran up the old wooden stairs would do the trick. For a man so slim with no sign of a beer belly in sight, he sounded like an elephant. Ben was right behind him, ready to fight a killer if he had to. He'd rather not, but there wasn't much else he could do. It wasn't that he was getting soft in his old age; it was more that he had someone he loved and cared about waiting outside for him that made him cautious.

Marc flung open the door to the first room. 'Christ, what a mess. The place has been ransacked.'

Ben peered over his shoulder. 'Nah, it was like that yesterday.'

'It was?'

The only place someone could hide in here was under the bed or in the old wardrobe. Ben pointed to them both.

'I'll take the wardrobe; you look under the bed.'

He hated looking underneath beds. It was some deep-seated childhood fear that had stuck with him into adulthood. As a kid, he had always been afraid someone would be hiding under his bed, ready to grab his ankle should he throw it out from underneath his covers. It used to take him ages to fall asleep, and he always made sure the covers were tucked underneath his feet. The first bed he bought for himself was a divan with a solid base.

He leaned down and lifted the duvet, then exhaled; the only things under there were dusty boxes that had been opened by the team. Marc threw open the wardrobe door that was full of clothes and more boxes. He rifled through the rail just to be sure, but it was impossible for anyone to be hiding in there.

They moved on to the next room, the one full of books, and as he stood looking around it, Ben realised that this had been the baby's room. The walls had faded blue paper with teddy bears and toy cars on it. A wave of sadness washed over him. This baby had never asked to be born and had suffered immensely at the hands of his mum. Was it that she hadn't been able to cope with him, had needed help that she either hadn't sought or didn't realise she should seek? For a moment he felt a deep sorrow and a sense of understanding... had she been abandoned and had that completely fucked up her way of thinking? And he could understand why this poor boy might want to punish Margery and George for what they did to him, what they put him through, but he didn't condone it.

'She was a bit of a hoarder, wasn't she?' Marc asked.

'Looks that way.'

Marc strode in. There wasn't anywhere to hide in here either. There was a small built-in cupboard in the corner, and stacks of books in front of it that were covered in dust. Ben didn't need to look under the cot in here – it wasn't big enough and there were more books underneath that. Haphazard piles of wonky book stacks made it impossible to move in here at all. The last room was the bathroom, which was empty. That left the small trap door to the attic, which Ben pointed out to Marc. He'd be surprised if anyone was up there now, as they had bolted it from the outside when they'd searched it yesterday.

'Why put a bolt outside of it?' Marc was staring up.

'I imagine this house is cold and very draughty, being on its own so far up the fell. The bolt was probably to stop the door blowing open in a storm and causing a wind tunnel.'

'Well, nobody is up there now, are they? Unless they can slide bolts across with the power of their mind.' He laughed. 'We better check it to be sure, then go downstairs and we can call off the backup, no point having them travelling at speed through these bloody narrow lanes for the sound of the wind blowing through an old cottage.'

Ben crouched down and cradled his hands to give Marc a boost up, so he could balance on the top of the railing underneath the attic. They watched as he struggled to loosen the bolt. 'It's rusted shut and stuck solid, did they open it yesterday?'

Ben shook his head.

'There's no way anyone is up there, it needs a hammer to knock it open and there would be fresh marks in the metal where the rust had given away.' He jumped down.

. . .

Ben knew Morgan wouldn't have mistaken the wind blowing for the sound of a floorboard creaking. He turned to give it one last glance before going downstairs and felt a cold shiver run down the full length of his spine. This house gave him the creeps. So many people had died in here, not just died, had been murdered. He imagined them all lined up along the landing, watching him like something out of that TV series *Ghosts*. He gave a curt nod to anyone who might still be hovering around then followed Marc downstairs, where they checked the rest of the house.

The kitchen door was locked from the inside, so no intruder could have escaped that way while Morgan had been talking to them outside the front of the cottage.

'The only person inside here is him, and he isn't moving around anytime in the foreseeable future. Morgan must have been hearing things.'

'Boss, Declan heard it too. They both did.'

'I'm not saying that they didn't, but it's an old house, old houses make funny noises, they groan and creak. I'm saying it's a false alarm, nothing to be concerned about other than him.' Marc was pointing at George. 'Poor bastard looks like he put up a fight, bad for him but good for us. Should we let Wendy get on with it, then we can get him moved?'

'Yes, we should. I was thinking, we're going to have to keep a watch on this place in case he comes back again. Providing he's not dead in the front of the car that's smashed to pieces halfway down the hill.'

Ben knew what was coming next; he could have bet a round of drinks down at The Black Dog for the entire pub on what Marc was going to say.

'Why do we not know if there is a body inside the car?'

And there it was. Not for the first time did he wish that

their old boss Tom hadn't retired. He missed the old sod more than he had ever missed anyone he'd worked with, apart from Morgan. Tom wouldn't be acting like some action man on speed. He'd be happy to go with whatever Ben decided and not argue at all. He never pushed any of them to breaking point, had trusted their decisions without any doubt whatsoever. He was a great guy and he missed him.

'It's down the side of a steep fell where the ground is precarious after yesterday's storm. Mountain Rescue are on their way to take a look.'

Marc strode towards the back of the cottage; Ben came out and gave Wendy, who was sitting in the van with Declan, a thumbs up. Then he turned and followed him to the edge of the drop where the car had driven off.

'I can get down there, might be a bit tricky but I'm sure I can make it to go take a look. I'm a bit shocked that Morgan hasn't already been down. I mean I get why you haven't, you have to be careful with your heart and all that, but she's young and fit.'

Ben felt his fingers curl into tight fists, and he stuffed them inside his coat pocket in case he got the sudden urge to either punch or push Marc off the end of the drop.

'I wouldn't let her, but she offered. I'll chase up mountain rescue and see what their eta is.'

He turned and looked at Ben. 'I'm not being personal, but do you think you are just a little too overprotective of her? If it had been Cain that had offered, would you have let him go down?'

Ben's fingers curled even tighter. 'No, I would not. There's too much risk of them slipping and hurting themselves, and I would suggest that you don't go down either and wait for the professionals to come and help. These fells are unforgiving should you lose your footing, sir, you could break an ankle or much worse; it's not like walking around the pavements of the inner city streets of Manchester.'

Marc shrugged. 'Have we got any rope?'

What for? To strangle you with? Ben didn't say this out loud – thinking it was enough. 'I have a tow rope in the back of my car, but I doubt it's long enough to get you down to the car though.'

'It will do. The hardest part is the first thirty feet. It's not as steep after that.'

Ben turned to go back to the car. He was angry and hoped to God that Marc went skidding all the way down the side of the fell. It would serve him right.

He watched as Marc strode back towards him in a pair of almost new walking boots that he must carry around in the back of his car. Morgan had followed behind him curious to see what was going on. He could tell by the expression on her face she was not happy that Marc was about to attempt what he had forbidden her to do. He gave her a half smile, shrug type of thing, and she rolled her eyes in Marc's direction.

Marc had a pair of gloves on, and he carried the rope passing one end to Ben who tied it tightly around his waist, but Marc who had the other end didn't test it to make sure it was secure as he knotted it around his own waist before he began to lower himself off the edge. Ben realised too late that Marc hadn't tied the rope tight enough; the knot was never going to hold him if he slipped.

'Maybe it will help soften Marc's ego,' Morgan whispered.

There was a huge pull on the rope as Marc lost his footing on the slippery grass, his boots unable to find purchase at the same time as a loud yell and then the rope went slack as Marc did indeed lose his grip on the rope he hadn't tied properly as it slid from his grip and despite the boots he went arse over tit down the steep side of the fell.

'Oh crap, I told Marc,' was all Ben could say as the pair of them watched in horror as he tumbled down, gathering speed and rolling around like the big purple thing off the children's show *Teletubbies*.

Morgan was shaking her head. 'That's going to hurt his pride more than his backside.'

Ben felt bad, had he wished this on the bloke? Morgan was always telling him to be careful what he wished for. Still, he couldn't stop the grin that had spread across his face. Marc had come to a standstill not too far away from the car and was trying his best to jump up as if he hadn't just done an Eddie the Eagle but on a mud run instead of snow.

'I'm okay, I'm okay.' He was on his feet, but bending over, and Ben knew he'd winded himself and was trying to catch his breath.

'Are you sure, boss, that was a nasty tumble. Do you want me to get the paramedic back?'

Marc shook his head and held up a hand.

'What an idiot,' said Morgan. 'I wish I'd caught that on bodycam. We could watch it every time he gets on our nerves.'

Ben nodded and watched as Marc cautiously made his way to the smashed-up car, his entire rear covered in wet, sticky mud from the back of his head to his feet.

'He's not going to save that designer suit; he's going to have to throw it away.'

Morgan took out her phone zoomed in and took a quick snap of the mud splattered across his back. 'One for posterity and to cheer us up when he's being a pain, plus it's not fair if Amy and Cain don't get to see it.'

He didn't argue with her or tell her to delete it.

Finally, Marc was at the car peering into the wreckage. He turned to them and shouted, 'Nobody inside.'

Ben sighed; he should have known it was never going to be that easy. Morgan patted his back then walked back in the direction of the cottage, and he knew she was going to share

Marc's spectacular fall with Wendy, who would tell Claire and before long the entire station would know about it. It was the little things that made it all worthwhile, and Ben knew that Marc would never be allowed to forget it once it got out, and he didn't care. If the guy wasn't such an idiot, it would be a whole different story.

Walking further and feeling the chill of the cottage once again, Ben was reminded that they were back at square one, with no strong suspect, only now they had two bodies.

22

They gathered back at the station. There was no sign of Marc who had borrowed a set of crime scene overalls from Wendy, getting changed in the back of her van out of his ruined suit and driving away from the scene without so much as a wave. Morgan knew he'd gone home for a shower; he wouldn't have walked into the changing rooms at the station looking like that for anything. Too much chance of anyone seeing him – he wouldn't want that. He was for all of his sins a very well-turned-out guy, his designer suits, smart haircuts and expensive cologne made him quite the catch with a lot of the women who worked there. She was pretty sure if they got to know him, they'd see through his suave facade and realise he was a control freak who didn't particularly like women who stood up to him.

In the office Amy and Cain were sitting at their desks working away. They both nodded at her as she sat down at hers. Morgan lasted approximately five seconds before she grinned at them. 'You missed the fun.'

Amy shook her head. 'If you class finding a dead body as fun you need therapy.'

'Not that part, the part where the inspector decided he was

better at climbing down the side of a slippery fell than the mountain rescue team.'

Amy was grinning now. 'Please tell me he did, tell me that he went down it on his bottom?'

Morgan nodded as Cain and Amy broke out laughing. 'Oh, I wish I'd have seen that.'

She felt a little bad about being so mean, but he hadn't cared when he'd sent her to Barrow to work, splitting her up from the team and putting her life at risk. She showed them the picture, which made Cain laugh so loud down her ear she jumped.

'It was funny.'

'Where is he now?'

'I think he went home to have a shower; there's no sign of him here.'

Cain was still laughing when Ben walked in. He frowned at the three of them. 'You better not let him hear you or let him know you've been showing a picture of him around not looking his best, or you'll be on his hit list.'

'Even more than I already am?'

He nodded. 'Absolutely. Delete it, Morgan, it will save me the heartache.'

'Okay, but only because you asked.'

She deleted the picture, and he nodded. 'Thank you. I need an address for David Lancaster like five minutes ago. Amy, have you got anything for me?'

'I tried social services, but they aren't playing ball. Still nothing back from forensics and yes, I phoned the lab myself to check. Al had some papers and stuff in the back, he also had an ancient packet of rat poison that he said was half empty.'

Ben's eyebrow arched at the mention of the poison. 'He did? That's good, it might be what David Lancaster ingested, I guess we're waiting on tox results to come back too.'

Amy smiled. 'You guessed right, boss, none of the solicitors want to give any information over the phone either, someone is going to have to visit them in person and use their persuasive skills to get someone to talk.'

Ben looked defeated and more than a little stressed.

'Let me go see Angela, she might be able to help.' Morgan smiled at him. 'I'll bring food and coffee back with me.'

'Get out of here. Do you want to take Cain with you?'

She shrugged.

'Wow, thanks, Morgan, it's nice to be wanted.'

'Come on, Cain.'

———

As they walked into the corridor Cain lowered his voice. 'You can get that photo out of the deleted items, you know. Send it to me and I'll keep it safe.' He winked at her, and she laughed.

'And you'll get us both in trouble, no thanks. I know I can retrieve it; I'm not going to.'

'You are such a teacher's pet, Brookes. When did that happen? I thought you had more balls than that. You don't owe Marc anything. Have you forgot what he did to you?'

'No, I'll never forget that, but I don't want to cause Ben any more hassle than he's already got. I didn't like George Lancaster, the guy we visited yesterday, but it was bad, Cain. He put up a fight.'

Cain reached out and put an arm around her shoulders, pulling her towards him. 'You got the fuzzy end of the stick.'

She pulled away. 'I got something. Do you believe in ghosts?'

He looked at her. 'You're being serious, this isn't a trick question?'

'Deadly serious.'

He smiled at her. 'Nice pun. Let me see, I'm kind of torn on the whole subject. I want to believe because it's better than not.

I want to think that when I leave this handsome body there is something better waiting for me and it's not the end of this.' He flexed his arm with a smile on his face. 'Why are you asking, do you believe in them?'

She nodded. 'Yeah, I do. I used to love watching all those ghost-hunting shows when I was a teenager, they'd scare the crap out of me.'

'Most of them are fake.'

'I know, but I still enjoyed them, and I do believe in ghosts. Have you ever been to a crime scene and come across one?'

'A ghost?'

'Yes.'

'No, definitely not. Have you?'

'Not until today. I don't know if it was a ghost but at that cottage, I heard something on the stairs when I was alone in there, then both me and Declan heard a loud creak, yet when Ben and Marc searched up there, they didn't find anything. We deal with so much death and there have been so many brutal murders in that small cottage. It makes you wonder that's all.'

He nodded. 'It certainly does. I wouldn't want to be alone in that place when it gets dark. Come on, I'm hungry, let's go see this social worker and get lunch.'

'Retired social worker.'

'Same thing, bit like a retired cop, once a cop always a cop.'

She smiled at him, that was probably very true. She couldn't stop thinking about the family murdered inside that cottage. Speaking to Angela would be a welcome distraction from spending any more time on the fells.

23

Morgan knew Angela's house in Kendal very well – it was the only one on the street with a pink front door. She already loved her for that. It was cute, there was an evergreen wreath with touches of white berries hanging from it, simple but classy.

'Nice door,' whispered Cain as she knocked.

'It is, I love it. I'm tempted to tell Ben to get one.'

This shocked Cain more than she could ever have imagined. 'You like the colour pink?'

She grinned at him, unable to answer his question because the door opened and standing there with matching pink hair the same colour as the door was Angela. Her hair had been grey the first time they had met a couple of years ago and Morgan approved of this change it suited her.

'Morgan, how are you? Come in.'

'Hi, Angela, thank you. I'm great. This is my colleague Cain.'

'Hello, Cain.' She held out her hand to him, and he took it, shaking it.

For the first time Cain looked kind of awestruck, and Morgan knew why. He'd been expecting a grey-haired old woman not the vibrant, beautiful Angela, who was dressed in a black polo neck, wide-legged trousers and a pair of vintage Vans; she had on a pair of oversized chunky black glasses. She was the epitome of cool in Morgan's eyes.

'Hello, Angela, it's lovely to meet you,' Cain said.

'The pleasure is all mine.' She winked at Morgan who had to stifle a laugh. Cain was a good-looking guy, a little rough around the edges, but he had a heart of gold and she realised that he had taken a liking to Angela.

They followed her inside the house that Morgan liked second best after her aunt Ettie's. This one was all shabby chic, painted furniture with lots of antique paintings adorning the walls. Cain couldn't take his eyes off Angela, and Morgan knew the feeling; she was striking.

'Tea, coffee, water?'

'Coffee would be amazing, please, for both of us.'

'Good, I got myself one of those fancy Nespresso machines and it makes life so much easier. Take a seat and I'll be back in a moment.' She pointed to the sofa. 'Unless you're happy to slum it in the kitchen.'

Morgan nodded. 'More than happy to slum it in your kitchen.'

Angela laughed. 'Follow me then.'

They did, into a cloud of Chanel Coco. The back room had been extended since the last time Morgan had visited and was now an open-plan kitchen-diner with pink cupboards and beautiful pink island topped with white and gold marble. 'Oh my, slum it in here. Angela, this is amazing, I love it so much.'

'Thank you, Morgan, I do too. Pretty much cost most of the retirement money I had left from my lump sum but what the heck, you only live once. Did I tell you I'm writing a book?'

'No, that's so cool. About your time as a social worker?'

'Dear God, no, I'm not sure who the hell would want to read about that. No, I'm writing a romcom, bit of a cross

between *Bridget Jones* and *Notting Hill*. My two favourite films.
I watch them with a bottle of wine whenever I feel sad or
lonely, and thought I'd give it a go. I mean I spent years writing
long, detailed reports, but writing for fun is so much easier,
wouldn't you agree? I bet you're the same.'

Cain was staring at the woman, his mouth hanging open,
and Morgan nudged him in the side.

'Not so much as writing by hand anymore, ours are all done
digitally. I can't wait to read it when it's finished.' She paused.
'I'm afraid this isn't a social visit though; I have some questions
about a case that you may have worked on.'

'Ah, the days of my misspent youth. Has it got anything to
do with Maggie Lancaster's murder?'

Morgan nodded.

Angela smiled at her. 'Such a sad case, let me finish the
coffees and we'll chat. I'll tell you what I know.'

Morgan couldn't respect Angela more; she was a good
woman, with a good heart, who cared about the kids she'd had
to rehome.

She turned around, and Morgan realised Cain was
watching her every move. He fancied Angela, and Morgan
couldn't blame him. She was a strikingly beautiful woman, and
Cain's last girlfriend had pink hair, too, although Angela's was a
subtle, paler pink and it really suited her.

The smell of fresh, hot coffee filled the air, and she could
have cried with relief. She had spent the last two days
freezing her fingers to the bone out in the storm that had
been raging all around the Lakes, well apart from her too
short visit to Ettie's house that was. Angela took a packet of
Rich Tea biscuits out of the cupboard and opened it, passing
it to Cain.

'Help yourself, I only buy these because I love to nibble on
them when I'm writing, and I think they don't have as many
calories as the chocolate-coated digestives I adore.'

She passed them ribbed glass mugs filled with lattes, along with gold spoons to stir them.

'Sugar?'

They both shook their heads.

They all sat at the table, and Angela smiled at them. 'This is nice, I don't get a lot of visitors you know, even if it is about work.'

'Do you live on your own?' Cain asked, and Morgan felt her cheeks turn pink at his question.

Angela nodded. 'Yes, I do, Cain. Do you?'

He laughed. 'Unfortunately, I do, my wife left me because I worked too much.'

Angela reached out her long, slender fingers and patted his hand. 'That's so sad when your partner doesn't understand. I'm sorry to hear that.'

'It was a blessing to be fair, we weren't getting along.'

Morgan sipped her coffee and wondered what the hell was going on. Was he hitting on Angela, or did he just feel as if he could talk to her?

'Maggie Lancaster, did you deal with the case?' Morgan asked, bringing them back to the topic at hand.

Cain seemed to break out of his slight hypnosis.

Angela nodded. 'It was horrid. That poor baby, he deserved so much better. I don't know why she didn't just take him to the hospital or the police station, anywhere really, and tell them she couldn't cope, that her husband was a violent bully who beat her regularly. Of course, we didn't know about any of it until the baby and husband were rushed to hospital with suspected poisoning. I remember thinking how terrible it was, but I try not to judge too much. No one knew the full story; she was a strange woman. She didn't confess what she'd done at first, not until the baby was going blue and looked as if he might die. She broke down in tears in the waiting room and told the nurse that she'd tried to kill them because she hated the pair of them.'

'Wow, that's awful.'

'It was, it really was. Everybody could understand about her wanting to hurt George. When the police got her hospital records there was nothing on there, but when she was examined they found so many fading bruises. She had burns on her leg that were going septic, and her X-rays showed quite a few old broken bones that had healed not too great. It was clear that George used her as his own personal punching bag. By the time social services spoke to her the baby was stable, but very poorly, and had been rushed to Manchester Children's Hospital. George was put into intensive care; he was in there for three weeks and it was touch-and-go if he was going to make it.'

'Margery was arrested. Was she remanded, do you know?'

'Not at first; they didn't want to send her away before they knew the full circumstances of what had gone on. She was a victim of domestic violence and suffering from late-onset postpartum depression that had never been treated. It was so sad. If she'd gone to see the GP there was a chance none of it would have happened. She was a very quiet, private woman afraid to ask for help, scared to tell anyone about George. Thankfully, they both survived so she didn't get charged with murder. I wasn't shocked to see the headlines this morning. I've kind of always thought that something bad would happen to Maggie.'

'Because of what she did?'

'I know you can't tell me but was it George? I always thought one day he would take his revenge on her; I'm just surprised it took his this long.'

'We don't know if he had anything to do with Margery's death, but he was found dead at the cottage earlier this morning.'

Angela's face froze in horror. 'He was? Well, I'll be damned. I can't say I'm sorry about that, he was a horrible man. He was having an affair you know, constantly leaving Maggie on her own with the baby to sleep with another woman. I think she was called Dawn and there were rumours she emigrated to Australia after this all came out. He must have known Maggie wasn't coping.'

'What a bastard,' Cain muttered.

'Exactly, he is, or he was. I can't see many people being upset about his passing or Maggie's to be honest. They were like the town's dirty little secret that nobody talked about.'

'Do you know what happened to David?'

'I do, he was fostered by a lovely couple who lived in Grange-over-Sands. They were both teachers, took early retirement and had been fostering for many years. They ended up adopting him. I believe he's a doctor now. The last time I spoke to Rose she told me he was working in Lancaster Royal Infirmary.'

This shocked Morgan; she had not expected that. She had been waiting for Angela to tell her that he was up to no good. 'That's amazing... we need to speak to him though. Did they ever tell him about his real parents?'

'Yes, they were very honest and transparent with him. He knew that he'd been adopted and the reason why. Rose didn't want him to find out any other way. She asked my advice, some time after, and I told her I agreed with her; he was a clever boy, and it wouldn't have been too hard for him to find out about his childhood. She took him to visit Maggie, once, but she didn't want to see him. Rose said she cried the entire time he was there, and Rose felt terrible about it, wished she hadn't bothered. She said Maggie showed not one little bit of love towards the poor lad. Her husband took him to visit George as well. Rose's husband Harry was a black belt in karate. She said she didn't trust George and wanted to protect David as much as possible. It turns out George was quite a changed character by the time of their visit. He was happy to know their son had been looked after, but still wanted nothing to do with him.'

'Ouch, that must have been so hard for David. What an

awful position for him to be in and for him to have to live with that, knowing his upbringing had been so terrible.'

Angela was shaking her head. 'On the contrary, he had the best upbringing he could ask for. He had loving, supportive parents who adored him and he is now a doctor. He could have gone off the rails, but he didn't. He is a very level-headed man who adores Rose and the late Harry. Rose told me that he'd said he was glad he had been brought to live with them and hadn't had to live with his birth parents.'

'Wow, that's amazing. How lucky was he to find Rose and Harry. Does he still go by the name of David Lancaster?'

'No, he's David Hawthorne and I believe he is a cardiac specialist. I can give you Rose's phone number and address. You can speak to her, although Rose lives in a nursing home now. Sea View, on the outskirts of Grange, big red-brick building; you can't miss it. She has early Alzheimer's, or you could speak to the hospital.'

'Thank you so much, Angela, this is brilliant. Once again, you've been so helpful.'

She smiled. 'It's the least I can do, and it's a pleasure to see you, Morgan, you really need to come here and have a bottle of wine or two with me when you're not working. I get the impression you don't have much of a social life and it's all work; you need a break now and again.'

Cain nodded in agreement. 'She doesn't, it's all work and no play, isn't it, Morgan?'

She felt her cheeks begin to burn. 'I do, well not much but that would be lovely. We'll do that when we've found the killer.'

Angela patted her hand. 'Good, I'd like that. You too, Cain, you're very welcome to come for a bottle of wine with or without Morgan.' She winked at him, and his cheeks turned redder than Morgan's, which made her smile.

'I'd like that, a lot. Thank you.'

'Why don't you come over tomorrow night? If you're free that is, I could cook us some supper.'

He nodded. 'You could, yes. That sounds amazing, thank you.'

They stood up, and Angela wrote the name of the nursing home on a slip of paper, and the phone number, passing it to Morgan.

'Take care, both of you, thank you for everything you do. It's a thankless job at times, but I want you to know I appreciate you all.'

She walked them to the door and waved them off, and Morgan waved back. Cain still looked as if he was in shock, and she couldn't feel any happier for him. He deserved a bit of good luck, and she thought that Angela might be good for him even if he didn't know it yet.

24

Morgan tried not to mention Angela first on the car journey back; instead she waited for Cain and after around three minutes, he said, 'She is amazing.'

A huge grin spread across Morgan's face. 'She is and I'll tell you something, she would be great fun to take out on a date. You know what they say about older women.' She winked at him.

'I mean, she's very attractive and I can't believe she asked me over tomorrow. Should I go, do you think?'

'You most definitely should, unless your diary is filled up with dates for different women.'

It was his turn to laugh. 'It's not, I haven't had a date since I broke up with Isabelle, and to be honest, I only had a handful of them anyway because she lived too far away.'

'Then you should go. Take her some nice flowers, a bottle of decent wine and enjoy yourself. I think you two would get on really well, and she's so lovely.'

He smiled all the way to The Coffee Pot, where he parked outside. 'You said lunch was on you.'

'I said I'd bring it back; I didn't say I would pay for it.'

'Same thing: don't make promises you can't keep, Brookes. Use Ben's credit card; he can pay.'

'I can't and won't do that, and besides, I don't have his cards. I have my own. I'm not a kept woman. I'm an independent woman. Have you no shame?'

'Not when it comes down to the very serious issue of food: I have no morals whatsoever. I want a tuna savoury baguette, no salad, cheese and onion crisps, peppermint traybake and a latte.'

'Not much then.'

He waved her out of the car. 'I'm starving, get a move on.'

She tutted and left him waiting there to go and order the mountain of food to feed all four of them, and wondered, briefly, if she should get Marc something then decided against it. He'd probably eaten while he'd gone home to get changed.

———

'How did you get on with Angela?' Ben was there, opening the door for her as if he'd known she was about to walk through it. He glanced down at the tray of coffees she was carrying and leaned over to kiss her forehead.

'Come on, boss, none of that funny business in public.'

Cain was laughing. Morgan slipped past Ben into the office and left him staring at Cain who was carrying the food. Ben leaned forward to kiss his forehead too, and Cain pushed him away.

'I'm so happy to see you both with refreshments. I'd kiss Amy, too, if she was carrying food.'

Behind him Amy stuck two fingers up, waving them in his direction.

Ben grabbed a coffee from the tray, took a sip and sighed. 'How did you get on?'

Cain was grinning. 'Amazing, Angela was so helpful, and

she gave us his details. He was fostered to a couple in Grange who ended up adopting him. He's now a cardiac specialist.'

Ben almost choked on the mouthful of coffee. 'What's his name? It's not David Hawthorne, is it?'

Morgan nodded. 'Yes.'

'He's my heart consultant, he's a nice guy and very good. I also think he went out with Declan for a little while.'

'Oh my God, I thought that name sounded familiar.'

Ben was shaking his head. 'I can't see it being him. Why would he risk everything he has to kill his parents? Did Angela say if he knew them?'

Morgan began to explain everything Angela had told them in between bites of her sandwich.

'Maybe it would be better for you to sit this one out. Me and Cain could go and speak to him. It would be awkward for you to have to go question the guy who saved your life. Do you still have to see him?'

He nodded. 'I go for a review in six months. Yeah, I don't know whether it's a good idea for me to be involved in initial questioning. God, I hope it wasn't him... he's a great doctor; this would be a huge loss if we had to arrest him.'

Marc walked in, looked at their food and pouted. 'You could have asked if I wanted something.'

'I would have if we'd have known where you were, you disappeared.' Morgan smiled sweetly at him.

'Had to go home, couldn't walk around the station covered in mud.'

Cain was grinning at him. 'How was your trip? You didn't send a postcard, sir.'

Marc turned to glare at him. 'Have I just stepped into an alternative universe? Am I back at school or am I working in a police station?'

Amy was rolling her eyes at Morgan, and Cain had to cover his mouth to stifle the laughter that she could tell was about to break free. He muttered through his fingers. 'I don't know, have you?'

'Childish, it feels like it. Yes, Cain, I fell on my arse down a steep banking, so you can get it out of your system now. Have a good laugh and then move on. Where are we up to? Have we got any leads on the son yet? He can't be that hard to find surely. I mean it's not as if we're looking for some terrorist cell hiding in the mountains, it's one man.'

Ben tore his baguette in half and offered the other half to Marc. He shook his head. 'No, thanks. I'll go see if there's anything left in the canteen.'

'Morgan and Cain have got a name, and I was just saying that I know him. He is my heart specialist which makes it a bit awkward for me.'

For once Marc looked concerned. 'Ah, no way. What a small world it is. Do you think he's capable of killing his parents?'

'Anyone is capable of murder under the right circumstances. I only know him through my appointments. I don't know what he's like. I couldn't imagine he'd kill them the way they've been killed though, or that he'd be bothered about what the cottage is worth, or the half a million pounds she had in the bank. He will be on good money, he's not desperate.'

'Maybe he's in debt, has a lot of bills to pay, has an ex-wife who is taking him to the cleaners for every penny and half of his pension.'

Morgan realised that last statement was about Marc; he never discussed his home life with them, and thought maybe the divorce he was going through was very messy.

'Maybe,' said Ben.

'What's the plan then? Because I want him speaking to like an hour ago. Morgan, do you want to come with me, and we'll go interview him?'

Morgan thought she would rather stand out on scene guard

in a hurricane than sit in a car all the way to Lancaster and back with him.

Ben was shaking his head. 'No, I don't think that's a good idea. We don't want to alienate him before we've had a chance to talk to him. Morgan and Cain should go.'

Marc crossed his arms across his chest. 'They should?'

Ben nodded. 'It looks like we're accusing him if you go; a senior officer might make him lawyer up. The forensics that came back were nothing to shout about, the footprint was from a generic brand of walking boot sold in every Mountain Warehouse in the country and online. Margery's fingerprint samples were mainly dried dirt and fibres from the rope, what little blood there was, it wasn't sufficient to give us a full profile.'

'Ben, we *are* accusing him. He's the main suspect, the forensics would have been nice if they had tied to him directly but we can't discount him because they didn't. He has motive because of what they put him through, revenge is a dish best served cold or so I'm led to believe. He's clever, he could have been plotting this since the day he realised he was adopted.'

'I just don't see him killing them like that, so brutally, when he could have done it much easier with his medical knowledge; it doesn't make sense.'

'And I think your loyalty to him for saving your life is clouding your judgement; but I'm happy for Morgan and Cain to go if you think it will be better.'

Morgan could see Ben was trying his best not to tell Marc to go screw himself. Ben nodded, picked up his latte and went into his office, slamming his door behind him.

Marc shrugged. 'What's up with him? God, you lot are worse than a class of teenagers. Sort it out. I want David spoken to ASAP and if he so much as gives you an inkling that he could be involved, cuff him and bring him in. I don't care if he's the Pope; if he's a suspect, I want him arrested whether Ben likes it or not.'

He stormed out, letting the door slam even louder, and Amy stood up to go check he wasn't listening outside. He'd disappeared up the next level to the canteen.

'What the hell was that about? Just because you didn't buy him a sandwich? He's hangrier than Cain gets, that was unreal.'

'I think he's having a rubbish time, and the coffee was the last straw.'

'I don't care, we all have problems, but we don't take it out on each other like that.'

Morgan felt bad. She should have brought him food, and she wouldn't make that mistake again. Picking up her coffee that she hadn't touched, she left the office to see if she could find him and make a peace offering.

25

Marc was sitting in his bland, white walled office with scuff marks and remnants of Blu-tack left over from when it had been Tom's. Now there weren't even pictures or posters with the latest crime stats or a community policing poster tacked to a wall to remind him who covered which area should he need their assistance. When Tom had used this office there had barely been any space on the walls, he had almost everything tacked or taped. Jokes were his speciality and quotes, he loved a good quote. He'd quite often print out the newsletter back in the day full of sarcasm about the local criminals and Morgan had loved his dark sense of humour and easy-going manner. She was sad she hadn't worked with him for long before he decided to retire. Marc's back was to the door and he was staring out of the window down onto the car park. Morgan knocked; he didn't even turn around to see who it was.

'Come in.'

So she did, and sat down in one of the chairs opposite his, placing the coffee on the desk.

'Sir, there's a spare latte here for you.'

He took a few moments as if he was composing himself before he turned around to look at her.

He looked tired, and his eyes were a little bloodshot.

He glanced down at the cup. 'I don't want your drink, thank you.'

She shrugged. 'I don't want it either. I didn't touch it, so you can have it, or it can go in the bin.'

He nodded, then leaned over and picked it up, taking a huge gulp. 'Thank you.'

'I'm sorry we didn't get you food.'

He held up his hand. 'It's not your fault.'

'Oh, I thought—' She stopped. It didn't matter what she thought because she hardly knew him; none of them knew him, but that was because he never let them get close enough.

'I'm having a crap time, that's all. My wife is trying to take everything in our divorce, including the shirt off my back if I'd let her. The girls don't want to visit me, my dad has been diagnosed with terminal cancer and there is a fucking lunatic running around killing people that we don't seem to be able to get a grip on. I'm not particularly hungry, stressed most definitely.'

'I'm sorry.'

'For what? None of this is your fault, and it's me who should be sorry for snapping at you all the time. I know I'm not the easiest of guys to work with, but since I came here, I've had nothing but enough stress to give me a heart attack. I guess you could say I'm a little fed up with all the curve balls that keep getting thrown my way.'

Morgan suddenly felt terrible for the photo she'd taken of Marc on the ground. 'Why don't you take a couple of weeks off and have a break? Go on a holiday and spend time with your dad, forget about this place and put your feet up. If you tell HQ they can send someone down to cover for you.'

'You're that sick of me you'd rather I buggered off for a couple of weeks in the middle of a double murder investigation than mucked in?'

'Do you want flattery or the truth?' She couldn't believe she was doing this, but it was about time somebody did.

He took another large gulp of the lukewarm coffee. 'The truth.'

Morgan inhaled deeply. 'You sure about that?'

He nodded.

'You're not going to send me to Carlisle to work or Barrow?'

He laughed. 'Christ no, absolutely not, been there, done that and you're still here. I can take it; it might seem that I can't, but I can.'

'Sir, you are a pain in everyone's backside. You are so moody we don't know how to deal with you, but that's not the worst of it. You come and go, are always disappearing, giving orders out then we can't find you for ages. You need to leave your crappy home life at home when you walk through the doors like the rest of us do. We might be struggling, in pain, feeling sad, lonely or whatever, but we leave that at the door and focus on the next eight hours of work. When we leave we pick up that excess baggage on the way out and sometimes depending on what we've been dealing with that day our problems don't seem that huge anymore, especially not when you look at the body of a woman hanging from a tree in her front garden, or a teenage girl beaten about the head with a block of wood and left for dead in a cold, damp cellar.' She was thinking about Beatrix Potter, Bronte's sister, and the first dead teenager she'd ever seen.

His lips were slightly parted, but he nodded. 'You know what, you're right and I never used to be this miserable and angry. I think I'm going through a mid-life crisis. Is there such a thing as the male menopause?' He smiled.

Morgan laughed. 'Probably, you need to go find yourself a

date, have a little or a lot of fun and blow off some steam. I mean, you already bought the sports car, didn't you?'

He laughed even louder. 'Yeah, I did that. I only got it back from the garage last week after you managed to get the door ripped off.'

She shrugged. 'Technically that wasn't my fault, and I still feel bad about that.'

He smiled at her and for once it reached his big brown eyes that she thought could be irresistible to the right person if only he'd lighten up a little. He always dressed so smart, and he definitely gave off a bit of a Luther vibe, only he was like his polar opposite. While Luther was a rebel and went against the rules to get results, Marc couldn't see a life outside of them.

'Basically, I'm a boring arsehole then?'

She shrugged. 'Nobody can say you're boring because nobody knows you. You don't let anyone know you. You might be the boss, but you still need friends. I don't care how happy anyone is saying they can manage on their own, it's still good to have someone to talk to.'

He leaned back, downing the rest of the coffee, before launching the cup at the wastepaper bin. 'I'm just an arsehole then?'

She smiled at him.

He looked down at his hands then looked her in the eyes. 'You're right, I need to lighten up more, talk about myself more and maybe we could have a team night out when this is over. Go to the pub quiz at The Black Dog? We couldn't do any worse than Ben's team, could we?'

Morgan grinned at him. 'Nope, considering Declan and Theo are both super clever, you would think that just now and again they'd come first place.'

She stood up. 'If you want food, you have to let one of us know, send a text or something. None of us are mind readers.

We live in each other's pockets that's why we know each other so well. You're stuck up here in your office, and you don't see us all the time, so it's hard to know what's going on.'

'Got that. Thank you, Morgan, for your honesty. As painful as it is, it's refreshing to know you care enough to come and talk to me. I appreciate that, I really do.'

Smiling at him she felt a little better that she'd made the effort. 'Do you read much?'

He nodded. 'I read a lot of autobiographies, motivational stuff.'

That figured; he looked like the kind of guy who was always trying to better himself. 'Why don't you give some gritty fiction a try and change it up a little? I adore reading. It's the best escape, and it sounds like you need to learn how to switch off.'

He smiled at her. 'What do you read?'

'True crime.'

He laughed so loud it made her jump. 'I'd have never figured that one out. Do you read gritty fiction too?'

'I read lots of fiction, depends on what mood I'm in. I'm currently reading an excellent psychological thriller called *The Lodge* by Sue Watson. I'll bring it in for you when I've finished.'

'Thanks, I'll give it a go.'

'Oh, one last bit of advice that is probably the best advice anyone will ever give you, and I may have already told you this, but I'm going to tell you again because it's important. If you really want to make an impression, bring cakes in.'

'For what reason?'

'Erm, you don't need a reason to eat cake, boss. Has nobody ever told you that now you're all grown up you can eat cake whenever you want?'

He shrugged. 'I'm not a forward thinker in that department.'

'Obviously. When I was on section, if you screwed up you

got a cake fine and had to bring enough in for everyone on shift, or if it was your birthday. Did they not do that in Manchester?'

He nodded. 'I never really got it.'

'Well, you need to because cake is the way to your team's heart and will hold you in good stead.'

She left his office feeling much better than when she'd walked in. It was time to go and speak to David Hawthorne.

26

Ben was sitting on her desk when she came back in, Cain and Amy were both staring at their computer monitors, everyone doing their best with nothing to go on. Amy had the phone in one hand as she chatted to someone about David Hawthorne's car.

'Where did you go?' Ben asked and she wondered if she should tell him, then decided it wasn't her fault he was in a bad mood. If he didn't like it that was his choice. 'I went to speak to the boss.'

'About what? Him spitting his dummy out because nobody bought him a cheese baguette?'

She shrugged. 'Basically, yes.'

Amy who had hung up the phone began to laugh. 'Oh, you didn't. Morgan, why didn't you bodycam it and give us all a laugh. I bet you made him even angrier.'

'No, I told him he was an arse and needed to lighten up, join in more and read some books.'

Ben who had been sitting with his arms crossed, his mouth in set in a straight line, began to laugh. Cain was shaking his head.

'See you then, nice working with you, Morgan. Do you want a hand to pack your stuff in a box and carry it to the car?'

'He was okay and actually I think we should be a little nicer to him.'

'Why?' asked Amy.

'He's going through a lot of personal stuff.'

'Like what?'

'I'm not gossiping about him, but he said he'll try.'

Ben stood up. 'Yeah, pigs will fly before he does anything that benefits the team.'

Morgan shrugged; she'd tried, that was all she could do. 'Who's going to speak to David Hawthorne?'

'Me and you.'

'But I thought you said there was a conflict of interest, and you wouldn't feel comfortable?'

'I did, but I can be impartial. It's my job after all and Cain is going to speak to the building society about the deposit and charm his way to some answers so it's me and you. Come on, Morgan, before you decide to start offering your agony aunt services to Cain and Amy.'

She looked at him and shook her head. All she had done was try to make their working lives better.

The rain had started to fall again as they'd driven into Lancaster, causing huge puddles in the well-worn roads. By the time they reached the hospital and parked it was pouring down and the pair of them were soaked. Ben led Morgan to the cardiac outpatient's department and headed for the reception desk. 'Can you tell me where I can find Doctor Hawthorne, please. Is he in clinic today?'

The man behind the desk nodded. 'He is, have you got an appointment?'

Ben placed his warrant card on the counter. 'Detectives

Matthews and Brookes. It's urgent. Can you let him know we'd appreciate him taking the time to speak to us?'

The guy studied the badges then looked at Ben and shrugged. 'I'll message him, can't promise you anything though.'

'Thanks, we'll wait over there.' Ben pointed to the row of empty chairs at the back of the busy waiting room, next to the vending machine. They took a seat and waited.

Morgan lowered her voice. 'What if he won't see us?'

'He will.'

'How can you be so sure?'

'He's going to know that we know who he is, and he should hopefully want to clear things up quickly and without too much fuss.'

After twenty minutes, Morgan looked up from the book she was reading on her phone. The waiting room was empty. The last patient must have gone in, and it was just the pair of them. Ben was playing *Candy Crush*, which totally tickled her; to think that he could have been reading when he was wasting time on a pointless game amused her, and she nudged him in the side with her elbow. 'I don't know how you can play that.'

'I don't know how you can read all the time.'

She shrugged. 'Touché. Where is he? I thought you said he'd want to speak to us.'

'I suppose he's getting his patients out of the way.'

'What patients?'

He looked around and realised it was just the pair of them and went to the desk. 'Is the doctor ready to speak to us now?'

The guy who looked even more bored than they did shrugged. 'I messaged him.'

'Did he reply?'

'I'll check.'

Morgan watched Ben's fingers curl into fists at the side, and she knew he was getting angry.

'He read it as soon as I sent it but didn't answer.'

'Is he in with a patient?'

His head shook. 'No, she left five minutes ago.'

'Right, thanks. We'll go find him then.'

Ben strode off, and she followed him. He was muttering profanities under his breath. He stopped outside a door, rapping on the wood with his knuckles a little louder than needed. There was no reply, and he looked at Morgan.

'Maybe there's been an emergency and he had to dash off to theatre or a ward?'

Ben twisted the doorknob, but it was locked. He knocked again then pressed his ear to the door.

'Anything?'

He shook his head. 'I don't think he's in there. Go get that guy to come open the door, Morgan, or tell him to get whoever has the keys.'

Morgan rushed back to the reception desk, where the unhelpful guy was zipping up his coat.

'He's not there. Can you open his door so we can see if he's not answering us on purpose.'

'I don't have the keys; the sister has them.'

'Well can you get her to come open it then? This is very important.'

'He's not in there.'

'How do you know?'

'His car was parked outside; I saw him driving off before.'

She stared at him. 'And you didn't think to let us know? We are investigating a double murder; you have just wasted our time, which puts this community in danger. Where has he gone?'

The guy's face had paled at the mention of murder, but he was still an idiot. 'I don't know, I'm sorry. He didn't go out this way; he must have left by another exit.'

'My boss is going to be furious; you better wait there in case he wants to press charges against you for wasting police time.'

He dropped onto his seat, his forehead scrunched up as he frowned at her.

'Don't go anywhere.'

She jogged back to Ben. 'He's gone, left by the side door. The guy at the desk saw him driving off. I told him you might arrest him for wasting our time.'

'You did?' Ben smiled at her. 'I'd almost forgot how feisty you could be, Brookes. He's an idiot but I haven't got time for that. Come on, David's given us no choice. I'm going to have to put a wanted marker on him and the car and get him pulled over. We gave him the chance to talk to us and he left before he had to. I'm not happy with those actions. They don't exactly give off innocent vibes.'

They went back to the desk, where Ben looked down at the guy who had taken his coat back off. 'What kind of car does he drive?'

'A Porsche Cayenne in silver. Look, I'm sorry, I didn't know it was so serious or that he'd leave before speaking to you. It's not my fault. You can't arrest me for that.'

'I'm not, at least not this time. Do you know if he's on his way to another hospital for a clinic?'

'He hasn't got another clinic today. I'm sorry, I don't know anything else.'

Ben waved at him, and they rushed out to get to Ben's car. He began to pass instructions over the radio to the Control room to put an alert out for David Hawthorne, and asked for a PNC check on his car and home address.

Ben threw the car keys to Morgan. 'Take me to his home address in Grange-over-Sands. If he's driving a silver car it could be the same one on that awful CCTV still that Cain got.'

Morgan hoped it was for both Cain and all of their sakes, it would make it so much easier for them if they could pin the murders of his birth parents on him.

'What about Declan? He could know where to find him.'

'Phone him.'

As if summoned by magic, a tall figure came into view. He was waving at the pair of them with a huge grin on his face.

Ben glanced at Morgan. 'Well, that was quick. How did you do that?'

She shrugged; Declan gave them both a hug. 'How did she do what?'

Ben shook his head. 'Nothing, do you know where David Hawthorne lives, hangs around, if he has somewhere he could be?'

Declan crossed his arms. '*My* David Hawthorne?'

'Who else?'

'Well, the entire gastric department for a start but we won't go there. Why do you need to find him?'

'You did post-mortems on his birth parents. When we came to speak to him, he walked out and took off before we got the chance.'

Declan gasped. 'No way. I mean, he's a mean, arrogant arse but you don't think he killed them, do you? I mean I slept with the guy and to think he could do that.' He shuddered.

Morgan realised that although David was a suspect, there was no evidence linking him to the crime scene. The honest answer was that they had no idea if he killed his parents. But by taking off like this he'd just put himself in a difficult position, making himself look a hundred per cent guilty even if he wasn't. 'We don't know yet.' Was the only answer she could give Declan.

Ben patted his arm. 'Thanks, and I'm assuming you haven't got the tox results back?' he asked, hopefully.

'Still early days for those, my friend.'

Ben shrugged. 'Damn, got to go. We'll catch you later, mate.'

They began to hurry towards Ben's car and were just getting inside when Declan jogged over to them and opened the back door. 'Sod that. I'm coming with you. Be quicker if I show you his house; it's a bit remote. I'm not missing out on a real-life cop chase. Although with you two there's a chance it's all going to go horribly wrong, but I'm here for it even if it does.'

Morgan laughed as she sat behind the wheel and snapped her seatbelt in.

'Oh God, Morgan, nobody said you were driving. Please Lord, have mercy on our souls, she knows not what she does.'

'Changed your mind?'

'Nope, I needed a little excitement to get me out of this afternoon slump. If me and Susie eat any more donuts this week on our mid-afternoon break, I'm going to look like one.' He patted his stomach, which was as flat as it had ever been. 'Please try not to kill us all, my life is only just beginning, and Theo is taking me out for supper tonight to that new Indian restaurant that opened last week. If we survive, you should come. It would be nice, and I bet you haven't been eating properly.'

Ben waved a hand at the pair of them to shut up as his phone call connected and he began to relay the information to Marc, updating him on the AWOL Doctor Hawthorne.

27

Morgan turned off at the roundabout before Lindale Hill following Declan's directions. 'What if he didn't come home?' She spoke loudly, voicing her thoughts.

Ben answered. 'There's a good chance he hasn't because the ANPR camera hasn't picked up his car passing this way. If it had, Control would have notified us with an update.'

Declan shook his head. 'He could have taken the back roads though, bit winding and longer but it's another option. Just a thought, why do you think he's going to be at home?'

Ben looked at Morgan. 'Yes, why do we think that?'

Declan looked at the pair of them. 'You haven't got a bloody clue, have you? Hahaha, oh my, what a laugh. He could have just gone to get some lunch in Lancaster at Sainsbury's and you're driving all this way.'

'It's a logical conclusion that he's gone home, if he's trying to hide. He may have come here first to grab his stuff,' replied Ben.

'He keeps a gym bag with clean clothes in the back of his car, underwear, toiletries, trainers, in case he gets the chance to sleep with someone. He's always prepared, so can't see him coming home for that. He has a bit of a reputation for sleeping around.'

'And you're just telling us this information now after we've driven twenty-five minutes towards his home address?' Ben was incredulous.

'Sorry, I didn't think. You're the coppers, not me. I'm just here for the ride.'

'Declan, I'll make her stop the car and dump you at the side of the road.'

'Ouch, that's not very policeman like or friendly of you, Ben. I thought we were BFFs.'

Ben turned to him. 'What the hell is a BFF?'

Morgan was smiling to herself but was keeping out of this conversation.

'Best friend forever. I've been meaning to ask you if you want to get matching BFF tattoos, be so cool, you and I branded at the same time in friendship. Sammi at Aurora Tattoo will fit us in, she's the best.'

'Have you lost your sanity? No, I don't want a matching tattoo. Have I been sucked into a different universe? Declan, can you please be quiet for five minutes while I try and think.'

Morgan glanced at him in the rear-view mirror, and he had a hand cupped across his mouth stifling the laughter. 'I'll get a matching tattoo with you.'

He leaned over and high-fived her, then whispered, 'Well, you better not kill us then before I can message Sammi.'

Ben was glaring at them both. 'Really?'

Declan leaned back and mimed pulling a zip across his mouth, which made Morgan grin, but she held in the laughter because Ben was getting more stressed by the minute.

'Take the next left, then after about a mile there's a hidden driveway on the right. I'll tell you when to slow down so you don't miss it.'

'There.'

Morgan saw the driveway and turned into it, thankful there were no huge gates blocking access to it. She really wasn't in the mood for scaling the camouflaged wire fence covered in ivy and vines. She drove a short distance and nodded in approval at the very modern-looking house that was sitting in the middle of the plot staring back at them.

'Nice house.'

Declan nodded. 'It's a very nice house; and he's mortgage free because his parents had it built for him.'

Ben tutted. 'No car. And it doesn't look as if he needs what money High Wraith Cottage or Margery would have brought him.'

She parked up anyway, stopping directly outside the front door. 'Might as well have a look around. There's a garage – he could have put his car away.'

Ben nodded as he got out. He turned back to Declan. 'Wait here, under no circumstances do you get out of this car.'

Declan pulled a face but didn't argue with him and stayed put.

Their feet crunched on the pea gravel as they strode towards the garage. The double door was locked. Ben went to the side door and tried that handle, but it was locked too. He knelt down on the gravel. 'Pass me your phone torch.' She did, and he lay almost horizontal on the damp gravel to see if he could see the car inside.

'Anything?'

He got back up, pulling a face at his now damp knees, and shook his head. 'Let's check the house; we might as well now that we're here.'

They walked the perimeter of the house. The front was all tall glass windows making it easy to see straight through into the open-plan downstairs. There was no sign of life; and they hadn't passed his car on the way here.

'Imagine you're David. You're born to two not very nice

parents, and greatly affected by that. You witness abuse from a
very young age, are poisoned by your own mother, and the man
who could have protected you abandons you in your time of
need. But you are fortunate enough to get fostered, then
adopted by a wealthy, loving couple who make sure that you're
well taken care of. Would you still focus on your parents?
Wouldn't you think that you got lucky, and leave it at that?'

'I would say so, yes. What's his motive? I mean there's the
money, but he's doing okay, so I can't see that being much of a
factor.' Morgan's theory that the killer was doing it for the inher-
itance wasn't tying up well with David Hawthorne.

'Why did he run though? I don't get that part; it's made him
look guilty as anything. He must have seen it, that must be the
reason why he exited the hospital so suddenly. Unless it was a
coincidence?'

'Imagine if he was guilty.' Morgan smiled at him, and Ben
laughed. 'I don't want to; I'd be really upset.'

'There is another option.'

'What?'

'Declan could phone or message him and see where he is
and if he's okay.'

'He could, but do we want to get him any more involved
than he already is?'

She shrugged. 'That's your call, boss, but I have a feeling
that he will already have done it or be planning on doing it.'

Ben, who was almost at the car, turned and looked back at
the house. She felt bad for him. They had no reason good
enough to go inside without a warrant and definitely not
enough evidence for a judge to sign off on one either. This had
been a complete waste of everyone's time, except for Declan
who was practically bouncing up and down off the back seat.

'Tell me I can, tell me you want me to, please.'

Morgan stole a glance at Ben as she asked Declan, 'Have
you already messaged him? Be truthful.'

'Might have done a teeny bit of an online stalk, checked his location and that kind of thing on Snapchat.'

Ben closed his eyes. 'Could you not have done this before we came here?'

'Well, I could, of course I could, but I didn't think about it.'

'Where is he? Did you find out?'

Declan shook his head. 'Nope, his phone must be turned off. I've been thinking and you know, I don't think he would purposefully run away from you guys. Maybe he didn't get the message and had a prior appointment.'

'Well, if he did then he's bound to show up sooner or later.'

'Wait, why don't we go visit his mum? She's in a home around here: Sea View. She might know where he is. Better yet, what if he wanted to go and see her before we got hold of him? He could be saying goodbye to her.'

28

Sea View nursing home was a huge, rather grand building, with a row of flags flying in the wind from the flagpoles that lined the drive. The grounds were well kept and there was lots of patio furniture stacked up for the residents, waiting for a nice day. Morgan parked in the visitor section.

'Did you ever come here with David? Would Rose recognise you, Declan.'

He shook his head. 'No, I only slept with the guy a handful of times before he dumped me for his next conquest. We didn't get that close despite my best efforts; I really liked him, and he broke my heart.'

Morgan reached over and patted his hand. Ben's phone began to ring, and he clamped it to his ear looking relieved he didn't have to console Declan.

'You two go and speak to Rose.'

Declan's eyes looked as if they were going to pop out of his head. 'But.'

'Matthews, can you hold on a second,' Ben said to whoever was on the other end. He turned to Declan. 'Look, this isn't official, it's a visit to ascertain if he's been here or when he might

come back. You know him better than we do. You can chat to
his mum about him make small talk.'

'I could, do I get an honorary police badge for this?'

'No, you get a thank you.'

Declan looked at Morgan. 'Did you not feed him today?
He's awfully cranky.'

They got out of the car, and he turned back to wave at Ben.
'I never thought he'd ask me to do this. I feel like I might be a bit
out of my depth. I don't want to mess anything up.'

Morgan smiled at him. 'Don't worry, you don't need to. I
can manage and trust me we are all winging it. I had no idea
what I was doing when they threw me out on my own that very
first day and I found the Potter family.'

Declan wrapped his arm around her shoulder, squeezing
her tight.

'Nope, I'm part of the team now; he just made it official, so I
can handle it, although Susie is going to end up eating all the
donuts if I'm not back soon.'

Morgan could just eat a sticky donut. She rang the doorbell,
which was answered instantly by a young girl in a green and
white striped uniform.

'Can I help you?' She smiled sweetly at them.

'Yes, we're here to speak to Rose Hawthorne. I'm Detective
Morgan Brookes and this is Declan.' She decided that she
wasn't lying to them; he was called Declan.

'Come in, Rose is in the craft session. Is this about something terrible?'

Morgan shook her head. 'It's not, we're just trying to find
her son to speak to him about an incident, but it's nothing to
worry about.'

'Oh, that's okay then. It should be fine, but I better check
with the nurse in charge though, just in case.'

Morgan read her name badge. 'Jessie, do you know Rose's
son David?'

She nodded. 'We all do, he's gorgeous and drives a nice car. He's so sweet. He takes her out every week and always brings her flowers; he brings the staff chocolates too which is so kind of him. Everyone fancies him; he's not married either because he doesn't wear a wedding ring, so you know, we all kind of flirt with him a little.'

Declan's gaze was burning into Morgan, and she ignored him.

'Could you just wait outside here, and I'll go speak to the nurse. I won't be a minute.'

She knocked on the door and slipped into the office. Morgan knew what was coming as Declan leaned across and whispered, 'Should I put them out of their misery and tell them he's gay?'

'No, that's not for us to disclose.'

'Spoilsport.'

'Besides he might not want Rose to know.'

'What? You think she hasn't figured out that her son who brings her flowers every week and is loyal and loving isn't gay? C'mon, how many straight men would do that? We are in a class of our own.'

She grinned at him. 'You most certainly are, but please don't. It's not relevant.'

'I suppose not, but he treated me bad, and Karma is a bitch.'

'That may be, but his mum deserves better.'

The door opened and a much older woman was standing next to Jessie. She smiled at them, and Morgan's shoulders relaxed.

'Hi, I'm Amanda, Jessie said you need to speak with Rose. Can I ask what about?'

'Hi, Amanda, Morgan and this is Declan. We're trying to find her son; we don't want to worry her and he's not in any trouble; we just need to speak to him about an investigation and something he may have witnessed.' Morgan felt bad, but she knew how gossip spread like wildfire and she didn't want to risk Rose hearing anything bad about David unless it was true.

'That's fine, come with me. Some days Rose is a little more lucid than others. Jessie said she's having a good day today which should help.'

They followed Amanda along the corridor to a room where there were tables covered in card, felt, coloured paper, glitter, crayons, and the men and women were sipping their hot drinks, while bent over studiously sticking all manner of things onto their folded pieces of card. The woman leading the crafting session looked at them and smiled.

'Have you come to join in?'

'I wish we could, this looks so much fun,' said Declan.

Morgan knew he was being serious and smiled, it did look pretty fun. It reminded her of art class back in school and she'd loved art, even though she wasn't very good at it.

Amanda crossed the room to go and speak to the cutest old lady Morgan had ever seen. She was wearing a candy pink sweatshirt with matching joggers; her hair was pure white, tight curls. She looked like a stereotypical grandmother, and when she looked up from the card she was making to smile at Amanda, her eyes crinkled at the corners full of warmth.

'Rose, you have a couple of visitors who'd like to chat to you about David. Is that okay?'

Rose turned to look at them, giving the same cute, warm smile to her, and Morgan smiled back, waving her hand at her. 'Hi, Rose.'

'Hello, dear.'

Amanda helped her up from the chair, linking her arm through Rose's. As they were leaving Rose stopped at the table of each resident and gave them a little clap. 'Good job,' she said to everyone before they were taken to a small office next door. Declan was holding his heart and whispered, 'I love her, do you think we can adopt her?'

Morgan nudged him with her elbow to shut up, but she completely agreed. Once they were all seated, Amanda sent Jessie to get a pot of tea for everyone.

Rose smiled at Morgan. 'What would you like to know about David?'

'We wondered if you had seen him today?'

Rose frowned. 'Who are you again?'

'We're detectives and we're investigating a serious crime that David might have witnessed and not realised.'

Rose thought about this, and she was still smiling at Morgan when she replied, 'You came all this way to ask if I'd seen him. Why didn't you just phone?'

Morgan couldn't help it, she laughed. 'It's been one of those days, Rose. We thought we'd come and speak to you ourselves.'

'He's a wonderful boy, he always has been. We are so proud of him. He's a heart specialist you know. Saves so many lives. He's a credit to us both and we were so lucky the day he came to us.' She paused and a look of sadness crossed her face. 'I forget, you know, most days, that Harry isn't here and it's a blessing really because I never thought that I'd be able to go on living without him by my side. He was my everything. We got married when I was eighteen and I never regretted a single day. Are you two married?'

'No, we're not, but we are good friends.'

Rose winked at her. 'Friends is good, then you can get married, although nobody wants to get married these days; it makes me sad.'

'Do you remember the last time you saw David?'

She nodded. 'Last night, he was here until late. He brought me pizza and we watched Netflix in my room. We both love *Schitt's Creek*, terrible name, but a funny show.'

'Is that allowed? Would he have been here late?' Morgan looked at Amanda, who said, 'We can check the visitors book. We have open visiting, and David often brings his mum pizza, and they stay up late watching comedy shows.' She turned to Rose. 'You like the comedies, don't you, Rose?'

'I do, I don't like all this crime and horror stuff, life is cruel enough without that.'

'Then he helps her get ready for bed, tucks her in and goes home. He's a loyal son.'

'Sounds cute,' said Declan.

Amanda turned to look at him, and Morgan made a mental note to check CCTV in the area to confirm David's arrival and departure.

'Rose, we know that David was adopted. Did he ever talk about his birth parents?'

'No, they are horrible people,' Rose said sadly. 'I felt bad for his mother. She was having a hard time with that brute of a husband, and she just couldn't handle David; it was all too much for her. But to do what she did to her own child, it makes my blood run cold. Poor little thing didn't stand a chance; but we were blessed to be able to give him all the love that he needed, and look at him now. He's so clever and we are so proud of him.'

Morgan realised that Rose had no idea that Margery and George were dead. Would David not have told her about their murders? She supposed he might not have wanted to upset her and as far as Morgan was aware it hadn't it hit the headlines yet.

'Harry took him to meet George; he didn't want anything to do with David, wished him well but basically told him that he wasn't interested.'

'How did that affect him?'

'He was a bit quiet then. After a day or so he told Harry he was glad he didn't have anything to do with George. He didn't need him when he had Harry. It was true, he never wanted for anything. We've been blessed and we love him so dearly that we gave him everything he could ask for. And he never once threw it back in our face.'

'What about Margery, how did he feel about her?'

'Why do you want to know that? You should ask him your-selves.' Her tone was no longer that of a sweet old lady, she was full on defensive.

'We will when we find him. He's busy and we haven't had the chance yet. Do you know where he would be if he wasn't at work or at home?'

Jessie came in with a tray of tea and passed a cup to Rose, who took it with both hands and sipped it slowly. Morgan and Declan both declined, and Amanda poured herself a drink. Rose put the teacup and saucer down on the table then turned to Morgan.

'No. Now, I might be a bit senile but I'm not stupid. Has something happened to those horrible people? Because I feel as if there is something you're not telling me. You come in here asking questions, but are not telling me what it's about. If you want any more answers from me, you need to tell me what's going on.'

'I didn't want to upset you.'

'You won't, trust me.'

Amanda shrugged in Morgan's direction.

'Both Margery and George Lancaster are dead.'

Rose smiled. 'They are? Was it a horrible death by any chance?'

Morgan nodded.

'Good, it's nothing more than what they deserve, and you are here looking for David. Do you think he had something to do with their deaths?'

The sweet old lady was piercing Morgan's gaze with her blue eyes, but Morgan didn't look away; she met her fierce stare. Rose had gone into protective mum mode and Morgan respected her for her loyalty.

'I don't know. I don't think he did, but I need to find him to ask him, and I don't know where he is at the moment.'

Rose picked the teacup up again and began to sip at her tea. When she'd finished, she spoke slowly. 'David had all the reasons in the world to want to see those vile people dead, but he didn't do this, he wouldn't do it. He was brought up better than that. He wouldn't risk throwing away everything he worked so hard for on those two guttersnipes. They are not worth him going to prison for. I'm sorry to say this but you're wasting your time chasing him when you need to be chasing the person who did it. I can't and I won't help you anymore. Amanda, can you take me back, please.'

Rose stood up and smiled at Morgan. 'I'm sorry I can't help you. If I thought that I could it would be a different matter.' Then she was being led out of the door, back to the card making.

Declan stood up and began to laugh. 'Saint David, eh? Who'd have known it. I'm glad he treated Rose and Harry with more respect than he treats the people he sleeps with.'

'Do you still want to adopt Rose?' she asked, and he shook his head.

'Looks can be deceiving. She looks so damn cute but she's a feisty one.'

They waited for Amanda to come back. 'I'll show you the visitors book and you can see what time he arrived and when he left.'

'Thank you.'

'Do you really think he had anything to do with it? I mean, is he a threat to Rose or any of the staff? because if you think he is, I will ban him from coming inside.'

'No, I don't believe he is, but it would be really helpful if you could let me know if he turns up. We'll attend quickly if you see him, as we're keen to get his alibi.' She gave her a huge smile and hoped it had put any concerns to rest. She didn't think he would hurt anyone here, but at the moment, he was still their only suspect.

29

David Hawthorne had driven to the busy garden centre in Ambleside and was currently staring out of the terrace window in the café at Wansfell Pike. Low clouds covered the top and he watched as rivulets of water ran down the window, distorting his vision. He stared down at the hot chocolate he was stirring – it was a hot chocolate kind of day – and occasionally glancing over to the kitchen to see if he knew he was here. Eventually he came to his table carrying a bowl of soup that David hadn't ordered and placed it in front of him.

'What's this?'

'I need an excuse to come talk to you, this is it. Please eat it so it looks like I'm doing my job. The supervisor is in a right mood today; she's gone for a fag break, so I have a couple of minutes. We're short staffed, half of them phoned in with a sickness bug.'

David had taken a couple of mouthfuls of the creamy vegetable soup, and he looked at it in disgust, pushing the bowl away.

'They're not sick, they were on a night out last night and too hungover to come up here. You can eat it, it's okay, none of us are ill. What do you want? Why did you drive here? Couldn't you have messaged me?'

'The police are looking for me, which means they're also looking for you. I thought you'd want to know, and if I get arrested it won't look good if I'm messaging you telling you this, will it? It will look incriminating for the pair of us.'

'Why? We haven't done anything wrong.'

'I haven't, but what about you? Are you sure you haven't?' David arched an eyebrow at him.

He shrugged. 'Why would I do anything? It's not like it's in my favour to, is it?'

'Is it not?'

He leaned over to swipe a cloth across the table. 'You are the only one who stands to gain from Margery's death. Eat the free soup, go speak to the cops. You have nothing to hide, tell them that and stop panicking.'

'I have you to hide though. Was it you? I need you to be frank with me, did you kill that woman?'

He grinned at David, that boyish grin that made his blue eyes crinkle and David's crotch go tight looking at him, even though he knew it was a definite no. It was wrong, but he'd never wanted anyone more than he'd wanted him, and it was ridiculous because the pair of them could never be anything more than friends. If he had anything to do with his birth parents' death, did he even want to be associated with him? The answer was no, absolutely not.

'No, it was not me. What do you take me for, some raving psychopath? You don't have to tell them about me, there's nothing to tell. I'm just a mate who likes going for rides in your fast car and has the same interests as you, that's it, so don't go spouting your mouth off about me to them and dragging me into something that's your problem and not mine. I wouldn't drop you in it, if it was the other way around, Doctor Hawthorne.'

He walked away, and David broke the crusty roll into

pieces, smearing it with butter. Be damned with the cholesterol, he was hungry and worried about talking to the cops. He had a feeling that his friend may be involved but no proof of this, just his gut feeling, and he couldn't always trust that, it had steered him into some bad relationships in the past and was an unreliable source. Once he got to the station they might keep him for hours. When he'd finished the soup, he blotted his mouth with a serviette and continued staring out of the window, wondering if his life was over. He was the logical suspect.

He would go to the police station when he left here and talk to them. He probably should have spoken to them at the hospital instead of panicking and running. He'd made himself look guilty. But he just wanted to protect his friend. He always worried his past would hurt someone he loved one day.

As he stood up, he glanced through the serving hatch into the kitchen and saw him watching him, smiling at him. He winked at David, smiled and gave a little wave, mouthing the words 'it's all okay' at him before a woman walked in front of him and blocked his view.

David went back to his car. Rydal Falls police station was only a few minutes away. He needed to get this over with.

30

Ben nodded as Morgan and Declan relayed Rose Hawthorne's conversation to him. 'She doesn't believe he's guilty then?'

Morgan sighed. 'Not one little bit. I checked the visitors book, and David signed in at eight fifteen and back out at eleven last night. George left his flat around eight to go and meet someone. I don't think it was David he was meeting. The timings are too far out. It's a good ten-minute drive from the cottage to the nursing home; it doesn't fit our timeline. He wouldn't have hung around for a few hours waiting for him to turn up? I can't see George being the sort of person who had that kind of patience; he would have driven away if whoever he was meeting wasn't there on time.'

'Who contacted George then? Why did he turn up at the cottage?'

'His car has been taken away for a full forensic search, so hopefully his phone will be inside,' Ben replied. 'We can look at his call log and messages.' He felt his own phone vibrate and checked it. 'Sam just messaged; they've been around the few hardware shops in the area that sell chains. There's a possible match at Musgraves in Windermere; they sell all kinds of chains, but to be sure they've given them samples to compare them to. She's asked if they can look back and find out when they last sold some and see if they have camera footage, but they only have cameras on the entrances.'

'Still, that's good, right? It would show the person who bought the chains coming in and out.'

'It's an excellent lead and Amy messaged to say that the huge lump sum paid into Margery's bank was from a company called Hachette, she's been through the documents the search team brought back and found a letter from an editor there offering her a large amount of money to sell her life story to them.'

Morgan felt her mouth open and murmured a silent. 'Oh.' Then nodded. 'I guess that is quite a story to tell, someone must have known about the case and thought her story would sell.'

Before he could answer, Ben's phone began to ring. 'Matthews.' There was a slight pause as the animated voice on the other end that clearly belonged to Mads chattered away. 'On my way, can you ask him to take a seat, give him a coffee or something, but don't let him leave.' He hung up. 'David Hawthorne has turned up at the station.'

Morgan let out a whoop of delight, and Declan laughed. Ben turned to face him. 'Do you need to get back to Lancaster straight away, or can we go back so I can go speak to him, then Morgan can drive you back?'

He nodded. 'I'm in it to win it now. Susie will have definitely eaten my donuts by now anyway, so there's no point rushing back. That's great. Can I come see him with you? I'd love to watch him squirm his way out of this one.'

'No, sorry. As helpful as you've been, I can't let you do that, it's unprofessional and I'm afraid I no longer require your services.'

'Spoilsport.'

Morgan smiled at him.

'Only kidding, Ben, I know you're busy and have a job to do. I'm pushing my luck. Morgan, you could take me to Theo's instead, save you having to drive back to Lancaster. I may as well call it quits for the day.'

'What about your car, won't you need it to get home later?'

'I can slum it on the train, if there are any running; or if Theo's heap of crap that he bought starts, he can drive me back. Have you seen the monstrosity? It's awful, he bought it because it was cheap. They should have paid him to take it off their hands.'

Morgan shook her head.

'You'll hear it before you see it. It's this awful purple souped-up joy boy, Vauxhall Astra. I'm waiting for him to get speakers on top so he can go around preaching the Bible to everyone from inside. It's awful, in fact you should arrest him next time you see him in it for being offensive to other road users.'

That did it and she doubled over with the giggles, thinking about Theo driving around in a purple car blasting out Bible quotes. Even Ben laughed, briefly, before turning serious again. Declan smiled to himself and sat back, determined to keep quiet for the rest of the journey back to the station.

'Please can I use the toilet?' Declan asked as Ben parked the car outside the main entrance to the station.

'Of course, there's one by the front desk, help yourself.'

All three of them got out of the car, Morgan to show Declan the toilet and Ben to go speak to David Hawthorne.

As they walked into the reception area Brenda pointed to the side room. 'He's in there but he's not very well. He keeps running to the loo, and he looks awful. I asked if he wanted me to get him a doctor and he laughed, told me he was the doctor.' She shrugged then lowered her voice. 'Bit of an arse, but hey ho.'

Ben went straight into the room, leaving Morgan and Declan outside. Declan opened the door to the toilet then shut it straight away. 'Erm, no thanks. I'll hang on till I get to Theo's. Can you take me there now, please?'

Morgan nodded.

They were about to get back into the car when Ben came running out and yelled, 'Declan.' He waved at him, and both of them ran towards Ben who looked worried. 'Something's wrong with him.'

He led them into the small interview room, where David was leaning across the table, perspiration pouring from his forehead and struggling to breathe.

Declan knelt down beside him. 'Get an ambulance now.'

Brenda rushed to the office to ask the Control room to contact them.

'David, can you talk to me, what's wrong?'

David's eyes were pleading with Declan. A violent spasm racked his body, and he clenched up into a tight ball. Declan pressed his fingers against his pulse, and his eyes widened.

'David, talk to me.'

He opened his mouth to speak and vomited all over himself. Declan jumped up and ran to the toilet to grab some paper towels. He placed them on top of the stringy liquid that covered the table and David's shirt.

David opened his mouth and said a word that none of them caught.

Declan leaned closer.

'Poisoned.'

Then he lost consciousness, and his entire body began to shake as he had a seizure. Declan gently lay him down on the floor, kicking away the chair. Ben dragged the table away to give him plenty of space, so he didn't hurt himself on them.

'He said he'd been poisoned?' Declan's voice was strained. All of them were staring down at David, unable to do anything to help him other than to wait for the ambulance.

31

He told his supervisor that he was sick, he needed to go home, and she exploded, calling him every name he'd ever heard of and more. Then she'd pointed to the door and told him to get out. He apologised to her and left. He could have told her to go fuck herself and probably should have, she was horrible to everyone, but he'd held his tongue.

He didn't know how long he had before the great David Hawthorne began to feel the effects of the ancient rat poison he'd found in the pantry at High Wraith Cottage. It had been an unexpected bonus when he came across it, and he'd known he would find a use for it as he'd tipped some into one of Margery's tiny, vintage Tupperware containers. If Jackie thought she had problems now, boy was she in for a surprise when the environmental health or whoever would deal with the problem came and told her someone had been poisoned in the garden centre café. He had to cup a hand across his mouth to stop the grin that was stretched across his face as he left through the staff exit in case the cameras were watching him. His pickup was a wreck compared to David's car, and it was true he did enjoy being driven around in his older model Porsche. Who wouldn't? Boys and their toys was a real thing and not just some made up crap. He was glad he'd never put his real address down on the job application form, otherwise he'd just led the cops straight to his door.

He was tempted to drive past the cottage one last time. He still couldn't believe he'd gone through with it.

As far as he knew, he was the only person who ever gave Margery the time of day. He told her all about his life and asked about hers. They would swap recipes, and he made her smile, sometimes he even got a laugh from those thin, straight lips of hers that seemed to be permanently set to miserable.

He had started bringing homemade cakes with him, or at least he told her they were. Sometimes he'd bring her flowers, and she asked him once why he was so kind to her, and he'd told her it was because he liked her a lot. She reminded him of his mum who had died, and he missed her. She'd liked that; it had made her feel sorry for him and she spent even longer chatting to him than she usually did.

The day he broke in and was alone in the cottage it had made every hair stand on end as he moved through the rooms. He'd wanted to feel closer to her. And that's when he found the will. It was sitting in a locked tin box under the bed with the key still inside the lock. It was an old document; there was one name on it that he'd never heard of.

He shuddered, he didn't really get the whole ghosts and haunted houses thing, but when he'd stepped inside of that place on his own into the shadows, he had heard whispers from upstairs. He had heard creaks and thuds from above him, and scared in case anyone was up there, he had left in a hurry with the hairs on his arms standing on end and goosebumps covering his flesh. He had no idea if the place was haunted or if it was his imagination, but he knew its history. Not many people did because it happened so long ago, but Ada had told him all about High Wraith Cottage as soon he was old enough to understand,

and it had always stuck in his mind. He could make a small fortune from it if he rented it out to ghost-hunting groups; he could let them go in and investigate, scare the crap out of each other while he got rich off their fears.

As he drove home he felt a tiny pang of regret about David. He had liked him a bit and he didn't deserve to die a horrible death. He hoped he'd given him enough of a dose of the poison that it would be fatal and not have him lingering in a coma for days before he finally succumbed because he wouldn't even be able to visit him. There would be police crawling all over the place looking for him; he had to keep a low profile now.

He knew that if he kept out of trouble and carried on as usual, he would be okay. He had done all the hard, brutal, nasty work. Now it was time to sit back and be patient. Even if the police traced him to David there was nothing to tie him to Margery and he'd taken great care not to leave any forensic evidence behind.

32

The paramedics rushed in, took one look at David with blood now seeping from his nose, and did a double-take. They kneeled on the floor, moving his body into the recovery position. He was still convulsing. Declan was holding his hand, and he stood up to give them room to work.

'He mentioned poison before he collapsed.'

'Has he ingested it, do you think?' one of the paramedics said, examining David's mouth.

Declan shrugged. 'I wasn't with him, I couldn't say but it's possible.'

'We need to get him on a stretcher and blue lighted to A&E, we don't have any time to waste.'

One of the paramedics rushed out to get a stretcher.

As the paramedic returned with the stretcher Morgan and Ben stepped out of the room to give them space, Declan followed and they watched as a still convulsing David was lifted onto the stretcher and rushed out to the ambulance.

'I feel so bad.'

'Why?'

'I couldn't help him; I don't know what to give him to make him better. It's not what I do.'

'What does he need?' Morgan asked him.

'Intravenous fluids, oxygen, blood tests.'

'You don't have access to any of those things here. There is nothing more you can do than you have already.'

'I think I should go with him to the hospital?'

'And do what?' It was Ben who asked the question this time.

'I don't know, be there for him.'

They had followed the paramedics outside and were watching them frantically working on David.

'Is he likely to regain consciousness anytime soon?'

Declan stared at the paramedics busy working getting a line in. One of them glanced at him. 'Probably not.'

Ben's voice was hushed. 'Then the best thing you can do is go to Theo's. You've been a huge help today, and you don't need to hang around a hospital on your own for hours when there's nothing you can do.'

He nodded. 'I know, I feel bad though. He was poisoned as a baby and now it's like history is repeating itself. I mean, what are the chances of the same thing happening twice? It's unreal and so tragic for him.'

Ben took hold of his arm, leading him away. 'You don't have anything to feel bad about, this isn't to do with you and yes it's terrible, but he survived being poisoned once, I'm praying he'll survive it again. I'll be sending an officer to sit with him and keep me updated. I'll keep you updated too as soon as I hear anything. Let Morgan take you to Theo's, Declan.'

'Okay, you're right. You'll let me know when there's an update?'

'Of course, I will.'

Morgan wasn't so sure the update was going to be a good one judging by the state of David Hawthorne.

'Come on, I'll take you now.'

She led him away gently back outside, but not before she glanced at Ben and felt bad for him too. His face was ashen. That was Margery, George and, if David didn't survive, the whole Lancaster family wiped out in forty-eight hours. Who had done this? David had been their most likely suspect. But would he poison himself?

Once Declan was inside the car she ran back to Ben and whispered, 'Ask them to test his hands, fingers, for traces of poison; we're going to need to go inside and search his house. What if he did this to himself?'

'When you get back, we'll search his office too. Ask Declan if David encounters any poisonous medicines or prescribes tablets that he could have used.'

'I will. What about iron tablets, could they have done this to him?'

'I'm no doctor, but if you find any then yes, probably.'

As she rounded the corner to the vicarage, Morgan let out a gasp at the awful lilac coloured car sitting outside the church gates. 'Oh wow, that's worse than I ever imagined. I thought you were exaggerating.'

Declan laughed at that. 'I wish I had been, but it's his pride and joy. Who am I to take that away from him?'

'I guess a priest is on much less than a pathologist. My car isn't much better but at least it's black.'

'It's discreet, your car – that is something else.'

'Ben said to ask if you think there's any medication David works with that could cause what's happened to him?'

'As in he thinks he tried to kill himself?'

She nodded.

'All medication is poisonous taken in the wrong dosage; I couldn't say unless we get blood tests done ASAP, which they will do in A&E. I can't see him being the kind of person who would do that, though; he's not the type. Not that there is a type. You never know when someone is so tired of living that they feel death is their only escape. Most people who do take their own lives, it comes out of the blue, and it is a terrible shock to their families. I still can't see David doing that unless he had no other option and did kill his parents. I suppose I can't say no because who am I to judge is what my head is telling me, but my heart is saying he didn't, that someone did this to him.'

He got out of the car. 'Thank you, it's been interesting, but I think I'll stick with pathology and not be joining the police; at least I don't get involved in stuff like you do and get to work from the mortuary and my office with the occasional court appearance. It's easier; the fact the patients are already dead when they get to me and I know that sounds terrible, but to see them sick and not be able to help them is far worse than dealing with their bodies. At least their souls have left and it's just the shell.'

She never expected to hear him say this and suddenly she loved him even more, knowing that he truly believed when a person died their souls didn't. She had spent so many hours pondering this after her adoptive mum Sylvia died, and then Brad her school friend had died far too young. 'Have you considered what will happen if he doesn't make it, Declan? He looked in a bad way. Will you let someone else do the post-mortem?'

He shook his head. 'He's a colleague; he could have been a lot more if he'd wanted but he didn't. If it comes to that I'll deal with him as I deal with all my other patients. I'll just be feeling even sadder that it's such a waste of a brilliant doctor, because for all his faults he is a fantastic heart surgeon and that would be such a great loss for everyone, especially his patients and poor, feisty Rose.'

He came around to her side of the car, opened her door and kissed her cheek. 'Be careful, Morgan, I hate that you and Ben are out there putting yourselves at risk chasing these sick people. I love you both very much.'

She smiled at him. 'And we love you too.'

He grinned at this. 'Enough to get matching tattoos? Tell your man he owes me big time, so we all need to get them.'

Winking at her, he walked towards the vicarage, but his shoulders were down and head bent. He looked so fed up that she wished they had never let him come with them in the first place. If they hadn't, he wouldn't have had to see his friend that way. She was going to have nightmares about David Hawthorne's convulsions, and Declan definitely would too.

33

In the past three years, Morgan had seen more bodies than she cared to count. She remembered every single victim she had dealt with, their names all stored in the little compartment she kept at the back of her mind. She knew what they looked like alive, full of life, and sadly she knew how they looked after they had died. Most had died far too young, had their lives cut short. Even Evelyn who had been in her nineties had been too young to be murdered. Rarely did she deal with someone who she didn't feel any empathy towards, yet she struggled with George Lancaster.

When she thought about what Margery did, she leaned towards the probability that she had been pushed to do what she did by him. Margery had thought there was no other way out of her dire situation so had decided to get rid of the problem. She must have considered David a problem too. Had she only ever seen George when she stared down at his cot and not seen the potential in her own child? Not that she was an expert on kids. She had very little experience with them; the only kid she ever really got to know had been Macy, and she had a real soft spot for her, but she didn't know if she ever wanted any of her own. She knew that Ben did. He'd said once he would love a family, but she knew that he would never push her. It would be her choice and maybe in a few years she would, especially if she didn't have to chase killers for a living, as Declan put it. But what scared her was the thought that deep down inside, what if she couldn't love a kid and felt the same way as Margery had? Morgan's biological father and brother were both killers, definitely sociopaths and probably psychopaths too. Gary had killed their mum in front of them when they were kids, and the fear that she was going to turn out just like them was all too real. There had been a couple of times when she'd been confronted with killers that she hadn't cared about how much she hurt them and had fought hard to win. What did that mean? that she was a borderline sociopath too.

The front desk was closed, it was now a crime scene and there was a piece of blue and white tape tied across the front entrance. It would cause chaos for anyone needing to come in and report a crime, but thankfully there weren't a lot of tourists around this time of year. It was the tourists with their lost phones, wallets, pranged cars that seemed to fill the reception area in the summer. Through the double glass doors she could see Wendy and Ian moving around in white crime-scene overalls.

She parked near to David's car and got out, peering through the windows to see if there were any discarded pill bottles on the seat or floor. It was clean, there was nothing, not even an empty coffee cup or water bottle. Unlike Morgan's car, which usually had an assortment of both in the cup holders and on the floor. She wondered what would happen to the car if he died, would it be left to someone, did he own it or was it leased? There were so many questions swirling around inside of her head, she had given herself a headache with them. Looking up she saw Ben's face pressed against the glass of the third-floor window, his lips pursed blowing her a kiss, and she grinned at

him, giving him a little wave. She wished they could go home,
pack a suitcase and get out of this rainy, miserable little town to
fly somewhere warm.

He was waiting for her by the lift doors.

'Was Declan okay? That was a bit of a nasty shock. I feel
awful for dragging him into this.'

She nodded. 'He's fine, a bit sad about it all, but aren't we
all?'

Ben looked around, then pushed her back inside of the lift
before the doors slid shut. Once they did, he wrapped his arms
around her and pulled her as close to him as he could. His body
heat and the subtle smell of his aftershave made her feel safe,
not to mention loved. Tilting her chin up he bent down and
kissed her with far more passion than was reasonable for a rainy,
wintry, Wednesday afternoon, and she kissed him back even
harder.

'Put her down, you animal; you two have a problem.'

Cain was standing in front of the open doors that had slid
open so quietly neither of them had heard. They broke apart as
if someone had just jolted them with a cattle prod. Ben grinned
at him, and Morgan felt her cheeks heating up.

'You must really like each other.'

They laughed, and Morgan realised that was probably the
understatement of the year. She loved Ben so hard it would
crush her if he ever decided to stop loving her back.

'Should you not be doing something useful, Cain?' Ben said
this with a straight face, and Cain's mouth opened. 'What, like
you two? Cheek of it. I'm always doing something useful. I was
going to offer to take Amy to go search the doc's house.'

'That would be useful, but I think me and Morgan will go;
we know where it is as it's a bit remote.'

Cain arched an eyebrow at them. 'I bet he has a big bed.'

'Cain, don't be so flippant.'

He shrugged. 'Just saying, boss. What is it with that family and secluded houses? Were they born hating people so much they couldn't live near them? If you and Morgan are going there, what do you want us to do?'

Morgan thought he had a fair point. Margery lived in a remote cottage, and David's house was hidden away from view and down a secluded lane. They didn't like having their privacy invaded, that was for sure.

'Search the car for anything obvious If there was a chance I thought he might regain consciousness soon, I'd send you to the hospital, but the paramedics are not so confident he will. They said it's likely he'll be put in an induced coma and into intensive care.'

'If not, do you want us to go home then? Get an early finish for a change.'

Ben paused. 'We still have a killer to catch.'

'What if he's the killer and poisoned himself to make him look like a victim?'

'I'm not discounting that, there is a chance he is, but I wouldn't have thought he'd make himself that ill.'

'Not unless he couldn't cope with the guilt.'

'Looks good, plenty of witnesses for a start.'

'But why would he do it here of all places?' Morgan asked.

'Good question,' Ben said.

They headed back towards the office, something wasn't right.

'Where was he before he came here? We were looking for him when he left the hospital while we were sitting there like idiots, and he had a good twenty-, thirty-minute head start on us. He didn't go home, so he had to have gone somewhere. To see someone maybe? We went to his house and then we went to the nursing home, so that's probably at least thirty to sixty minutes unaccounted for. We need to check the ANPR cameras again. Did they have the right number plate? Because one of them should have picked him up.'

Ben was nodding. 'That's right, he did. Cain can you check the log and make sure they had the right VRM? Come on, Morgan, we'll go to his house and have a quick look around then I'll send a full search team in if we don't find anything.'

Glad she hadn't bothered taking her coat off, she waited for him to grab his and then they were heading to the back yard to grab a van.

'You better make sure there's a whammer in before we set off.'

'No need.' He held up a keyring. 'Paramedics passed me the car keys before they took him away, and it looks like a house key on it too. I told them we needed access to his car. We'll take the house key and leave the car keys in the Sgt's office so they can lift the car.'

'That was forward thinking.'

'It is and that's why I'm a DS. It's also the kind of thing you usually do, and it's also why you should be a DS too.'

———

They got into the van, which smelled of fish and chips. 'It stinks in here.' Ben was wrinkling his nose.

'Why do we need a van?'

'It's got a full search kit in the back; I borrowed it from Al who said they'd come down as soon as we're finished. I thought it made sense and would save time getting ours together.'

She nodded. 'I don't want to be a DS, I keep telling you that.'

'You might not want to now, but you should be thinking about it.'

'I wouldn't get to work with you if I did that.'

He grinned at her. 'Would that be such a bad thing?'

'Yes, it would. I love being a part of this team. I enjoy working with Cain and Amy, with you. All right, Marc I could happily never work with again and not feel a moment's regret, but I don't want to be separated from you all, at least not yet. I tried it once and didn't like it, remember?'

'I do remember, you still got yourself in even more trouble down in Barrow than you do up here. I suppose I should keep you where I can keep an eye on you. It makes sense.'

'I'm not a child who needs babysitting.'

'Never said you were, I'm not implying that at all. I think I should shut up.'

'I do too.'

He laughed. 'Only about you, it's my job to make sure you are working on your self-development.'

'Ben.' She growled his name at him, which made him laugh louder.

'Where do you think he went?'

'Maybe we have this all wrong. What if he wanted his parents dead because he just hated them and it's nothing to do with the money? Maybe the poison was his way of taking his own life.'

'Still can't see that being a motive. He really fell on his feet with the Hawthornes. He was one of the lucky kids who got a loving family home and doting adoptive parents who loved him and nurtured him.'

Morgan was adopted, and she had done okay too. Well, in her younger years, Sylvia and Stan had been great parents; she hadn't known about Sylvia's struggles with her mental health or the fact that she needed support until she'd come home and found her slumped with her head in the gas cooker, dead. Stan had tried but he'd fallen to pieces and turned to alcohol, preferring to drown out his sorrows at the pub than spend time with her, but she'd forgiven him and then he'd been murdered and taken away from her too. Life was truly shit at times.

'I give in, I thought it was about money or revenge. Maybe

that cottage is just cursed and anyone who lives in it dies eventually.'

Ben laughed. 'I agree it's had its fair share of bad luck, but cursed or not, someone had to physically kill Margery and George, a curse didn't do that.'

She stopped talking, trying to think where David had gone in that lost bit of time between his leaving the hospital and turning up at the police station. It didn't look as if there had been evidence of him ingesting the poison in his car, so what did that mean? The fields all flew past in a blur, the rain on the windows distorting her view, as Ben drove down Lindale Hill a little more cautiously than usual towards David's house.

'How do you get someone to ingest poison without knowing they have?' she asked.

'What?'

'He must have gone somewhere for lunch, had a drink, maybe something to eat and somebody laced his food with it, just like Margery did when he was a baby. That's why there's a period of time unaccounted for. He stopped off to get something to eat, and it has to be somewhere he either goes regularly or somewhere whoever wanted him dead works and knew he was going to call in at some point, so they had whatever it is they gave him ready to put in his food or drink.'

Ben was turning into the drive of David's house. 'We need to find out where he went. Surely there must be a single camera out there that picked him up. What about his phone? Sometimes it updates your parking and tells you where your car is.'

Morgan typed a search into her phone and let out a whoop. 'Location services on an iPhone: if we can go on that it will tell us the two most recent ones. I'm sure it would be the same on other phones. His last location will be the police station, but it should also tell us where he was before he came to us.'

Ben held up the palm of his hand and she high-fived it. 'He

must have had his phone on him or it's in his car. There is no way a doctor who is working wouldn't have a phone with them.'

'What kind of phone did he have?'

He shrugged. 'That I can't tell you. I never saw him using it and had no reason to look at it. I was there for a check-up, nothing more than that.'

He stopped outside of David's beautiful home once more.

'This is so sad. He has it all. He's a good person. Okay he might not be the nicest of people to his lovers, but he does good in society, and he's a valuable human being; he saves lives; he contributes; he doesn't deserve to die a horrible, painful death.'

Ben nodded. 'You just said it, we need to find out who his past relationships have been with and if anyone he's been involved with had a reason to kill all three Lancasters. Declan, we know he had a brief fling with, but he's not our killer. I would stake my life on him not having anything to do with it.'

'Besides, he's moved on. He's with Theo, and he was finishing up a post-mortem at the time of George's death, I asked him what time he finished work that night in a non police talk manner just to be clear.'

'It's not Declan.' Ben blew out a long breath. 'Now I don't feel so bad about dragging him with us. We're his alibi for David Hawthorne. It saves us having to ask him embarrassing questions about what he was doing this afternoon.'

They got out of the van and got suited up. If they didn't find anything they would send the task force search team in, who would tear the place apart looking for evidence. Someone must have got close enough to poison David, or know him well enough to want him and his birth parents dead. Would the clue to that person's identity be in David's home?

Morgan was hoping that they would find something so they could wrap this case up without any further deaths, but deep down she had that feeling inside of her gut that told her it was far from over.

34

Cain answered the phone to Ben and was nodding intently while Amy stared at him wondering if they were ever going to get home tonight. This had been one long shift, and she was tired, more than ready to call it a day. Cain hung up.

'What did he want?'

'We're to find David Hawthorne's phone ASAP, and you're to bag it up but see if you can get onto his location services first, to see the last two places he's been or something. Is that even a thing?'

She nodded. 'Yeah, but if I haven't got his passcode, it's going to be a waste of time, but I can try.'

Cain was grinning at her. 'Where do you think his phone is right now? And you could always use his Face ID if he's got that working.'

'How the hell would I know that?'

'Let's ring it and see if anyone answers.'

'That's brilliant, you should be a detective.'

He laughed, his big hearty laugh. 'And you, my angry friend, should have been a night club comic.'

'Yeah, I should. Regular hours too I bet, not shifts that run on for days. Have you got his phone number then?'

Cain's cheeks flushed the tiniest bit pink, and it was her turn to laugh. 'Oh, what a conundrum we are in.'

'I beg your pardon, what does that even mean?'

'What a predicament. We have a decent idea but can't follow it through. Too complicated for you, Cain.'

'Well can you just speak normal then, so I don't feel as if I'm stupid.'

She smiled at him. 'You're not stupid, this is a really good idea. What about Declan? He would know; he went out with him, didn't he?'

He nodded. 'Where is he, at the hospital?'

'I think Morgan was taking him to Theo's. Ben mentioned it earlier. We could drop by and see if he's got it. Worth a shot, don't you think?'

'Yep, should we check his car first, in case it fell out of his pocket.'

'And the hospital. Who's with him? I'll call them and see what they bagged up as evidence.'

A few minutes later, they were in a car heading to the vicarage. David was still being worked on, and Amber who was waiting to go sit with him, hadn't been allowed in yet. She said she'd ask one of the nurses as soon as it was appropriate about the phone.

Cain looked at Amy. 'You know him better, you go ask.'

'I do not, come with me.'

'Why, are you scared?'

She glanced over at the prettiest church for miles around that held the worst memories of her life. She had never got over seeing Des's dead body lying out across the steps leading up to the altar; it haunted her worst nightmares.

Cain followed her eyes in the direction of the church, and he gently touched her arm.

'Sorry, I'm such a dick at times. Bad memories, I get it. You wait here and I'll go knock.'

She nodded. 'It's just the viciousness of it. It was so bloody, so gory and so unnecessary. He was a pain, but he was one of us.'

'Bit like me?'

She smiled. 'You're just a pain in my arse.'

He laughed and got out of the car; she watched him walking down the path to the vicarage. Cain was the best partner she'd had. Des had been lazy, there had been no getting away from that, whereas Cain was always ready to jump in and do his fair share. She hoped that his date with the social worker went well tomorrow, because he deserved to be happy. This job was thankless at times; they worked all hours to find the scourge of society and lock them away so they couldn't hurt anyone else. Lately it seemed as if it had been nothing but murders. She was beginning to miss shed break-ins and burglary investigations – that was something she had never thought she'd ever say. Feeling bad she got out of the car and followed Cain, who was knocking on the door. He looked at her but didn't say anything.

'They might make us a brew; Theo has a fancy coffee machine.'

The door opened and the vicar was standing there, shirtless, in a pair of faded jeans.

'Oh, hey, guys. I thought you were the delivery driver.'

'Delivery of what?'

'Food, what else is there to get delivered this time of night around here?'

'Hey, Theo,' said Amy, ignoring Cain's rude comments. 'Is Declan here?'

Theo nodded. 'He is but is this a call-out? Because he's had a bit of a shock.'

'God no, it's not. Oh, sorry about that.' Amy felt her cheeks turn red, and Theo laughed.

'I don't care if you take my supervisor's name in vain, don't worry about it. I won't thrash you with a whip or make you say a hundred Hail Marys. Come in, be kind to him though; he looks a bit worn out. We were supposed to be going out to that new Indian restaurant, but I figured he wasn't in the mood so we're getting it delivered, hence the reason I thought you were the guy.'

Cain smiled at him. 'I've heard great things about that place.'

He nodded. 'Me too. Come in, he's in the kitchen. I was just getting changed.'

Amy was staring at his six pack. 'Don't get dressed on our account, we won't be here long.'

Theo grinned at her and flexed his muscles. 'Can you tell I've been working out?'

She nodded. 'I can.'

He high-fived her. 'Got to try and make an impression.' He rolled his eyes in the direction of the kitchen, and she lowered her voice. 'I'm sure he likes you for you, Theo, although I have to say I like what I see.'

Cain was staring at her in horror.

'What? He can appreciate a compliment, can't you? He's gay, but it doesn't mean he isn't human.'

'You're perving over him in public.'

She shrugged and pointed at Cain. 'He gets a little jealous.'

Theo pointed to the kitchen door. 'I'll go grab my shirt, save the pair of you arguing.'

He ran up the stairs, leaving Cain glaring at Amy, who shrugged. The kitchen door was closed, and she knocked before pushing it open.

Declan was sitting at the table with a large glass of red wine. His expression became sombre as he put down the glass.

'Is this bad news?'

'No, we have no news yet. Sorry to bother you, Declan, we're trying to find David's phone. Do you have the number?'

The relief made him pick up the wine glass, and he glugged a mouthful. 'I'll check, I might have deleted it.' He took out his phone and scrolled through until he said, 'Oh, I do.' He looked up at Amy, who had her notepad and pen out ready to write it down. He rhymed off the number to her.

'Thank you, that's a great help.'

'Is there any update on anything?'

'Not really. Ben and Morgan have gone to search his house. We're looking for his phone, and he's still in resus being worked on.'

'He's still alive though, that's good right?'

'Yeah, alive is always better than dead.'

'Most of the time anyway.'

Theo walked back in wearing a tight black T-shirt. 'Can I get you guys a drink? I don't suppose you can have a glass of wine if you're still working, but tea or coffee I can do.'

Cain smiled at him. 'No, we're good, but thank you.'

Amy wanted to kick him; she could do with a coffee if she was going to have to keep on working ridiculously long hours.

Theo looked at her. 'Amy, would you like a coffee?'

'Yes, please. I honestly really, really would.'

'You look as if you need a coffee.'

'I bet I do. Cain will have one too, he's just more polite than me.'

Declan was sipping his wine a little slower, but he smiled at them.

'I have some takeaway cups if you have stuff to be getting on with.'

'Perfect, got any biscuits?'

Cain could hide his shock no longer and turned to glare at her, but Theo laughed. 'I'm a vicar, of course I have biscuits.

Tea and biscuits are the tools of my trade. I have a whole packet of Custard Creams you can take with you.'

Amy put her hands in the prayer position. 'It's a miracle.'

'They happen every day. I keep telling everyone that they don't have to be life changing.'

'Coffee and biscuits are life changing for me though, especially after the shift we've had.'

'It's the simple things that often are.'

He made their drinks and passed them over. Opening the cupboard he took out a packet of biscuits and passed them to Cain. 'Can I get you guys anything else?'

'No, thank you. We're good, enjoy your takeaway. We'll see ourselves out.'

Theo smiled at them, his gaze falling on Declan who was on his second glass of wine, his eyes a little glazed. He waved at them but didn't speak, and Amy felt sad for him. He was always so full of life, always joking, but he looked heartbroken as if today had wiped every last bit of joy out of him.

———

Back in the car they sipped the coffee, ate the biscuits then drove back to the station to stand next to the car while Amy rang the phone number. Cain frowned, then pressed his ear against the glass. 'Ring it again.' She did, and he let out a whoop. 'It's in there, must have slid between the seats. Who has the keys?'

'Sergeant's office, it's probably to be lifted to be taken away for a full forensic search. I'll go get them – you wait here.' She passed him her phone.

She came back wearing gloves with a set of car keys dangling from her finger. She clicked the car open and opened the rear passenger door so as not to contaminate any evidence from the driver's side. 'Can you ring it one last time, please?'

Cain pressed the call button, and she saw it light up underneath the driver's seat. Picking it up she put it into an evidence bag. The iPhone had Face ID enabled.

She looked at Cain. 'I think we should go to the hospital and use his face to unlock it, and then I can do a quick look at his location services before sending it off to headquarters for the tech unit to do the same.'

'You're the boss, as long as we're not going to get in trouble.'

'Well, I'm only following my boss's orders, so we're good.'

'Let's hope they'll let us in to see him when we get there.'

'They will, you can charm whoever is in charge while I try and get it unlocked. We're not doing anything criminal; we're trying to catch one.'

Amy sounded confident, but she knew that it was risky. There was a chance the hospital staff wouldn't let either of them get near enough to David Hawthorne, but it was worth trying.

35

The search of David's house yielded a single, black pillowcase that Ben had found in the linen cupboard and nothing else. For a guy, there was a surprising lack of guy stuff around. Morgan had searched downstairs and hadn't found anything. The kitchen didn't have a single dirty cup in the sink; a plate, couple of mugs and cutlery were in the dishwasher and sparkling, the sides had nothing on them, not even toast crumbs from his breakfast this morning. The only crime that had happened here was one of a life not lived before it was almost taken away from him.

Ben sauntered downstairs pillowcase in an evidence bag; his cheeks pinker than when he went up there.

'Anything?'

'This. No idea if it matches the one found on Margery's head but it was out of place in a cupboard full of white and cream bedding. The only other thing he had was a few adult toys in his bedroom drawers and some magazines that you wouldn't want your mother to find.'

Morgan laughed and the sound echoed around the large, open plan, empty house. 'Very little happened here, except maybe for wild sex. Do you think it's from the same set?' She pointed to the evidence bag and Ben shrugged. 'I'm hoping so, but then again it's so out of place it makes me think that it may have been planted here by someone else. Would David be so reckless as to keep the other pillowcase in full view for anyone to find? It just doesn't sit right with me. This is not our crime scene, and there is nothing to suggest anything untoward happened here. I don't think we'll waste Al's time unless we find something else that leads us back here.'

He phoned Amy. 'Did you locate his phone?'

'Yes, on our way to the hospital to try and use his face to unlock it, to check the location services.'

'You are? Christ, whose idea was that one? Don't tell me, I don't want to know. Whoever it is, well done for using your initiative and good luck. Try not to get in any trouble while you're there.'

He hung up and turned to Morgan. 'You will not believe what they are about to do.'

She was smiling; judging by Ben's reply it wasn't strictly above board. 'Face ID?'

'How did you guess?'

'The look on your face.'

'I'm that readable?'

She nodded.

'Come on, let's get out of here. I feel like I'm snooping where I have no business to be snooping. The poor guy has had nothing but pain in his life if you ask me. If he survives this, imagine how he's going to feel knowing that two people have poisoned him, trying to kill him.'

'It's awful. He didn't ask to be born; he didn't ask to have parents who didn't care. He didn't ask to have someone who knew so much about him and wanted him dead.' They were walking out of the door. 'Somebody knew all of this; they must have known everything about him, so is it a lover or a friend? I wonder if Margery ever had a pregnancy and maybe lost the baby before he came along, something like that would have brought about a lot of unresolved issues, especially if George wasn't a sympathetic husband.'

Ben locked the door behind them, and she stopped, turning to stare at him. 'Jesus, how did I miss it? I can't believe I didn't think of it before. Damn, he probably wouldn't have been poisoned if I'd thought about this sooner.'

'Thought about what?'

'Angela said that George had an affair with a woman in the village while Margery was stuck at home with the baby. What if she is the one who got pregnant and there is another Lancaster out there who we don't know about? What if he or she is out for revenge? Working with David and then turned on him? I think that when we find out who David went to see before he came to the station, we will find out that it's George's child.'

'That's a big leap. Did Angela tell you the name of the woman George had an affair with? It can't be that hard to trace her and her kid.'

'I need to speak to Angela.' Morgan phoned her and it went to voicemail. 'We could go see her if she doesn't ring back?'

Ben looked at his watch; it was almost seven and they had been working nonstop. She knew he was torn: she was tired, and he looked exhausted. 'Okay, let's go see if she's in.'

'There's also the grocers on the high street. Ettie said Margery got food deliveries off the young lad who worked for them before he went away to uni. We could speak to the new owners and see if they have any contact details for him, to ask him what he knew about Margery. If she knew George had another child.'

They got in the car, and Morgan sighed. 'I wonder if there was anyone else she was friends with. Oh God, Ettie, she knew her, and she visited her once a month.'

Morgan phoned her aunt, who answered.

'Morgan, is everything okay?'

'We're trying to trace that delivery boy who went to Margery's that you told me about. Did you know his name?' She had her fingers crossed, hoping her aunt could save them lots of running around.

'It began with D, Duane, Davy, Darren maybe. I'm sorry, I only saw him on the odd occasion.'

'That's okay, did you know George was having an affair?'

Ettie sighed.

'I suspected as much, he was full of himself was George Lancaster, loved himself more than he loved anyone else.'

'Do you think he could have another child with whoever he had an affair with? Did you ever hear rumours?'

'I knew he was all over the young girl who worked behind the bar in The Black Dog, a little bit besotted with her. She left one day and didn't tell anybody where she was going, didn't hand her notice in. Just never turned up for work. Rumour has it George was bereft. He moped around for months, and I think that's when he started to get really nasty to Maggie with his fists.'

'Do you know her name, Ettie? It's really important.'

'I do, but it's been a long time since I've thought about her. I only heard the gossip and rumours that were flying around, and I never gave much heed to them if I'm honest. One of the reasons I moved out here when I found out the old woodsman cottage was going on the market. You can bet I whipped around to that estate agents quicker than anything to make them an offer. I couldn't stand the way the women in the village were too quick to judge everyone but what went on behind their own doors. Let me see, was she called Dawn? Maybe, that rings a bell. Dawn Stephens maybe, but if you go ask the guy who owns The Black Dog, he will be able to tell you; he should remember her. You know, I'm not sure if she came back to the village a good few years later, had a kiddie by then.'

Morgan felt the stirrings of excitement as her stomach began to churn a little. She was on the right track. She was annoyed with herself for not thinking about this before, but at least she was working on it now.

'Is there anything else, sweetheart?'

'No, no, thank you, Ettie. That's a huge help. I'll see you soon.'

Ettie laughed.

'I hope so, please don't make me wait too long. I love you, Morgan, be careful.'

Morgan smiled at the screen as Ettie ended the call. Why did everyone tell her to be careful.

'Did you catch that?'

'Most of it, let's go to The Black Dog, eh?'

She nodded. It was a lot nearer to home than Angela's. Maybe they were finally heading in the right direction. All they had to do was to find the angry, jealous, devious love child of George and Dawn. Surely it wasn't going to be that hard? They had to catch a break at some point in the investigation, and she felt that this was it.

36

He was sitting cross-legged on the floor of the one-bedroom flat, one of three units on the top section of the large, detached house in Ambleside, with a view of the cemetery at St Mary's churchyard. In almost total darkness. He had a solitary candle burning to give him a little light. Bright enough he could see the piece of paper in front of him, but not light enough that from the outside it looked as if there was anyone home.

On the floor next to him was the cheap, pay-as-you-go mobile phone he'd picked up at a car boot sale last year. It was ancient, had no internet, no camera, nothing but the ability to make calls and send text messages, which made it perfect for what he needed it for. He had gone to the police station to see if David had turned up like he said he would, and oh boy had he arrived there in style. His precious car was in the car park, and the front doors that led into the entrance of the building had been taped shut with police tape strung across them, sealing off access to anyone. Pretending he hadn't noticed, he'd pulled into the car park next to an ambulance with the rear doors wide open, catching a glimpse of his half-brother being worked on in the back of it by two very stressed-looking paramedics. Two coppers were standing at the rear of the ambulance glaring at him, and he'd mouthed 'Sorry' to them as he pointed towards the front doors. They both shook their heads at him, and he smiled, driving away as they turned back to see what was happening inside of the ambulance.

He knew he'd been reckless, stupid; they were bound to have cameras on the car park, but he had to know who had been inside. He'd seen David's floppy hand and recognised the gold signet ring he wore on his little finger as it trailed lifelessly against the metal trolley he was on.

Now he was staring at the phone, wondering if he should make the call to the A&E department to see how he was, if he'd been taken there and if he was still alive. It was okay if it was busy and he got a receptionist who didn't care less, but there was a slim chance his phone call could set off alarm bells and they might just go tell whichever copper was with him about the weird guy on the phone.

It was only a matter of time, he supposed, before they caught up to him. He could cut his losses and run. He had a small amount of cash that he'd saved up, the handouts from David, who if anything was a very generous half-brother. A part of him knew that he should leave before they came looking for him. What did they have on him really? Very little was his honest answer; he had been careful. He had never brought any attention to himself, had never been in trouble with the police, which he thought was admirable with his background and upbringing.

He stared down at the folded piece of paper; this was the problem. He unfolded it to stare down at the only name on the last will and testament of Margery Lancaster who was to get everything she owned, the money, the creepy cottage, and the land around it. Just who the hell was Esther Jackson? And what had she been to the murderous Maggie to deserve every penny the evil, old bitch had in her bank account?

Did he leave now and hope that the police never realised he existed? There was a good chance that they wouldn't. He wasn't confident they were that good. Or did he kill her too and get his final revenge?

He had his scrapbook next to him, so old the pages were falling out, but he had spent hours at the little library researching High Wraith Cottage, the Lancaster family, and the land around it. Using his pocket money he had paid to photocopy every article there was about the poisonings, the arrest, the trial, what happened to Margery Lancaster aka The Iron Lady. It had been like his own personal bible; he had studied it and could probably repeat every article word for word, and then he'd found out after months that David Lancaster hadn't moved very far at all and was nearer than he ever imagined.

In a way, he supposed he had kind of groomed the guy into believing he genuinely cared and was lonely, wanting to get to know his family better. It was his own fault. He'd seen the look on his face when they'd first met – he'd been a little drunk and had tried his best to seduce him, but he'd told him he couldn't, there was no way on this earth the pair of them could be together, and that had been the biggest challenge that David had ever faced because he had made it his business to find out why they couldn't.

He had felt bad when he'd finally caved in and told him it was because they could be related. David had been so angry, he had punched a huge hole in the wall of the kitchen in his fancy house, and he'd had to get someone to come out and repair it. They hadn't spoken for weeks after that, but he knew he would get in touch. And he had. He'd texted him: *I miss you.* And that had been all he'd needed to bring David back into his life.

Now he had a whole section in his scrapbook of David: pictures, articles, you name it; if it had his name attached to it, he kept it. He picked it up and turned to the last few pages, where there were pictures of one Esther Jackson. She lived in a cottage in the woods; she wore a velvet cloak and sold jars of herbal teas at the market a couple of times a week. She was easy pickings, but he didn't know how he felt about taking out an old woman who probably didn't even know that Margery Lancaster had left her a small fortune. What he wanted to know was why she had, and then destroy any chances of Margery's final wishes coming true.

37

The Black Dog was busy. Mark, the owner, waved at Ben as he walked in. 'Missed you at the quiz last night.'

'I'll bet you did, someone else had to come last for a change.'

Mark nodded. 'Yeah, Brian and his team were gutted to take your title. Can I get you both a drink?'

Morgan shook her head. 'I'm good, thanks.'

He turned to Ben.

'I'm okay too, we're here on work stuff. How long have you owned the pub?'

'Is this a trick question? Because it feels like forever, but probably around fifteen years now.'

'Ah, I don't know if you were here then. Did you know Dawn Stephens?'

He shook his head. Two guys in their early seventies walked in; one of them had a black Labrador on a leash that headed straight to sniff Morgan's leg. She smiled, bending down to scratch behind its ears, and it sat down by her feet.

'Sorry, she's a bit overfriendly at times. Come on, Bess.' He tugged at her leash, but she wasn't having any of it and was now sniffing her trouser leg.

Morgan smiled. 'She can probably smell our cat, Kevin.'

The man nodded. 'Happen she can. Strange name for a cat.'

She laughed. 'It is, not my first choice but he kind of looks like a Kevin. Have you been coming here long?'

The guy holding the leash looked at his friend, and they both laughed. 'Too long, we keep him in business, don't we, Mark?'

Mark nodded as he was pulling their usual pints of bitter.

'Do you remember a Dawn Stephens?'

They both said, 'Aye,' at the same time, and Ben turned his attention fully on the men but didn't say anything, letting her continue.

'Is she still around by any chance?'

They shook their heads. 'She died last year. Dropped down dead, foaming at the mouth. They thought it was a seizure, poor lass. She was a nice girl, grew up into a nice woman; don't know where her son is now. He doted on her; wouldn't know him if I fell over him though, but I think he moved away.'

Morgan felt deflated, all roads were leading to nowhere. 'Do you know her son's name?'

Both men shook their heads.

'Where did she live?'

This time they shrugged. Mark passed over their pints.

'We're not much use, are we? Probably as good as your quiz team, Ben.'

Ben laughed so loud it made the dog bark.

The owner of the dog took a long sip of his pint then sighed. 'I'll tell you who she was friendly with though, the woman who has the general store on the high street, Joanie. She knew her very well; you'd be better talking to her. She probably knows where her son is too. She's that nosey, she knows everything about everyone.'

'Thank you, we'll go talk to her.' She bent down to give the dog one last stroke, and they left.

'That was another dead end.'

'Not completely, if we get to the shop and it's still open by some miracle, we might have a name and address, fingers crossed.'

Ben smiled at her. 'I love your optimism, I really do. That dog liked you.'

'I like dogs, always have done. More than cats really.'

'I don't like either, well Kevin is okay, but I wouldn't have chosen to have a cat like him, especially not with those white cat hairs, but it wasn't his fault he ended up with us, so we have to give him a break.'

'Talking about Kevin, did you refill his feeder this morning?'

He nodded. 'I did, those Dreamies cost a fortune.'

She stared at him. 'You filled his feeder with Dreamies?'

'Yeah, we're out of them now.'

'Jesus, Ben, that's like giving him caviar. They're a treat, not a food. No wonder he likes you so much.'

'He's a spoiled kitty. What can I say? He deserves the best.'

Morgan laughed. 'Spoiled, he's spending most of his life in a Dreamies coma.'

'Lucky sod, I wish I was. Come on, let's get to the store and see if we can at least catch one break today before we go home. I wonder how David is doing?'

'No update from the hospital. I suppose no news is good news; he must still be alive.'

'I hope so, he doesn't deserve this.'

Nobody deserved this, nobody deserved to die horrible painful deaths, but they did.

The grocer's shop had old fashioned tiny windowpanes, each one cast an orange glow out onto the pavement. It was probably one of the few shops that had its original windows from when it was built, it was like stepping back in time and Morgan was relieved to see it was still open. Through the rivulets of rain that were running down the glass. As they stepped into the warmth a woman was leaning across the counter reading a magazine, a huge cup next to her that she picked up and sipped while simultaneously looking in their direction and running a hand through her hair. She straightened up. 'Still raining, it's never ending. Can I help you?'

Morgan smiled. 'Detectives Brookes and Matthews. We're looking for Joanie?'

'Whatever it is I didn't do it, but please take me away from here before I die of boredom. I'm Joanie's daughter. She's upstairs in the flat. Should I go get her?'

'Yes, please, we just need a quick word with her. It's nothing to worry about.'

'Ah, that's a shame, be fun to see the old bird get dragged out of here in handcuffs. She's been a right pain.' She picked up the phone next to her. 'Mum, the police are here wanting to talk to you. What did you do?' She was laughing and hung up. 'Sorry, she's been a cow all day, so this kind of serves her right. I wanted tonight off to go see this band in Kendal and she wouldn't work late, then Cath rang in sick, and I'm stuck here for another hour.'

A woman appeared in the doorway behind the counter, making Morgan jump. She hadn't made a sound approaching unlike her daughter who was loud and chatty, she reminded her a little of Cain who could gossip and chatter until the cows came home.

'Don't listen to her, she's in a bad mood because she had to work for her wages.' Joanie gave her daughter a look. 'I'm Joanie Green, how can I help?'

'We were wondering if you could tell us about Dawn Stephens and her son. It's in relation to an active case.'

Joanie tilted her head slightly. 'I can, come on through to the back.'

They followed her along a narrow corridor that was stacked floor to ceiling with crisp and chocolate boxes into a staff room. She pointed at the chairs, and they sat down.

'She was a good woman, worked hard and didn't deserve the lot she got in life. It broke my heart when she collapsed. I knew by the look on her face she wasn't going to make it. Her eyes were glazed over as she went down. It was horrible. They said it was a massive stroke, there was nothing anyone could have done. She was foaming a bit at the mouth, that bothered me, but the docs know their stuff and she'd been to see the doctor the day before about headaches, so you know there was a warning sign, I suppose. You never know the minute, do you?'

'I guess not, when was this?' Morgan asked, thinking the foaming sounded suspiciously like poison.

'Last October, poor Andy was beside himself. He adored his mum; it had always been just the two of them.'

'How old is Andy?'

She shrugged. 'Around thirty, thirty-four, maybe older, I'm not sure.'

'Where is he now?'

'Last I heard he was in a flat in Ambleside. He never married, and I don't think he has a girlfriend.'

Morgan wrote *Andy Stephens* down in her notepad and looked up. 'Was his dad around?'

Joanie shook her head. 'I'm tempted to ask what this case is about, asking me these questions when I know you can't tell me anything. I watch the TV shows, they always say they can't disclose any information and are on enquiries, is that true?'

Ben nodded. 'Unfortunately, most of the time it is, we have to be careful what we say before anything goes to court.'

'I get that, I suppose. Should I tell you why I think you're here?' She smiled at them slyly. 'I think you know that miserable bastard George Lancaster had an affair with Dawn, and that Andy is his son. Now George and Margery are both dead and you're looking for their killer.'

Morgan smiled at her.

'I'm on the right track then?'

'Sort of.'

She nodded. 'Have you traced their son? The one Margery tried to kill off? Poor lamb, he was only a baby when she did that to the poor mite. I'd say he has more motive than Andy to want the pair of them dead, though I haven't seen him since the day he was taken away from that awful, haunted mausoleum.'

Ben looked confused; Joanie was truly an expert at keeping up with multiple strands at the same time, and he asked, 'The cottage is haunted?'

'Yes, one hundred per cent. I mean it has to be, there is no way that entire family could be murdered in such a small space and not still be stuck there. They say when you die unexpectedly that your spirit is stuck. It's going to be mighty overcrowded adding Margery and that big bully George to the mix, and before you ask it's all over Facebook. Imagine you're Margery and you now have to spend all of eternity stuck in the house you tried to kill your husband in. I have a friend who is a psychic, and she went there once at Margery's request. Only time the woman ever asked for help. She asked her to make it more peaceful. Well, my friend went there, didn't even get past the front door. She ran away and said she couldn't deal with the number of spirits stuck in that house, terrified herself she did.' Joanie actually shuddered, and Morgan found herself staring at the woman in fascination. She wondered if Ettie would know who this woman was.

'Oh God, I hope not, that would be awful.'

'Wouldn't it just? I have no idea what Dawn saw in George. I'd have to say she was young and daft, desperate for attention and he came along to give it to her, gave her a kid she didn't really want, too, she hinted as much when she talked about the past that she got pregnant far too young and wished she'd waited a bit longer, never regretted moving to Australia though. She had a distant cousin out there who she lived with.'

Morgan said, 'Dawn didn't want Andy?'

'Well, she never came out and said as much, but she upped and left the village pretty quick when she found out she was pregnant, and that Margery had tried to poison her own kid and George. She didn't come back until the kid was a teenager, probably thought nobody would remember her.'

'But they did?'

Joanie crossed her arms. 'It's Rydal Falls, of course they remembered, but nobody cared. Margery was a recluse when she was let out, so she was no threat. I don't know if she ever took up with George again. I don't think she did, but I don't know everything.'

This last statement surprised Morgan because she thought that the woman knew plenty. 'Thank you, you've been very helpful, Joanie.'

She nodded. 'Welcome, I would be looking for David if you want my opinion.'

'We know exactly where he is, but thank you.'

'I guess you better find Andy pretty fast then. He works in the kitchen at the garden centre in Ambleside. Gave me a huge portion of fish and chips last time I visited. He's a nice boy. He used to work here, loved mountain biking, and would bike it up to High Wraith Cottage with Margery's weekly groceries when he was younger.'

Morgan and Ben looked quickly at one another. Andy was the delivery boy.

'She hated coming into Rydal Falls and paid him a tenner cash to deliver her bits to her. Come to think of it, he probably spoke to her more than any of us. I wonder if she knew he was George's son? Makes you think, doesn't it? I was so busy at the time I didn't really give it the time of day, that was before all these flipping mini supermarkets began popping up every-where, taking all our business. Dorothy and her husband got out of here at the right time; they must have known what was going to happen.'

Morgan didn't need to look at Ben again. Ambleside was on the way to the police station. It would fit the timescale perfectly if David had called in to the garden centre to see Andy.

He stood up. 'Thanks for your help, Joanie.'

Morgan followed him. 'Yes, thank you so much.'

Joanie nodded. 'Good luck, I guess I'll wait to read about it in the paper.'

As they walked out of the shop, her daughter called out, 'Thanks for calling, could you not at least handcuff her?'

Ben ignored her, but Morgan laughed and shook her head. 'Sorry, too much to do at the moment.'

And then they were in the car just as Ben's phone began to ring. He put it on loudspeaker.

'Amy.'

'Boss, we got kicked out of the hospital. The matron caught us trying to hold the phone in front of his face. Cain only lifted his head off the pillow for a couple of seconds.'

'Crap, is she putting in a complaint?'

'Possibly, she was so pissed, and Cain was joking with her, trying to defuse the situation, only she didn't take it very well. She actually pushed him out through the doors with her bare hands. We're back in the car now.'

Morgan couldn't help smiling.

'I'll sort it, get yourselves home. There isn't much we can do tonight now; we have a lead that we can follow up on first thing.'

'We do, is it a confirmed lead?'

'It will be, hopefully. How is David?'

'Looks like death warmed up, but stable. They were taking

him down to intubate him and then he's going into intensive care. We tried, sorry.'

'You did, it's all I ever ask, and you used your own initiative which might have landed you in deep shit, but I've got your backs. Thank you.'

He hung up and began to laugh so much his eyes were watering. When he gathered himself together, he said, 'Fuck me,' which set Morgan off laughing. The pair of them were tired, stressed and on the verge of being maniacal but at least they could see the funny side of it.

'What now?' she asked.

'We need to find Andy.'

38

Morgan had stayed under the hot shower until her skin was pink and the bathroom was steamed up, and she couldn't see herself in the mirror. They'd arranged for a car to watch Andy Stephens' house. It didn't look like anyone was home, but they were all on hand to rush there if he left. Morgan hadn't been able to relax all evening, she wanted to force entry, to rush in there, but if Andy was their killer they might startle him, and lose him. She wiped the condensation away from the mirror in front of her. At least she was finally warm. As she rummaged around in the fridge looking for the contents to make something to eat, she discovered she needed to go shopping; the only beans they had was a tin that was pushed to the back, open, with a film of blue and green mould across the top. Grimacing she dropped the can into the bin. There was the curled-up bunch of spring onions that either one of them bought without fail when they shopped and never, ever used. It tickled Morgan so much it was like a family tradition. Apart from that they didn't even have any bacon or eggs left. She sighed. She didn't want to go outside in the rain again, to go to the shop, but she was starving. As she closed the fridge door, she saw the leaflet for Gino's and wondered just how bad it would be to eat takeout pizza again? Then phoned an order in anyway, they had to eat, and Ben wouldn't want to call in at the Co-op on the way home, although she knew he would if she asked. He really was that kind of guy, but she wouldn't make him when she couldn't be bothered herself.

As she sat down, she opened her laptop and began to search for Andrew Stephens. A whole list of them came up on Facebook. Not one of them looked as if they were local. She tried Dawn and nothing came up for her either, which was weird. Maybe they didn't like social media. She didn't blame them – it was hard keeping up with everything if you let it take over. She then searched both their names in Google. A small article had been written in the local paper about Dawn's sudden death, but nothing else. She sat back, it was strange. Had they purposely kept a low profile? She could understand Dawn: with all the press around Margery and George, she wouldn't have wanted anyone to know she was involved with him and had moved away. Would Andrew though? He had nothing to hide, and he was much younger. He would've struggled in school if he refused to get any sort of social media account. Plus, the past was well in the past and nobody would connect him to the Lancasters. Or at least she didn't think they would care, so why was he not easily found? The only thing that she could think of was that he knew for a long time that he would eventually do this, had planned it out thoroughly, which meant it was premeditated, so he couldn't go with a plea that it was on the spur of the moment. She wondered who it was that had found Margery's body. Had they ever taken a full statement from them? She didn't want to bother Ben, so she rang Cain.

'What's up dawg?' He drawled his words out.

'Did you really just call me a dog?'

He laughed.

'It's a saying, Morgan, I'm not insinuating that you are a dog.'

'Good. Did you or Amy go speak to the guy who phoned in Margery's death and get his statement?'

'Negative.'

'What are you watching?'

'Some US cop show, they have it much better than us you know, all those donuts and coffee shops open twenty-four seven.'

'Cain, why did nobody go talk to him?'

'I don't know. Benno said to but then he sent me to the farm on CCTV enquiries, and I kind of forgot about the guy who rang it in. Nobody else mentioned it, so he's probably waiting around on someone going to get his statement.'

'Crap.'

'Exactly that.'

'I'll mention it to Ben but not tonight. He'll be wired enough as it is without throwing that onto him. Cheers, Cain.'

She hung up before he could say anything else. The guy could have gone back home by now. Probably left the area, but at least they had his phone number on file. She would sort that out first thing while everyone else was getting ready to go arrest Andrew Stephens and bring him in. She wasn't sure that it was all Andy, David must have got pretty close to whoever had poisoned him. Trusted them, had he and Andy killed Margery and George together? Had David been at the police station to confess? Is that why Andy had tried to kill him? At least with all of the family dead or almost, there was no one left for him to focus on.

39

Coffee was life, there was no doubt in Morgan's mind that the cardboard cup full of magic set her up for the entire day. She had driven into work a little earlier, taking Cain's advice, and leaving Ben in the shower. There was no way that she was starting another day without a coffee. She realised that they were going to have to invest in a decent coffee machine for their kitchen. It would be the answer: since their other one had packed up, life had not been as fun. She stopped at The Coffee Pot, buying coffees for everyone and cakes, especially after giving Marc her little work advice about buying them. As she sipped her latte, Fleetwood Mac started to sing 'Don't Stop' on the radio, and she turned it up as loud as it would go and began singing along. Even though her windscreen wipers were swishing double time she didn't care. She had her waterproof coat on today, her thermal beanie hat, coffee in her cupholder and her eyeliner game was strong.

Morgan also had the feeling that today was going to be productive. Ben would get an arrest team together to go and get Andrew Stephens, and she would speak to the guy who started all of this by taking a wrong turn and finding poor Margery's body – and everyone would be happy. They might even get to work a normal eight-hour shift after tying up all of the loose ends. She turned into the car park and smiled to herself. There waiting for her near to the rear entrance was a lovely, empty parking space. 'Thank you,' she whispered, not sure who to, but she was grateful.

Cain and Amy came in a few minutes after she was at her desk, coffee and cake in each hand.

'Whoa, the breakfast of champions is that, Brookes.'

She pointed to the spare desk where there were coffee cups and white paper bags containing cakes.

He turned to Amy. 'Have I died and gone to heaven, am I tripping?'

She pushed him out of the way and grabbed the paper bags to see which cakes were inside and winked at Morgan. 'Thanks, cake for breakfast is living the dream. Where's the boss? I couldn't sleep last night waiting to find out about this lead he has.'

'Why didn't you just phone him and ask?'

'At like two in the morning. I'm not that mean, he might have thought it was a call-out.'

'Probably. He'll be here soon; but I'll put you out of your misery. We know that George Lancaster had a son to a woman he was having an affair with when David was still a baby. The woman, Dawn Stephens, moved away when she found out she was pregnant, not wanting Margery to find out.'

Cain spoke through a mouthful of cake. 'Don't blame her, was probably scared for their lives with her track record.'

'Anyway, to cut a long story short, she moved back when the kid was a teenager, and he worked for the grocers on the high street and would deliver shopping to Margery once a week. His mum died last year, dropped down dead of a massive stroke which possibly set him on this path to wipe out George, Margery and David.'

'Why, because he's jealous he never got to play happy families with his dad?'

'None of them played happy families. I've never known a family unit so distant. After what Margery did it was never going to be a happy family. He could have done it all *with* David and then turned on him.'

Cain was clearly trying to process everything she had just said. 'Did Margery know about him being George's son when he was delivering these groceries, because I'm not being funny, if I was her and he kept turning up rubbing the result of an affair in my face, I'd be telling him to bugger off and not come back.'

'Well, anyway, who knows what's going on inside his head because he clearly doesn't think like the rest of us do. We found out that he works in the kitchens at the garden centre in Ambleside, and guess where David Hawthorne's last location was that Ben was hoping you'd find?'

Amy glanced at Cain who was grinning. 'The garden centre?'

Morgan threw her hands up in the air. 'We are on fire today.' And all three of them burst out laughing. 'So, how mad was the matron in A&E on a scale of one to ten with you yesterday?'

'Ninety-nine, she was raging with us. Well, more with Cain really.'

'Why though?'

Amy smiled. 'Do you want to tell her or should I?'

'Be my guest.'

'Cain thought it would be a good idea to hold David Hawthorne's head up to get a better position to unlock it. I was waving his phone around in front of his face in an evidence bag, and Cain had one of his big hands holding the unconscious guy's head in the air. I never heard language like it, she was so angry.'

'Then he called her love and told her to calm down, that was it, boom.'

Morgan buried her head in her hands in disbelief, then looked at him. 'You didn't?'

'It slipped out. I was trying to defuse the situation only it got her even angrier. I told her it was for his own good, that we're trying to figure out who did this to him, but she wasn't having it and pushed me out of there with her bare hands. I was going to tell her I'd arrest her for assault, but Amy told me to zip it.'

Morgan tried not to laugh because it wasn't funny, but it also was. 'You are such a dinosaur; nobody likes being called love.'

'Erm, I beg to differ. The old dears love it. Whenever I used to go to jobs with a little granny-type woman who was the victim, they positively thrived off it.'

'Yeah, well they're a different generation. I hope you apologised to her.'

Amy shook her head. 'I did, on his behalf. He was too busy nursing his injured ego.'

Ben walked in, headed straight for a coffee, then looked at the three of them. 'Want to tell me why you called that matron love, Cain? She was not impressed.'

'How did you know, were you eavesdropping?'

'Where?'

'Here, I was telling Morgan.'

'No, I was not. I have better things to be doing than standing listening to you lot, who sound like a bunch of cackling hyenas from out in the corridor. I just took a phone call from an old friend called Alison, who was the matron on duty last night.'

'Oh.'

'I explained to her that you are a good guy, despite being a huge fuck up at times, and she said she wasn't putting an official complaint in if I told you not to address anyone as love in future. So consider yourself told, you idiot.'

Cain mimed wiping his brow. 'Phew.'

'Yes, quite. I want everything you can get me on Andrew and Dawn Stephens. Dawn is deceased, but we still need to know if she's got any previous, same for Andrew. He lives in Ambleside. Marc is getting an entry team together to go into his flat, then the search team will go in. We don't know if he's there, but we need to be prepared. Amy and Cain, I want you two with me; Morgan you can go to the garden centre and speak to the staff there before we go in. Get a confirmation he was working at the time David Hawthorne was there, then you're going to have to seize anything that belongs to him. If we find out he gave him the poison at the café, we're going to have to shut it all down for CSI, but I'll give you the go-ahead before you need to give them that snippet of good news.'

She nodded. 'We never got a statement from the guy who rang it in. Do you want me to get that sorted first? The garden centre isn't open for another hour.'

'We didn't, how did that get overlooked?'

'It was a mess, wasn't it? The weather, the scene, everything was the wrong way around.'

'I suppose so, but we're going to need that so, yes please. Even if you only speak to him over the phone and get one, it will do for now.'

She scribbled down the man's phone number off the log and picked up the phone. It went to voicemail. 'Hi, this is Detective Brookes. I wonder if you could give me a quick statement regarding the body you found two days ago.'

The others were all heading out to the blue room, and she smiled at Ben who winked at her then let the door shut behind him. She hung up, and her phone began to ring. 'Brookes.'

'Oh, hi you just left a message for me. Sorry the phone signal around here is atrocious.'

'Yes, I did and yes, it's terrible, isn't it? Thanks for calling back. I really need to get a quick statement from you, if that's okay. I can come to you. I know you're on holiday, so I won't take up much of your time.'

'Yes, that's fine, but I'm about to go walking. I'm at a little car park near to a place called Covel Wood. Do you know it?'

'I do, very well. I can be there in ten minutes. Thank you, I promise it will be quick.'

'It's fine, honestly. I can't get that image out of my head. It's kind of the first thing I see in the morning and before I go to sleep.'

'I know, it's hard and it was awful. I'm on my way.'

Morgan finished her coffee and put her coat back on, tugging the hat out of the pocket. She might even have time to pay Ettie a quick visit while she was there.

40

The briefing was quick, Ben knew they didn't have much time. There had been an officer dressed in plain clothes in an unmarked car outside the address they had for Andrew Stephens all night, and there had been no signs of life; but if he was going to work this morning then he could leave at any moment.

They had no idea how violent Andy was, if he would come in without a fight. If he had killed Margery, George, and poisoned David then he was a sick and very violent individual. He'd sent Morgan out to go to speak to the Airbnb man purposely, to keep her out of the way. He'd been amazed she hadn't picked up on it, but then she'd been the one to suggest it and he wasn't going to turn down the chance to keep her at arm's length from this arrest.

Amy had found nothing on Andy on the system, just one grainy image of him on the internet that wasn't much good. How did he manage that, Ben wondered? For all intents and purposes Ben didn't do Facebook or Instagram, didn't even know what TikTok was about, though he'd heard of it, but he had no desire to spend hours on there. Yet his face was all over the internet when you typed his name in a search bar. He'd done it once when he was drunk after Cindy to read the reports on her suicide and had sobered up immediately. So many pictures of him at crime scenes, coming out of court, press conferences. With all the high-profile cases they'd worked the last few years he suspected there would be even more now.

Marc was buzzing, he loved the thrill of the chase, whereas Ben didn't find it quite so exciting anymore. He would be ecstatic to get a killer off the street, but until he was cuffed and in the back of a police van, he wouldn't feel happy.

Cain, who was door entry trained, was dressed from head to foot in black, with pads on to protect him should he have to use the metal battering ram to put the door through. He looked a formidable sight, and Ben noticed both Daisy, who was ready to go in as part of the search team, and Amber had both eyed him up with a look of pleasant surprise. This made him smile; Cain was walking around in front of them day in, day out in his chinos and shirt, but put the guy in an all-black uniform and make him look tough and the women were suddenly interested. Cain was oblivious which was probably a good thing, as he was easily distracted, and Ben didn't want his concentration ruined. It could lead to disaster if he didn't pay attention.

They parked around the corner in a small car park, and Ben wasn't happy that they didn't have a clear picture of Andrew Stephens to identify him. He radioed Amy. 'Can you go to the garden centre ASAP? I know it's not open yet but see if anyone is around and get us his employee picture to distribute to everyone. I'm going to hold off on going in until we know what he looks like. I'm not happy that the only description we have is brown hair, medium build and around five foot ten. That could be half of the men in Ambleside.'

'Yes, boss.'

She turned the car she was in around and left the car park at speed. He looked at the clock on the dash, it was almost nine.

Surely someone was inside and would let her in. Marc who was in the van with Al and the search team came over and opened the door.

'What's going on? What are we waiting for?'

'We don't know what he looks like.'

'So, we go in and cuff every person inside his flat. It's a one-bedroom flat, there can't be many people in there. We're wasting time, Ben, let's get this over with and get him into custody.'

He nodded. He kind of agreed with Marc, but there was this churning feeling inside of his stomach that was making him doubt his own judgement.

He looked at Marc. 'Okay, we'll do that.'

'You sure?'

Ben knew he was being sarcastic, but Marc hadn't lost a team member like he'd lost Des, and he certainly hadn't had to watch his partner get hurt the way Morgan had in the past over and over at the hands of violent killers. He was bound to be a little cautious. 'I'm sure.'

As the police cars and vans filled the street outside of the large house where Stephens' flat was, it occurred to Ben that the night shift officer wouldn't have known what Stephens looked like either, but then the doors were slamming and officers were heading towards the building, Cain leading the way, and he jumped out to follow them. He guessed they were going in blind, he just hoped it didn't end with anyone getting hurt.

The front door was unlocked, and they all piled in behind Cain, like a flowing river of bodies, one after the other, their movements fluid and anxious. As Cain, Ben and Marc stood on the small landing area with Daisy and Amber behind them, who were both taser trained, Ben held up a hand to stop everyone from moving. He walked up to the door and hammered with a closed fist on it, waited a few seconds then hammered again. He pressed his ear against the door, but didn't hear any movement. It didn't mean there was nobody inside; if Stephens looked out of the window, he couldn't miss the carnival of police vehicles in the front street. He'd have to be pretty stupid to not realise what they were doing there.

Ben stepped back and nodded at Cain. The door was an old-fashioned wooden door, thankfully, and not a modern composite one, otherwise they'd be standing here all day. It only took one hit with the universal key, as they called it, and the door splintered into twenty pieces. Hanging on by its lock, Cain lifted his size twelve Magnum boot and kicked it so hard the door flew inwards.

A guy from the flat below stuck his head out of his door to see what was going on, his mouth open at the sight of the gaping hole where the door should have been. He stood there in a pair of boxers rubbing his head.

'What's he done?'

Ben leaned over the railing. 'Nothing, we need to speak to him. Have you seen him lately?'

'Nothing? You need to calm it down, lads, if that's the result of someone doing nothing. I'd hate to see what you did if they had. In answer to your question, I saw him yesterday. He came home from work early, then went out again. Didn't hear him come back though. Are you sure you have the right man? Cos he's a nice lad. Doesn't deserve to come back to that mess to sort out.'

There it was that twinge of doubt that Ben had been feeling that something wasn't right. He looked at Marc, who shrugged. Then Marc turned to Daisy and the other task force officer standing behind her.

'Full search, please, looking for anything that could be used as poison, containers, medicines, you know the score. If it has a medical warning on the back of it, bag it, even if it's just paracetamol. I want the place turning upside down, find me something to prove that we have the right guy, please, and we didn't waste our time or this warrant. Amber, you can stay and scene guard in case he turns up; you have a taser, so use it if you have to.' He turned to Ben. 'We'll go back and reassess the situation, okay?'

Ben wanted to shake his head; it wasn't okay. What if they'd just messed up? But where was Andy and why hadn't he come home if he wasn't scared and hiding from them?

41

For a dreary, wet, January day, Covel Wood car park was busier than Morgan imagined it would be. She looked for a car with a family still inside, but there was only one and it had a guy in it. He was on his phone talking to someone. Morgan got out of the car and walked to knock on his window. He looked up at her and smiled. Ending his call, he leaned across and opened the door for her.

'Get in, it's freezing out there.'

She looked at his face, he looked nice, but that didn't mean he wasn't a weirdo. It started to rain, and she knew writing on the hand-held tablet would be impossible, so would paper. She sat on the passenger seat, even though every serial killer documentary she'd ever seen was playing across her mind, and she knew he could have automatic locks with the child locks on. Drive off with her and she'd never be seen again. *Stop it, Morgan, do your job and get out of here.*

'You are the detective who phoned me, right?'

She nodded. 'Yes, sorry. Detective Brookes and you are?'

'Johnson Stone.'

He sounded like an American private investigator. 'Sorry,

it's been a funny morning already. Yes, you are Johnson Stone and I just need an official statement from you about how you came across the body. Your baby was with you, you said. Can you tell me where it is now?' She glanced into the back and saw no car seat.

'My wife hates walking with a passion. She loves the lakes but only for the coffee and cake shops, loves the quirky little gift shops too, so they're having a wander around Ambleside while I came here.'

She felt her shoulders drop a little. He seemed like a nice enough guy. She opened up her tablet.

'I literally just need you to talk me through it and sign your statement, then I'll let you get on. I don't want to waste your holiday time. Where are you from?' He sounded local to her not like someone who was visiting.

'I'm from Barrow, grew up there on Barrow Island. My wife is from Liverpool, so we live near Aintree. Bit more going on than down in Barrow, and of course, no problem. Well, my wife wasn't with us, she stayed at the Airbnb, but the baby was unsettled, so I took him out a drive so she could unpack. Only I got lost and had no signal to put the satnav back on. He fell asleep and I ended up driving over all these narrow roads. I saw the house up the hill, had already tried the farm at the bottom, but that was all shut up and nobody was around, and thought I'd go ask them for directions. I wish that I hadn't bothered and just turned around when I could at the farm.'

'I bet you do; it must have been a terrible shock for you.'

'Well not at first because as I got closer, I thought it was a scarecrow or something like that. I don't know what kind of things people around here get up to, and I was thinking well, I'm in the middle of nowhere, maybe that's what they do. Then I realised it was a person. It was raining so hard, and the wind was blowing, I was scared to stop and leave the baby alone. Selfish of me, but you know, I panicked so I pulled over and phoned the police, and they told me they'd take it from there. I spoke briefly to the paramedics who turned up first, and then I left because there wasn't anything I could do; and because I never heard from anyone I kind of assumed they were okay or maybe it hadn't been a body and had been a scarecrow.'

Morgan's thumbs were tapping double time on the keypad, writing it all down. He paused to let her catch up.

'That's about it.'

Finally, she looked up at him and smiled. 'Sorry about the delay in getting updated. It's been a bit full-on, but someone should have been in touch with you before now. I appreciate you talking to me.' She passed him the tablet and the stylus. 'Could you just sign in that box?'

He scribbled in it and passed it back. 'What happens now?'

'Not a lot, you could be called as a witness to come to court, if it goes to court, but it's hard to say.'

'Was she murdered, or did she decide she'd had enough and do it herself?'

'She was murdered.'

'Oh, wow. I mean you wouldn't expect that, would you, not in the middle of nowhere like that.'

'No, you wouldn't. Thank you for your time. I'll let you get on. Have you walked here before?'

He shook his head. 'No, I wanted a woodland walk that was not too steep. I have a dodgy knee, and these woods seemed ideal.'

Her phone began to ring, and she got out of the car, excusing herself. She waved at him, indicating that he was free to go, and he waved back.

Ben's voice sounded strained.

'No sign of Stephens at his flat; apparently, he hasn't been there since yesterday. Where are you? We're heading back to the station to regroup and figure out what to do.'

'Just got a statement from Johnson Stone.'

'At least that went to plan. Can you come back here?'

'On my way.'

She got back into her car, relieved that Johnson had not turned into a crazed killer despite her internal alarm bells ringing repeatedly. Just to be sure she started the engine and locked her doors; he was at the boot of his car putting a pair of muddy walking boots on. As she drove past, he nodded and lifted a hand to wave. She smiled and was on her way back.

Ettie would have to wait another day for a visit; at least she hadn't phoned her aunt to tell her to put the kettle on. She felt a little deflated for Ben and the team. Why was life always like this? You caught a break, then it didn't work out, so you then had to carry on working like a blue-arsed fly to catch up again.

She was almost at Ambleside when her phone rang. She didn't have hands-free in her own car, as it was too old and knackered, so she pulled over to the side of the road as soon as she saw a place wide enough and looked at the local number.

She rang it back. 'Hello, I've just missed a call from this number.'

'Are you from the police? Did you leave a message for us about Margery Lancaster's estate?'

'I did, I'm Detective Morgan Brookes.'

'Morgan, it's Cheryl Walker, we went to college together. I work at Riley and Smith's solicitors in Windermere. How are you?'

Morgan laughed. 'Cheryl, it's been awhile, I'm good, how are you?'

'Oh, you know how it is, busy working and not doing much else.'

Morgan sighed, she knew exactly how it was. We do handle the estate for Margery Lancaster of High Wraith Cottage. I saw it in the paper yesterday and realised it was the same woman.'

'I don't know if you can help but I'm just looking to find out who her beneficiaries are as part of the murder investigation?'

Cheryl paused.

'Hang on, I'm not sure I can divulge that information, let me check with Mr Smith.'

As the line went quiet, an urgent email appeared on the screen of her tablet on the seat next to her, and she opened it to stare at the photograph of a guy in chef's whites staring back at her.

'Detective Brookes.'

'Yes.'

'Mr Smith said we can tell you there is only one beneficiary of Ms Lancaster's estate.'

'Thank you, are you allowed to tell me their name? It would be extremely helpful with our investigation.' She would bet a thousand pounds it was David Lancaster/Hawthorne and that Margery had felt bad about what she'd done to her only child.

'Yes, well I'm not supposed to but because it's you and because I know how good you are I can, but we couldn't disclose any other information unless you come in with a warrant.' She whispered Ms Lancaster's entire wealth, house and any land she owns are to be given to a Miss Esther Jackson.

Morgan's mouth dropped open; she had never in a million years expected to hear her aunt Ettie's name.

'Is that okay? Sorry to sound so rude, Morgan, I don't want to get in trouble. You won't drag me into it, will you?'

Unless there was another Esther Jackson. 'Yes, thank you, that's great and no, I'll keep your name out of this. Is it the same Esther Jackson who lives in the cottage in Covel Wood?'

'It is, or at least that's the address we have for her on file. Mr Smith will be pleased to know that she's still there and we don't have to go chasing around half of the country looking for her.'

'She's definitely still there. Thank you.'

Morgan hung up, then glanced down at the photograph Amy had sent. He had a look of the guy she'd just spoken to, only he'd had darker, shorter hair and his eyes had been brown;

the guy in the photo had blue eyes, but he could easily be wearing a pair of coloured contact lenses. Creeping fingers of icy cold began to wind their way along Morgan's spine up to the back of her neck. Stephens was missing. Would he have the audacity to meet her in a car park near to Ettie's house to give a statement? But then, serial killers often returned to the scenes of their crimes. They knew he'd been back to High Wraith Cottage to kill George. It was exactly the sort of brazen behaviour Morgan expected of a sadistic individual like this.

42

Ettie's umbrella had opened inside the house when she was getting ready to go out in the rain. She had picked it up and must have accidentally pressed the button or it was faulty, but it had shot open like some kind of weapon, scaring Max so much he'd taken off out of the window, and sent the cat running for cover. She wasn't a huge believer in all superstitions and old wives' tales but some of them did have meaning to her and this she felt was an omen not to go out in the rain maybe.

This had never happened to her before, and as she leaned on the kitchen worktop, staring out into her very soggy vegetable garden, she was considering the implications of whether she should be worried or not. Ever since she had heard about Margery Lancaster's terrible murder she had been unsettled, for no reason she could explain, but there had been something there, lingering at the back of her mind where there was no place for it.

George's death had come as a bit of a shock; if anything she had always thought he had taken his attempted murder very well for a violent bully.

She smiled at Max who was perched on the lowest branch

of the oak tree outside, watching; he was making sure she didn't throw any more ninja moves his way. She needed to go out. She was supposed to be at the farmers' market selling her jars of tea, but not in this weather. Nobody was desperate enough to brave the persistent rain that seemed to have taken up residence over Rydal Falls. Not even for her famous herbal teas to help with insomnia, anxiety and self-love – those were her biggest sellers and customers couldn't get enough.

About to turn away from the window, she caught a glimpse of black – someone was moving through the trees in the distance – and she paused. Who would be out in this weather? It didn't make for a pleasant walk when the paths were slippery underfoot; the leaves that blanketed them could be lethal if you weren't careful. Not to mention the mud that stuck to everything. But she was used to it. Always had a clean pair of boots in the back of her small van ready to swap into, but it wasn't walking weather that was for sure. Max had noticed them too because he had turned around to stare in the same direction, and then he took off into the trees. He was like a little guard dog, and she loved him dearly. He was on his way to check them out whoever they were. It wasn't Morgan, she knew that because she always got a tiny electrical sensation in her chest whenever she sensed her beautiful niece nearby.

She turned away from the window. She should really go out and get some shopping. She was almost out of milk and her biscuit supply was running dangerously low. Lately, with all this miserable weather, she seemed to have done nothing but drink tea and nibble biscuits as if they were going out of fashion.

The hammering on her front door scared her so much she jumped. Whoever had been out wandering the woods had found their way here, and for what reason she didn't know. She stared at her front door, wondering if she should ignore it, but she couldn't, and they might be lost or need help and she just couldn't turn anyone in need away. It wasn't in her disposition to be so cruel. She opened the door to see a young man standing there, rain dripping down the front of his waterproof jacket and running down his face.

'Can I help you?'

'I hope so, I'm lost and have no phone signal. I'm also soaked to the bone and not feeling very well. Do you have a house phone I could use, please?'

Ettie eyed him up. He was a tall, gangly thing, his teeth were chattering, and she knew she should turn him away; these woods weren't huge, and she could point him in the right direction of the main path out of them, but she wouldn't.

'Come in, yes, you can use my phone.'

He followed her inside.

She didn't see the sly smile which had spread across his lips as he gently closed the door behind him.

43

Morgan sped back to the car park. It was dangerous, the roads were wet, but she had to see if it had been the same guy and the only way to be sure was to check out his car. She parked behind it; he was nowhere to be seen. Taking her police radio out of her pocket she turned the volume up and waited for the airwaves to become clear. There was a domestic in Bowness and officers were updating the outcome. Finally, the chatter stopped, and she began talking before anyone else did.

'Control, can I have a PNC check in Covel Woods, please. Suspicious.'

'Pass the reg, Morgan.'

She read it out to them. A sickness was spreading through her stomach at the thought that it might belong to Andy Stephens.

'That's a white Vauxhall Corsa registered to a David Hawthorne with Andrew Stephens as a named driver...'

Her mind began to swim, and she took off running in the direction of Ettie's house, leaving the car abandoned in the middle of the car park. She didn't hear the rest of the message, she didn't need to, it had to have been Stephens – all roads led back to David Hawthorne and somehow if Stephens had found out about Ettie in Margery's will... she shuddered at the thought of what it could mean for her beautiful, gentle aunt. If David was killing anyone who had wronged him, surely the woman inheriting what he'd consider *his* family wealth would be at the top of that list.

'I need urgent assistance.'

Ben's voice broke through.

'Morgan, what's going on? I only caught the name.'

'The guy, the witness, it's got to be Stephens. His car is in the car park by Ettie's. Ben, Ettie is the sole heir to Margery Lancaster's estate.'

'Don't go in, wait for patrols to arrive. We're on the way.'

Morgan kept on running. She knew that if she had to go hand-to-hand with Stephens she would. Ettie was her everything.

A loud squawk above her made her look up to see Max flying to the left of the path. She nodded and followed him into the woods. He knew a shortcut and she was taking it. They looked a strange sight, the bird soaring above the out of breath woman who was trying to keep up with him as she pushed through the bushes and trees to reach the cottage. She found herself bursting through the trees at the rear of the cottage, skidding to a halt through the mud and detritus on the ground that had splattered her leggings and coat.

She saw movement inside and caught a glimpse of her aunt. She was in the kitchen, maybe Stephens hadn't gone after her after all and she'd panicked. Sucking in a deep breath she bent over slightly to catch her breath. Max let out a loud squawk and too late she realised that someone was behind her. Before she could turn to face them, she felt something heavy hit the side of her head and she swayed forwards as blackness threatened to take over.

Pressing the red button on the top of her radio, she managed to shout *help* before her knees gave way and she collapsed face down onto one of Ettie's herb beds.

44

Ben's heart was in his mouth when his radio began to make the vibrating noise that only happens when someone hits the small emergency button on the top, issuing an urgent call for assistance. He heard Morgan call for help and then... silence.

He followed Cain, who had the keys for a van, and shook his head. 'Too slow, need something faster.' Cain looked at the board and grabbed the keys for the 4x4. They ran to it, and Ben could hear Marc shouting after them, but he ignored him. Officers were already charging out of the back doors, and he heard sirens and knew they were on the way, but did they know how to get to Covel Woods car park? It wasn't the easiest of places to find and he knew a quicker way. They jumped in the car, neither speaking. Cain followed a van out of the gates down to the main road.

'Don't follow them, take a left instead and turn off at the second on the right.'

Cain did as he was told. Ben knew the way he was taking him was far too narrow and twisty for a speeding car, but he didn't care. He had to get to Morgan and fast. How had this all gone tits up in a matter of minutes? He'd thought he was sending her to safety, and it turned out he'd sent her straight into danger.

'You weren't to know, boss.' Cain read his mind.

Ben couldn't speak; his tongue felt as if it had grown to three times its normal size.

'I mean, only Morgan could find the guy we've all been out looking for all morning without even trying.' Cain paused. 'She's okay, she'll be okay. We'll make sure she is.'

He was rambling, and Ben wasn't sure if it was to make himself feel better or Ben. It had been a while since he'd been this worried about her. Since he'd had chest pains that scared him, and now he had both, and his cardiologist was in an induced coma in the hospital. He closed his eyes and said a silent prayer. 'Please, God, if you don't let me die and don't let Morgan die, I'll make it up to you. I'll do anything.'

Cain slammed on the brakes, and the car skidded to a halt, letting out a high-pitched scream as a tractor came trundling around the corner, narrowly missing them by centimetres but managing to take the driver's mirror right off with a loud crack and groan as it was sheared straight off.

'Fuck.'

'We're good, keep going.'

'The mirror.'

'Doesn't matter, please, Cain.'

Cain put his foot down once more. They were either going to get there in minutes or die in a fatal accident while trying.

Cain screeched into the car park; Morgan's car was there. Abandoned. They were both out of the car and running towards the path, giving a couple of walkers the fright of their lives as they charged in their direction.

Cain held up a hand. 'Sorry, have you seen a woman?'

They shook their heads.

Ben knew the path to Ettie's, but his shoes weren't equipped for this amount of mud and his feet were slipping from underneath him, making him slow down before he fell over and was no good to anyone. Cain had his boots on and overtook him. Ben had never been so thankful to Cain and his extra-long legs or the fact that he'd taken up running. He heard sirens as two vans pulled into the small car park, causing absolute chaos, and the slamming of doors as the officers headed towards the path.

He waited for them; they were no good to anyone if they got lost in the woods. Ettie's cottage was off the main footpath, and they could end up running around in circles.

45

Morgan opened one eye to see where she was and realised she was in Ettie's cottage. She looked around for her aunt and saw her sitting wide-eyed, tied to one of the chairs with chains that looked scarily familiar. Ettie was trying to tell her someone was behind her with her eyes, without speaking. There were heavy footsteps that came from the direction of the door as he quickly went to each window and drew the curtains. Then he was standing in front of Morgan, staring down at her. He prodded her with the tip of his boot.

'Just who the heck are you, Detective Brookes, are you some kind of super cop?'

She couldn't feel her radio in her pocket. Trying to move her hands she realised they were tied together. She looked up at him and smiled. 'Your worst nightmare.'

He laughed. 'What, you are mine? Sorry, you can't be and it's the other way around, mate. I'm actually your worst nightmare.'

Her head was throbbing where he'd hit her, and she shrugged. 'Swings and roundabouts, mate.' She emphasised the *mate*.

He laughed. 'Why are you here when you left me not long ago, and how long before the coppers you called show up?'

'Anytime, they're probably already here, out in the woods, watching the house with their guns. Any second now they'll red dot you and shoot you.' Morgan knew this wasn't strictly true; she had no idea how long it had been since she made the emergency call, but she needed to buy time.

'Maybe that wouldn't be so bad, it's all gone to shit anyway.'

'What has?' Morgan knew if she kept him talking it was giving Ben and the others time to get a plan together.

'All of it, seemed like a brilliant idea at the time. I hated how smug and rich David was, how he pitied me for being his poor, half-brother.'

'All the best laid plans do; you know that any minute now the door is going to get put through, so why don't you untie me and let us go?'

He shrugged. 'Well, I could, but what would be the point in that? I don't want to hurt you; I came for her.' He was pointing at Ettie, who had a look of confusion in her eyes as to why this guy was wanting to kill her. 'She is the last one left.'

He kneeled down to look at Morgan's face. He was inches from her and staring directly into her eyes when a loud bang filled the air. He looked up to see the big police man running towards him, the front door in pieces, and she knew this was her chance.

Morgan threw her head forward and headbutted him so hard in the face that she heard his nose crack with the force, a hot gush of blood spattering all over her face.

He didn't make a sound, just slumped to the floor unconscious. She managed to pull herself to her feet as the pain in her head intensified by the cracking of their heads, just as Cain reached them, closely followed by two coppers both with tasers drawn. Ben behind them. Cain took in the scene.

'Glad you're okay.'

A wave of dizziness washed over her, and she felt herself falling, then she felt Ben's strong arm around her waist.

'I've got you, it's okay.'

She glanced at Ettie, who was being untied by Cain, and she let herself fall into Ben who helped her onto the sofa. Andrew Stephens was coming around, but he was already in cuffs and wasn't going anywhere fast. She closed her eyes, waiting for the dizziness to subside.

'Move away, let me take a look at her, please.' She looked at her aunt Ettie, who was shaking her head. 'I knew that umbrella opening inside the house was the start of something awful. Now let me get you something to help with that bruising.'

She shooed Cain and Ben out of her way and went to the kitchen, coming back with a small first aid kit in a well-worn tin. She placed it on the pine chest in front of the sofa, then went to get a bowl of warm water. Max had taken up his usual position on the windowsill and was watching everyone intently.

Cain, who wasn't too fond of birds, kept glancing his way and keeping a safe distance.

'Should we get paramedics?' asked Ben.

'No,' both women said at the same time, making Ettie smile.

'It's nothing a bit of ice and arnica salve won't solve. Morgan dear, you're going to have an impressive black eye, but I think you saved that pretty little nose. I can't say the same for his nose.' She was pointing at Stephens, who was muttering incoherently on the kitchen chair. 'Do what you need to for him, because I'm not treating him, just Morgan.'

Ben smiled at her, and she nodded at him. 'I would like it if you could get him out of my house though. He's full of bad energy and messing up my vibes.'

Ben turned to the two officers. 'Let's get him to the van and take it from there while we're waiting for the paramedics to arrive. He's going to have to go to hospital, otherwise his lawyer will throw everything at us.'

Ben read him his rights, but Stephens wasn't taking much notice of him. 'When he comes around read them to him again and make sure he understands.'

'Yes, boss.' They hooked an arm through Stephens' and helped him to his feet. Morgan watched as he was half carried, half dragged towards the footpath. Ettie was holding a cold cloth against her forehead, and it felt good.

'Now, can someone tell me what the hell was his problem?'

'Revenge.' Morgan looked at her aunt, who was thoroughly confused.

'On me?' Ettie replied, incredulously.

'He's the son George had during his affair with the young girl from The Black Dog. And he wanted vengeance on the Lancaster family. You will be getting a letter or a phone call from Margery's solicitors. She left everything she had to you, the cottage, the land. So you were his final target.'

Ettie sat down on the sofa next to Morgan, shaking her head. 'That's just.' She paused. 'Flabbergasting. Why would she do that?'

Morgan took hold of her aunt's hand. 'You were the only person who ever showed her a little kindness. I suppose she wanted you to know how much she appreciated that.'

Morgan felt sad for Margery.

'What about her son? Didn't she want to give it to him?'

'It doesn't look like she did. He's currently in intensive care at the moment; he was poisoned too.'

Ettie stood up. 'Why the evil little bastard, what a terrible thing to do to him after everything he's been through. Is he going to be okay?'

'I hope so.'

'Me too.'

Morgan hugged her aunt and held on to her for a very long time.

46

TWO MONTHS LATER

Morgan waited in Covel Wood car park for Ettie, who arrived with Max soaring above her. 'Shoo bird, I'm busy today, got some important things to do.'

He took off, leaving her shrugging at Morgan, and she got into the car. 'He's such a worrier, he hasn't left my side since that day you know. He must have thought that was it, game over for me and he'd have nobody to feed him M&S shortbread biscuits.'

Morgan laughed. 'Are you sure you want to do this?'

'As sure as I'll ever be.'

Ettie had a big bag in one hand and a solitary key in the other.

'Have you thought about what you are going to do with the cottage once all the legalities are done? And please don't tell me you're thinking of living there.'

'God, no way would I want to live there. I'm going to sage the shit out of it and you're going to help me. We are going to set those poor tortured souls free once and for all, get them out of the shadows and into the light, although I don't know if my sage stick is big enough for all of them, but we'll give it a go. Once we've cleared all the negative energy from it, I'll get a house clearance firm in to empty it and then—' She stopped talking for a moment. 'And then I'm going to offer it to the women's refuge in Kendal, to see if they could make use of it for emergency accommodation for women in need of escaping violent relationships. It seems a fitting thing to do. Once the house and land have been cleansed, and the ghosts have been moved on, maybe it can do right by those women in need and become a sanctuary instead of a prison. I think Margery would approve of that, and I've spoken to David. He's doing very well. I asked him if he would like the cottage, but he flatly refused to have anything to do with it. He thinks it's a great idea. What do you think, Morgan?'

Morgan's eyes sparkled with tears as she nodded. 'I think that's a wonderful idea.'

Ettie sighed. 'Me too, I just wish that I'd thought of cleansing the house while Margery was still alive. She must have suffered in those negative vibes for such a long time.'

Morgan parked the car outside of the gate to the cottage. The warmth of the sun reflecting off the off-white walls made it look like a completely different place than when she'd first set eyes on it that dark, stormy January morning. She stared up at the upstairs window. The curtain moved slightly, and she didn't know if a breeze was making them move or if it was one of the many souls who had been stuck inside of there forever.

Ettie sighed. 'They know we're coming and they're excited, I can feel it. They are ready for this, Morgan. We can finally give them some peace after all these years of torture.'

She smiled, still not sure whether she believed in ghosts, but she believed in her aunt Ettie and would do anything to make her happy. If this was what she wanted then Morgan was here for that, no matter what because Ettie was like the mother she'd always longed for and now finally had.

A LETTER FROM HELEN

I want to say a huge thank you for choosing to read *Poison Memories*. If you enjoyed it, and want to keep up-to-date with all my latest releases, just sign up at the following link. Your email address will never be shared and you can unsubscribe at any time.

www.bookouture.com/helen-phifer

This book has been a challenge in more ways than one. There has been a lot going on and losing my gorgeous mum threw me off track. Please know that if you get to this point, I'm so very grateful for all of your support.

The story about Thomas Lancaster poisoning his entire family with arsenic in 1672 is true, and he killed seven people and made others poorly. He was found guilty at Lancaster Castle Assizes and was taken back to the farm where he was hanged in his own front garden.

It is just mind blowing to think that stuff like that happened, but we all know how cruel people can be. I recently did a very interesting, guided tour of Lancaster Castle which was fascinating, and if you're ever in the area I highly recommend it. At one point Lancaster Castle was known as the Hanging Court and more death sentences were passed there than any other court in the country outside of London. Including the Pendle Witches, but we'll save that story for another time.

I hope you loved *Poison Memories* and if you did I would be very grateful if you could write a review. I'd love to hear what you think, and it makes such a difference helping new readers to discover one of my books for the first time.

I love hearing from my readers – you can get in touch via social media or my website.

Thanks,

Helen

www.helenphifer.com

 facebook.com/Helenphifer1

 x.com/helenphifer1

ACKNOWLEDGEMENTS

The hugest thank you goes to my fabulous, patient, wonderful editor Jennifer Hunt who is just brilliant and a pleasure to work with. This book was a challenge and I can't thank you enough for shaping it into something that resembles a coherent story. I promise the next one will be easier!

Another special thank you to the brilliant Jan Currie for her hard work with the copy editing too.

Thank you to Shirley Khan for her proofreading too.

Where would I be without the wonderful Kim Nash who is just so supportive and always there to check in when things are getting a bit much. Kim, you are so appreciated and I can't wait to go for a posh coffee with you again next time we're in London.

Thanks to my wing gal the amazing Noelle Holten who always has my back and makes all the important dates go without a hitch. Thank you from the bottom of my heart Noelle for everything you do.

Thanks to the amazing Sarah Hardy and Jess Readett for their support too.

The whole team at Bookouture are just phenomenal, thanks to Jenny Geras, Peta Nightingale, Jen Shannon and Levke Kluge, off the top of my head. I'm so glad that the whole team will have their own acknowledgements, it takes a lot of people to put these stories together and I'm so blessed to work with them all.

A big thank you to the wonderful Paul O'Neill for his

surveyors report and all of his support over the entire length of my writing career. You really are my lifesaver, Paul, when everything has turned into one big blur.

I can never thank my lovely readers enough, you are the reason I get to write these stories and it's thanks to your never-ending support, love, and kindness that I'm still here doing what I love. I've said it before and I'll say it again, I wish I could give you all a huge hug.

The same to the wonderful book bloggers who take the time to read, review and shout about my stories. You are the unsung heroes of the book world and I appreciate your support more than you could ever know.

I'm sending so much love to my family, we lost our guiding light, the kindest woman who we were blessed to have as a mum, nanna and great nanna. I'm so proud of you all for being there for Nan when she needed us the most. To be so loved was a huge testament to how wonderful Patricia Corkill was, she is forever in our hearts, in the sunsets, the rainbows, the thunderstorms, the trips to Primark that she loved so much and the music that makes us smile and lifts our hearts when we think of her. I love you all.

Helen Xx

PUBLISHING TEAM

Turning a manuscript into a book requires the efforts of many people. The publishing team at Bookouture would like to acknowledge everyone who contributed to this publication.

Audio
Alba Proko
Sinead O'Connor
Melissa Tran

Commercial
Lauren Morrissette
Hannah Richmond
Imogen Allport

Cover design
Lisa Brewster

Data and analysis
Mark Alder
Mohamed Bussuri

Editorial
Jennifer Hunt
Sinead O'Connor

Milton Keynes UK
Ingram Content Group UK Ltd.
UKHW010335250624
444652UK00004B/222